CRAWLSPACE

ALSO BY ADAM CHRISTOPHER

STAR WARS

Shadow of the Sith

Master of Evil

THE EMPIRE STATE

Empire State

The Age Atomic

THE SPIDER WARS

The Burning Dark

Cold War

The Machine Awakes

THE RAY ELECTROMATIC MYSTERIES

Brisk Money

Made to Kill

Standard Hollywood Depravity

Killing Is My Business

I Only Killed Him Once

STRANGER THINGS

Darkness on the Edge of Town

DOCTOR WHO

The Dream Nexus

What Still Remains

The War Master: His Greatest Trick: The Blue Shift Ritual

WORLD OF WARCRAFT

Heartlands

The Doom of K'aresh

ELEMENTARY

The Ghost Line

Blood and Ink

DISHONORED

The Corroded Man

The Return of Daud

The Veiled Terror

Seven Wonders

Hang Wire

CRAWLSPACE

ADAM CHRISTOPHER

TOR PUBLISHING GROUP
NEW YORK

This is a work of fiction. All of the names, characters, organizations, places, and events portrayed in this work are either products of the author's imagination or used fictitiously.

CRAWLSPACE

A Nightfire Book
Published by Tom Doherty Associates / Tor Publishing Group
120 Broadway
New York, NY 10271

www.torpublishinggroup.com

Nightfire™ is a trademark of Macmillan Publishing Group, LLC.

EU Representative: Macmillan Publishers Ireland Ltd, 1st Floor, The Liffey Trust Centre, 117–126 Sheriff Street Upper, Dublin 1, D01 YC43

The Library of Congress Cataloging-in-Publication Data is available upon request.

ISBN 978-1-250-38128-6 (trade paperback)
ISBN 978-1-250-38129-3 (ebook)

First Edition: 2026

Printed in the United States of America

10 9 8 7 6 5 4 3 2 1

FOR SANDRA,
ALWAYS

CRAWLSPACE

1

OPERATIONAL TEST

This is Artemis Control to XK72," came the ever calm, ever patient female voice over the comms. "T-minus seventy minutes until Operational Test."

"XK72 to Artemis Control, acknowledged."

Colonel Josef Redway flicked off the comms and eased back in his flight seat, stretching his hands behind his head, arching his back as far as the straps would allow. Beside him, Liv Halliday, Mission Lead, glanced at him out of the corner of her eye from the co-pilot's position. The colonel actually had his eyes closed, looking like he was getting ready to relax at home on a cozy winter's night, instead of commanding an experimental spacecraft balanced in high orbit.

She wasn't sure if she should be jealous of the test pilot's calm head, or nervous that he was taking such a crucial moment so lightly.

"You can say it." Redway opened his eyes, his arms falling into his lap before he gestured to the forward view. "Let yourself go a little, come on. You've earned this. You'll feel better."

Liv pursed her lips. He had a point. The test flight of the XK72 was the culmination of years of hard work, of research and tests and experiments, of designs and redesigns, of invention; long hours and late nights at the Artemis labs for . . . well, Liv couldn't remember how many months it had been, the workload increasing almost exponentially as the launch date approached, her own dedication to the project, even she could see, bordering on obsession, and . . .

And here they were. Less than an hour to go until the culmination of her efforts—and those of her team, of course—and suddenly, it struck Liv just *where* they were. No simulation, no computer-generated projection could have prepared her for *being right here, right now,* for what she now had just a few precious moments to actually appreciate.

Because they still had a lot of work to do, and very soon. Getting *here* was only halfway. Maybe not even that. There wouldn't be another moment like this one. Redway was right. She had to grab it while she could.

Strapped into the flight seat next to her, the colonel turned his body around as far as he could to face her. Liv sensed the movement more than saw it, because now her attention was most certainly captured by what was outside the ship.

The flight deck of the XK72 was a sparse, functional module, one of several infinitely customizable units that made up the structure of the entire ship. The two flight positions themselves sat in a pod-like extension that jutted out from the front of the module, the rest of the blocky ship stretching out for one hundred meters behind it. The front half of the pod was constructed of an Artemis-patented transparent ceramic, the curved wall giving a clear view, ninety degrees top to bottom, one hundred and eighty left to right.

And what a view that was.

In front of the ship, at a distance of twenty-eight thousand kilometers, the blue marble of the earth revolved, the glow of its halo bright enough to blot out the star field beyond.

Redway gave a quiet chuckle. "Honestly, you can say it. Just go on and say it. Everyone does. Hell, even I do, and I've seen it more times than most. Really. It'll help clear your head. You want me to do a countdown? Because I can do a countdown. Here we go. Three, two—"

"Wow," she said.

"One." Redway paused. "What?"

Liv looked at him, saw his eyes narrow, his mouth open somewhere on the way to saying something else. Then he closed his jaw and ran one finger around the curve of his chin.

"Wow? Seriously? Is that it? All that and you give me a 'wow'?"

"Yes! I mean—" Liv gestured to the forward view. "Wow! This is wow! The truest, most accurate definition of *wow* there is."

The colonel's grin returned. "Well, okay, I'll admit I was expecting something a little more—"

"Expressive?"

"Colorful was what I was thinking. But sure, okay. *Wow*. Let's go with wow."

The pair laughed, and Liv sank bank in her seat, rested her head against the headrest, and went back to drinking in the view.

Okay . . . maybe *wow* wasn't quite right. Liv leaned forward in the co-pilot's seat, pulling against the straps that held her firm—as though moving a scant few centimeters forward would somehow bring the planet noticeably closer—and peered at the surface of the world, focusing now on the fine details. Africa spun lazily below them, much of the vast continent free of cloud, save for a smear of white across the lower third.

In a way, it was so . . . mundane. Anticlimactic, even. A view of Earth from space. Big deal. People had been looking at similar images for decades. Many had seen it for themselves—heavy industry was well established in the asteroid belt, the Earth-Moon loop had been a routine trip for workers and pleasure-seekers alike for years now, and the cooperative efforts of Artemis, Inc, and their military partners had seen more distant regions of the solar system explored thanks to the development of short-range hyperspace transit.

But despite the steady reduction of the magical to the everyday, despite her decade-long tenure at Artemis, Inc, the test flight of the XK72 was Liv's first actual trip into space. She might have left it longer than most, but here she was, and she wasn't going to let anything take away the thrill of seeing her home planet as a *whole* from this remarkable vantage point. She stared at the view, trying to absorb it all, trying to be aware of what she was thinking, what she was feeling, etching those emotions permanently on her soul. This was a moment she would remember—*should* remember—for the rest of her life, but a moment she was afraid of letting slip by. The XK72 was Liv Halliday's first flight as mission lead, and she was determined to never take what she did for granted, ever.

Below them, Africa had moved out of view. They were now over the Atlantic, the sky there thick with clouds, a cyclone forming in the tropics. Soon enough, that view would change again, as the planet rotated and the XK72, once the last prep was done and the final stage checks were complete and deemed satisfactory, exited its orbit and moved out to a predetermined distance more than halfway to the Moon.

"Systems are green for go," said Redway, his voice bringing Liv out of her reverie. She watched as he made another cursory check of instrument readings he had checked and rechecked five times already. "Operational Test and Drop in T-minus sixty-five minutes."

Drop. It was useful shorthand; an accurate, if unofficial, nickname for the XK72 test flight—or, more specifically, the Operational Test of the ship's prototype hyperspace engine, the SLIP drive. Single Linear Induction Pulse, as it was properly known, was a significant refinement of hyperspace tech, one developed to stretch the range of the limited drive systems that Artemis had been manufacturing for years. When the XK72 "dropped," the SLIP drive would draw power from the induction combs that studded the hull of the ship, break the laws of physics, push the limits of engineering, and send the ship across two light-seconds of space in two microseconds of time. The implications of making a successful first Operational Test, proving the concept of the new drive system, were actually quite profound, increasing the sphere of achievable human space exploration by orders of magnitude.

Now *that* was something that made Liv say "Wow."

. . . If it worked.

The science said it would. After years of development, the final build had gone flawlessly. The data was solid, the technology worked, and as far as Artemis was concerned, the risk-to-benefit ratio was good enough to allow a crewed Operational Test flight. And if Artemis was happy, then so were Colonel Redway's superiors. This, Liv knew, was key—the whole program was an expensive one, and she was under no illusions as to who was footing most of the bill.

"Well," she said, breaking the silence, her hands reaching to tug on her seat straps, an unconscious gesture she only became aware of when she saw Redway watching her, "if nothing else, the trip was worth it just for the view."

Redway grinned again. "You've seen one Earth, you've seen them all," he said.

"What!" said Liv, in mock outrage. "How quickly the glamor fades."

Redway laughed, and reached down to pick up his data pad from its storage slot in the side of his flight seat. He flicked through a few screens, making more pre-Drop checks. Then the communications deck pinged.

"This is Artemis Control to XK72. Acknowledged, all systems green, we have you at T-minus sixty-four minutes to Operational Test. All green for final prep."

"XK72 to Artemis Control, acknowledged," said Redway, thumbing the main comms off and switching to the internal. "This is Redway. All sections, commence final-stage prep for Operational Test."

At this, the comms chimed as the XK72's six other crewmembers acknowledged the request.

"Engineering. Astrid and Avery," said a male voice—Avery Cormack, answering for himself and Astrid Healey, the two down in the

Engineering module at the rear of the XK72. "Check, all green. And what a lovely shade of green it is too. A little chartreuse, a hint of pine."

"Acknowledged," said Liv, with a smile and a slight shake of her head. Avery had a tendency toward the verbose when he was excited, even in the middle of an official part of mission protocol.

Another female voice. "Data Monitoring. Check."

Mirai Ikeda was stationed in the lower module of the XK72, her dedicated station filled with measuring equipment that would record every single aspect of the test run: stresses, tolerances, performance parameters, the works. The data—collected, analyzed, and interpreted by Mirai, as lead data analyst—that could make or break the XK72 project.

Now it was Liv's turn. "Data Monitoring and Engineering, acknowledged. All sections ready. Auxiliary, report please."

"Aux, Deak reporting. All checks acknowledged." The deep bass rumble of Titus Deacon came from his position in the main passageway module outside Engineering, where he was now sitting in a fold-down flight seat. Liv imagined him sitting on the awkwardly low seat, legs outstretched, his hands gripping his harness, counting the seconds until the moment Redway gave the order and he could be up and about and getting on with his job. She smiled at the thought.

"Acknowledged," said Redway. Flicking off the comms, he turned his attention to his data pad. "Mission Lead, Z-axis stabilizer reading, please."

Liv turned to her console. Her control yoke was parked in a slot in the control panel in front of her, but around it, the readouts shone brightly. As she reached for her own data pad and began verbal confirmations of her readings as Redway read them out, she began to feel a pleasant, warm buzz grow inside her, the lights and sounds of the flight deck coming into sharp focus as her excitement built.

T-minus sixty-four minutes to Operational Test.

All systems green.

2

ONE, TWO, THREE

The ship was supposed to be called the HERMES, which stood for Hyperspace Experimental Research Mission–Extra Solar.

Instead, that was scrubbed, and the project went back to XK72, like it had been on the drawing board, and somehow nobody came up with anything better.

So XK72 it was.

Titus Deacon—Deak, as he liked to be called by those he liked in return—wasn't sure if this should annoy him or not, but the fact was he thought about the mission name more than he knew a reasonable person would. So, yes, in actual fact, it *did* annoy him. There was a certain poetry to HERMES, the way it went with Artemis, the way it implied mercurial speed, travelers moving as fast as thought.

HERMES. Hyperspace Experimental Research Mission—Extra Solar.

Well, okay, clunky maybe, someone forcing the acronym with every ounce of effort. Deak wasn't even quite sure what "Extra Solar" was meant to convey. Beyond the solar system, probably.

But hey, not his department, not his problem. XK72 it was (again) and he accepted that. He'd been with Artemis for long enough to see missions come and go, test flights succeed and fail. And during that time—what, ten years now?—he'd carved out a very particular niche for himself that he was rather pleased with.

Auxiliary specialist.

Which meant as much—or as little—as he wanted it to mean.

More power to Titus Deacon.

Truth was, he was good, and he was good at *everything.* Twenty years a military engineer, with stints as naval architect (and degrees to match, which he never mentioned unless someone asked, which was *never,* and that suited him just fine, thanks), then he specialized in hyperspace drive systems, reaching such rarified levels of expertise that he began running and then ended up actually *coordinating* official military training courses on the subject.

That was when he realized his mistake. Because as good an engineer as he was, he knew, plain as day, how hyperspace tech was changing and how he was becoming far too embedded in the training side of the job. Which was, on the face of it, fine—a good way of keeping up-to-date, right?—but in reality was a road to nowhere. He wanted to *do important things*, and that meant stepping out of the classroom and back into the real world.

At least, that's what he told himself. Maybe it was true, and maybe he was just bored and maybe he wanted a little bump in his paycheck.

Enter Artemis. Enter the role he had crafted for himself: auxiliary specialist.

Had a ring to it, it really did. And came with a nice salary, courtesy not of the military, but of Artemis, Inc, the largest global aerospace research and development outfit on planet Earth.

It couldn't have come at a better time. Deacon was looking for a way out, but he didn't want to leave what he loved—which was not the military, but the work of his life.

Because he had a gift. He could talk to machines, and machines listened, and there were no finer machines than those built by Artemis, Inc.

Machines which included the HERMES—sorry, scratch that, the XK72.

A machine in which he now found himself, lying on his back, staring at the embossed text on a metal panel that really, honestly, truly should have been larger and easier to read.

"Arrow A, to the front."

He raised an eyebrow, cursing his increasing age and decreasing eyesight.

"No wonder your skills are so keenly sought after, Deak. Your parents must be very proud."

Deacon craned his neck around and looked across the floor of the probe module. The only part of the person who had spoken visible from Deacon's position beneath the runner probe rack was a pair of Artemis, Inc, work boots, and a moment later those boots moved out of sight as Senior Engineer Astrid Healey continued with another task.

Deacon laughed and returned his attention to the job at hand. "Just remember to check that off on your little list there," he said. "Wouldn't want my vital contribution to this mission overlooked." He aligned the core of the runner probe into the slot beneath the device itself and clicked it home. "And now you need to send flowers to my mother's grave for taking her name in vain," he added.

The sound of Astrid's footfalls came to a stop, then she reversed and ducked down, appearing at an odd angle to Deacon, her long white-blonde hair completely immobile in its tight bun.

"Are you kidding?"

Deacon laughed again and pushed himself out from under the runner probe rack. "Yes. I'm kidding," he said as he got to his feet. "She's happily retired in Barcelona."

"Barcelona?"

"It's my father who is dead."

"Ah." Astrid didn't move, but her shoulders seemed to rise as she tensed up. Deacon enjoyed the moment, then pointed at the data pad in her hand.

"Checklist."

"Ah," said Astrid again, quickly looking down, perhaps glad of the exit from this awkward situation.

Deacon just hid his grin and turned away to check over the runner probe.

It was a standard piece of Artemis kit: two meters long, a rocket-like cylinder sitting in a complicated cradle in the middle of the XK72's topmost module. Once prepped, the probe could be launched ahead of the ship itself, should a final batch of test data need to be collected. The runner probe's core—the thing Deacon had just checked and reset manually—was a smaller, single-use version of a hyperspace drive. Once launched, the core would burn itself out as it dropped the probe into hyperspace, the resulting spike in output surfacing the probe just a few milliseconds later.

Useful things. Cheap, disposable, but enabling a plethora of data to be collected before, during, and after any larger engine test, which included the first flight of the XK72's experimental SLIP drive.

Truth was, prepping the probe was just busywork. Deacon could do it with his eyes closed—provided he got arrow A pointed in the right direction—and he doubted they would use the thing anyway. But test protocol was test protocol and he went along with it because that was the job, and if there was one lesson he *had* taken from his former military life, it was orders was orders and protocol was protocol.

Okay, make that two lessons.

You do it right, or you don't do it at all. A maxim also held by the rest of the XK72's crew, and that included Astrid Healey.

Astrid Healey was, for her part, a genius. Genuine, bona fide, and that was something that Deacon thought about a lot as well, because if there was one thing he admired it was hard work and professionalism and Astrid had both in spades, along with natural talent.

Fine, three lessons.

The XK72 was *her* baby. Astrid had designed nearly all of it, working closely with Mission Lead Liv Halliday.

Nearly was the operative word. There was just one small part Astrid hadn't had a direct hand in, and that was the SLIP drive. The fabrication and installation of that particular technical wonder had been the purview of Colonel Redway's masters.

Well, Captain *Jackson's* masters, actually, but he wasn't here and Colonel Redway was and Deacon also wasn't sure if that should bother him or not either.

And, actually, credit where credit's due. The SLIP drive might be a sealed unit, but of the XK72's crew, Astrid did know a lot about it. As senior engineer, she was also the project's military liaison, and over the last couple of years had been seconded for lengthy spells to the SLIP drive team, disappearing from the Artemis laboratories and workshops as she helped with the experimental drive's design and build.

There was a lot of secrecy around the mission—around the SLIP drive in particular. Deacon knew that wasn't unusual either. He'd been part of plenty of tests, flown several missions where the crew weren't entirely sure what it was they were testing. Par for the course, right?

And that was why, Deacon knew, Captain Jackson had been replaced at the last minute. It wasn't that he knew too much—nothing so dramatic—but perhaps his task as military test pilot was just to run through the program, make sure everything was fine and dandy on the Artemis side before stepping out and letting Colonel Redway, a pilot with the same experience but perhaps a higher security clearance, take his place.

Sounded fair to Deacon. Okay, so it hadn't happened before, but it had happened this time and . . . sure. Deacon assumed that someone somewhere knew what they were doing, and on Deacon's part he knew he had a job to do and he was going to do it to the best of his ability.

What did bother him was the SLIP drive itself. Because it sounded interesting and he really, *really* wanted to get a close look at it, but it was a single sealed unit and nobody aboard had any access except to the control systems grafted into the ship's mainframe computer.

Again, not unusual, however irritating it was. The military was paying for the SLIP drive, which meant they were paying for most of the mission, and to Deacon there was also nothing nefarious about that either. The SLIP drive was expensive. The military fronted the money, got first dibs on the data and probably on the tech itself, assuming the test flight was hunky-dory and everyone—engineers and accountants combined—were happy. Really, Artemis were getting a good deal. If things went wrong, if the test didn't go as it should or the SLIP drive underperformed, they could blame someone else entirely.

Of course, things were not going to go wrong, not with Astrid aboard, Deacon ready at her side to do whatever she told him to.

Orders was orders.

Deacon felt his grin returning. Oh, that was fine by him. Jack-of-all-trades, master of . . . actually, most of them. As aux specialist, he was free to provide assistance to any of the others should they need it, and was even qualified to pilot most Artemis, Inc, vehicles, the XK72 included. He may have had twenty years on Astrid—that was why he was here, after all, as one of most senior and most experienced hands-on crew in the entire company—but he was at her beck and call. And at the beck and call of her fellow engineer, Avery Cormack, who right now would be busy in his department, running through his own pre-launch checklist.

Satisfied with his work on the runner probe, Deacon stood tall and stretched, his huge muscles pulling the fabric of his Artemis T-shirt tight across his chest, and ran a hand over his buzzed scalp, the dark skin slick with a light sweat (hey, runner probes were heavy). "We done?" he asked.

Astrid tapped at her data pad. "We done." She put the data pad down on a nearby console, and the two of them stepped around to stand on either side of the runner probe rack. She leaned over and flipped two safety catches before getting a good grip on the folding mechanism.

Deacon did the same, and looked over at her. "One, two, three."

Together, they lifted, and the rack folded in on itself on a smooth, balanced mechanism, then shifted upward, taking the runner probe with it, and neatly slotted into the open launch bay in the ceiling of the module. Astrid stepped back and let the much taller and stronger Deacon do the final push to lock the probe into place. Then she touched her earpiece.

"Flight, this is Astrid. Runner probe loaded and ready, all systems green."

The comms chimed in her and Deacon's ears. "Acknowledged," came Redway's voice. "Runner probe ready. Thanks, you two. Proceed to your Drop positions and begin systems check."

"Acknowledged," said Astrid and Deacon in unison, then Astrid nodded at her colleague.

"Good job."

"Put me in for a promotion when we get back."

Astrid smiled. "I think we might all be in for a promotion after this. See you on the other side."

At that, Deacon and Astrid bumped fists, then left the module, and headed to their designated stations.

3

IS YES THE RIGHT ANSWER?

The Data Monitoring module was attached to the bottom of the XK72's hull; as spartan as the rest of the ship, it was accessible via a ladder and hatchway that led up to the main passageway. As such it felt detached, isolated even, from the rest of the ship. Quiet and cool, a space all of its own.

Exactly how Flight Analyst Mirai Ikeda liked it. Here was her domain, her *refuge*, where she could hunker down and get to work without interruption, focusing on the data as it came in, ensuring everything was monitored and logged and archived. And as that data came in, she could begin her primary mission assignment, analyzing flight parameters and performance outputs, comparing, contrasting, charting.

She loved her job. And not just because of the numbers and the math and sheer complexity of the task at hand, one that required every bit of her many qualifications and certifications to carry out.

She loved it because she was left alone to do her job. Here, in a module of her own, while the other five crew of the XK72 were busy over her head, she could tune out the universe and give all her focus, 100 percent, mind, body, and soul, to the *data*.

Right now, though, was the lull, that moment in time just before the work began, a moment that Mirai enjoyed, savored even. She was ready, and waiting, and in reality, she had nothing to do as she sat at her workstation in front of her keyboard and a bank of monitors that stretched away on either side. Around her, other consoles and panels slept, their lights dim, waiting, while against the wall behind her stood four thin blade-like towers that housed the Data Monitoring station's actual computer power and data storage.

Mirai turned her modified flight seat around and scooted it over to the towers, the seat running on a recessed track in the decking, allowing her access to every available panel and console and system in her module without unstrapping herself—useful if things got bumpy, although in all the Operational Test hours the twenty-five-year-old analyst had logged, there had never even been the slightest hint of turbulence.

That, or she had never noticed. She could have been buried in the data as all hell broke loose around her and she might never had known a thing about it.

"Nearly time," she said aloud, to nobody.

But while she had solitude, she was not alone.

Given the nature of her job, Mirai had been given dispensation to bring a small personal item to decorate her space: On the console next to her primary display was a photograph—Mirai and another younger woman, the pair standing in front of a huge reclining Buddha in green bronze—held in a small metal clasp that was itself magnetically attached to the frame of the screen.

Mirai turned to face the photograph. "I'm sorry if this bit is boring, Suki, but not long to go now. And then we can have some real fun, right?"

She pushed herself forward until she was back at the workstation, and reached across the desk, caressing the edge of the photo with long, pale fingers, imagining that she was stroking her sister Suki's face.

How long had it been? Two years? Three? Mirai had lost track of the time since her sister's death, but she had done it deliberately, a conscious effort. Mirai was afraid not of the future, but of the way time was passing so quickly. Every moment, every breath, took her further and further away from her sister. Mirai didn't believe there was anything after death—*show me the data and I might reconsider*—and she didn't really believe in the relativity of time, despite what her qualifications might have said on the matter. All she knew was that she and Suki were getting farther and farther apart, and that she would do anything, *anything*, to arrest the flow of time.

Having her sister here helped. Suki was gone but not gone, always alive in Mirai's mind, not just a memory, but a piece of herself and a past she wouldn't let go of, not now, not ever.

It was the metallic *thunk* that broke the spell. Mirai jumped in her seat, snatching her hand away from Suki's photo like it was electric. She turned, in time to see someone awkwardly descending the access ladder, the man's head bowed as he tried to look down to see where he was stepping.

Then he missed the last rung altogether and those boots hit the decking with another thud. He turned, adjusting his glasses as he peered around the module, like he wasn't quite sure where he was. Then he seemed to notice Mirai, and he straightened up, raising his head so the data pad he had balanced between chin and chest slipped. He grabbed it, then gestured to the ladder with both arms, like he was ready to go up and start again.

"Should I have knocked? Sorry. I should have knocked. Not sure on what. Sorry."

Mirai smiled as Avery dropped his hands, his mouth in an "O" like he had been surprised by something.

"You don't need to knock, Avery," said Mirai. She turned and grabbed her own data pad from the workstation. "Are we ready to start logging the output from Engineering?"

"Ah, yes," said Avery. "Logging, logging, logging. That's what I came down for." He lifted his data pad and peered at it, long and hard, before he started one-finger tapping on the screen. "I have the handshake PIN here . . . there . . . ah, somewhere. Ah, okay, PIN, PIN." He turned the pad around so Mirai could see the long string of numbers on the screen, the security code that would allow the Data Monitoring station a direct data link to the Engineering module.

As Mirai began entering the code, Avery stood and shifted on his feet—several times, like he was trying to get comfortable, like he was suddenly nervous of Mirai's attention, even though she was looking at the screen he was holding, not him.

Truth was, Avery McCormack, all of thirty-five going on fifty-five, was just nervous, period. Not anxious, not self-conscious, not awkward, just . . . nervous. And not about anything in particular, it was just his normal state of mind.

It was his work that calmed him. Engineering was more than a job, it was his lifeblood, his reason for being. It was the first thing he thought of when he woke up, and the last thing he thought of when he went to bed. Avery Cormack didn't have any family—partly by choice, partly by circumstance—and nor did he have any friends, because all of that pesky stuff called "basic human interaction" was a distraction from the work and a time sink he really couldn't afford to indulge in.

According to Avery, anyway. Because in reality he had both friends and family, and both of them were the team at Artemis, Inc, and more specifically the crew of the XK72.

Well. Not Colonel Redway. He wasn't entirely sure who Redway was, none of them were, but it didn't matter. He was just a pilot. Dime a dozen. Not part of the team.

Not part of *my* team.

And this mission, *ho boy*, it was a good one, because not only was Avery working closely with Astrid Healey, one of Artemis, Inc's best—and he included himself in that metric—but because she'd been seconded to the military for so much of the project, he'd been able to take the lead for much of the development period.

In fact, he was due to submit the next batch of monographs for the XK72's Technical Manual almost as soon as they got back, and he was looking forward to that almost as much as the Operational Test itself, and—

And that's when he found himself standing in the Data Monitoring module with his mouth in an "O" like he had been surprised by something, and with Flight Analyst Mirai Ikeda waiting patiently for an answer to a question he hadn't heard.

"Yes," he said. He turned his data pad around, peered at the screen like he'd never seen it before, then thumbed the device off and held it behind his back. Then he adjusted his glasses, just so. "Ah . . . is yes the right answer?" He leaned toward the module's access ladder, ready to leave.

Mirai sighed, but was smiling. "Data handshake complete," she said. "Engineering and Data Monitoring are synched." She turned her seat around and slid her keyboard closer. "You can go back to Engineering."

Avery nodded, paused as he considered the decking under his feet, then nodded again. When he left, Mirai didn't turn around, but there was still a smile on her face, and as Avery clambered up the ladder, there was a smile on his face too.

4

YOUR CALL, MISSION LEAD

T-minus three minutes," said Liv across the ship-wide comms. "All stations, report for preflight."

In her ear, the comms chimed as the rest of the crew began to sign in, the last official acknowledgment that everything was ready and the test flight could go ahead.

The XK72 was still facing the earth, but now the familiar blue-green planet was a fraction of the size it had been as they had moved to their test launch coordinates. Liv narrowed her eyes as she scanned the globe, but it was hard to make out any specific, recognizable land masses now. There was too much cloud, and nearly half of the planet had faded into the black of space. Her excitement had tempered, but now she felt something else, a buzz of anxiety. Only natural, she told herself.

"All sections, acknowledged," said Redway.

The comms beeped again. "This is Artemis Control to XK72. Acknowledged, all systems green. Countdown hold at T-minus sixty seconds. Runner probe is green. Do you require runner probe test launch? Confirm and initiation protocol."

The comms went quiet. Redway turned to Liv. "Your call, Mission Lead."

Liv glanced over the heads-up display that was now painted over the lower half of the viewing bubble, providing a tidy chevroned listing of every individual key system and check essential to the Drop. Everything was green. The XK72 was operating perfectly. To fulfill test flight procedure, Liv brought up both long-and short-range sensor readings. The mass of data they brought back was vast, but the mainframe filtered and analyzed it, and a second later chimed that no anomalies were detected.

But, even so, launching the runner probe would be that one final, positive check. It was programmed into the test schedule so would have no impact. The data it would gather would likely be superfluous to their needs, but . . . data was data and data was good.

Liv pursed her lips. From the corner of her eye, she saw Redway glance in her direction as she studied the HUD.

"All looks good to me," said the colonel. "Your call, but I would recommend a negative on runner probe."

Liv felt her jaw tighten. She had hesitated, and Redway had seen it, something flickering over his expression, just for a second. It didn't matter—she was being too hard on herself, she knew that, but still couldn't shake the desire for her first mission lead to run with absolute efficiency and perfection—but it bothered her.

She took a breath. Redway knew what he was talking about. As a test pilot, he had more experience than even Deacon.

The seconds continued, and Liv still didn't answer. Because something else bothered her—it wasn't the first time she had had these thoughts, but they came back to her right now, no matter how hard she tried to dismiss them. She glanced at Redway again, tried to read his expression like she had been able to read Captain Jackson's, but the fact was she didn't know what Redway was thinking because she didn't know him.

None of the crew did.

Colonel Josef Redway wasn't even supposed to be there. Their first test pilot had been Captain Matthew Jackson, a charming man with a square jaw and a glint in his eye, every inch the walking cliché. He had been impressive at the mission briefings and the crew were looking forward to carrying out the flight with him at the controls.

Until he wasn't the test pilot anymore. Three days before the mission launch, Colonel Josef Redway had been waiting for them at another briefing, and had explained how he was their new pilot. Captain Jackson was unavailable, his status, when asked, was classified.

Deacon was happy to go with the flow. He'd even said that to Liv, at that briefing and then more than a few times afterward. Liv hadn't been happy with the change, but Deacon's acceptance of the situation had set her mind at ease. Deacon was the most experienced of them all. Liv knew she could learn a lot from him, and followed his lead . . . without making it look like she did.

Avery was less happy, and bristled at Deacon's attitude—not for the first time—but he seemed to forget very quickly that Redway was the replacement. Whoever actually flew the thing wasn't important, was it?

Mirai hadn't been sure how to answer Avery's question, but perhaps Liv thought that, underneath the inadvertently brusque statement (typical Avery), he was right. Afterall, the XK72 was a joint effort, and the military—who were paying for it all and who had not only installed the SLIP drive but most of the equipment in Data Monitoring so Mirai could be comfortable with the responsibility of collecting the data output of the test flight—surely knew what they were doing.

Didn't they?

So if Mirai had doubts, she had never voiced them, and instead focused on her job with a tunnel vision that was typical Mirai.

To Liv's surprise, Astrid never said anything about Colonel Redway's sudden arrival at all. She had worked closely with the military on the SLIP drive, they'd even sent her away on confidential briefings about it. So perhaps she'd already met him and just couldn't talk about it.

So Astrid didn't say anything, and Deacon said he assumed it was because she was fine with it.

And if she was fine with it then Deacon was happy.

And if Deacon was happy then Liv was . . . *accepting* was probably the right word. She knew that Avery and Mirai both looked up to her to *lead the mission*, so perhaps, in the end, they saw Captain Jackson's replacement as something above their pay grade. He was only the pilot, just one, single—albeit important—component of the XK72's test flight.

Colonel Redway, for his part, seemed . . . fine? He was relaxed, like Jackson had been, like all test pilots seemed to be. Part of the job description, no doubt. He smiled and laughed along with the rest of them and in three days had integrated himself just fine into the crew.

"Okay," Liv said, every option considered, the crew waiting patiently for the mission lead to make the final call before the test flight proper. "Negative on runner probe."

"Acknowledged," said Redway. He thumbed the comms. "XK72 to Artemis Control. Negative on runner probe. Road looks clear from here."

"Artemis Control to XK72, acknowledged. Countdown resumes at T-minus sixty seconds. Colonel Redway has control."

"Colonel Redway, acknowledged." He grinned and flicked a sequence of switches at his position, then pulled his control yoke free from its cradle and gripped it with both hands. "Commencing test run in sixty seconds. Initiate primary sequence."

Liv unlocked her own control yoke. It slid forward, and sat between her knees, but she kept her hands clear and instead operated the button controls on her console, running through the initiation sequence that would switch the XK72 from its conventional ion drive to the experimental SLIP drive.

"Primary sequence acknowledged," said Liv. She leaned forward and flicked a switch. The HUD updated to the new status. Now, all but three indicator chevrons were filled green—a little chartreuse, a hint of pine, she thought with another smile. Everything was ready.

"Test run in twenty seconds," said Redway.

"Acknowledged, XK72," came the calm voice from Artemis Control. "Have a good trip."

Redway ran through a sequence on his console as Liv did the same. The last three chevrons on the display changed from orange to green. A humming sound came from somewhere far behind them, the steady background noise of the ship increasing in volume as the SLIP drive was engaged and made ready for ignition.

"Engineering," said Avery over the comms. "Check, all green, green, green."

"Acknowledged," said Redway.

Liv opened her own comm channel, then closed it. She wondered if now was the time, if it was even appropriate, to say anything that wasn't on the checklist.

Screw it. She opened her channel. "Good luck, everyone."

Nobody replied, but beside her, the corner of Redway's mouth curled into a lopsided grin.

"Ten seconds," he said.

Liv settled back into her seat. She wasn't sure exactly what the ignition would feel like. Hyperspace transit was nothing new. She'd been through it several times, and it felt like nothing at all.

The SLIP drive might have been experimental, but it was still a hyperspace engine. A new design, new tech, vastly improved and incredibly efficient, but it did the same thing that a regular drive did.

But still, she didn't know what it was going to be *like*. None of them did.

"Nine . . ."

As the final countdown started, the crew began calling in their own reports. It was overkill perhaps, given everything was now more or less running on automatic, the ship's passive (or "dumb", Deacon liked to call it, perhaps with a little too much enthusiasm) mainframe computer handling almost everything, save for the Drop itself, controlled by a switch Redway had the honor of throwing. But it was all part of the program, the verbal acknowledgments recorded in synch with the system output in Mirai's Data Monitoring station. It helped with compiling the project report for when all this was over. And if anything went wrong, it was good to have as much data as possible to scrutinize. There wasn't a black box as such, but everything was logged and recorded.

Avery: "SLIP drive primed."

"Eight . . ."

Astrid: "Induction power combs at eighty-four percent, charge steady."

"Seven . . ."

Liv's eyes flew over the HUD. Everything was looking good. "All systems green."

"Six . . ."

Mirai: "Data recording."

"Five . . ."

"Power combs eighty-nine percent."

"Four . . ."

"Power combs ninety-three percent."

"Three . . ."

"Power combs ninety-eight percent. SLIP drive engaged."

"Two . . ."

Beyond Liv's HUD, the half-shaded disc of the earth looked close enough to reach out and take. It pulled at Liv's gaze, and she found herself suddenly, desperately, terribly homesick. The feeling caught her by surprise, as did the fluttering feeling inside her chest.

"SLIP drive ignition."

It was fine. Everything was fine. This was just part of the project. They would Drop, fill every exabyte of data storage they had onboard, then return home. Return to that thing, that small ball floating in the deep nothing in front of the window.

"One . . ."

Her lips felt dry, so she wet them, but that somehow only made them feel worse. Beside her, Redway creaked in his seat as he reached forward and touched a control. She didn't know which one, but it didn't matter. As a test pilot, he would be checking and rechecking every single control, every single reading, over and over again, no matter whether they were now falling through an automated sequence or not.

And then—

Redway sat back and looked ahead. "Flight program engaged. Test protocol running."

And then—

Liv looked at Redway and then she followed his lead and looked dead ahead. The HUD was lit in neon green. All systems ready and operational. Flight program running.

The Drop counter in the middle of the HUD spun through a dizzying number of microseconds.

And then—

There was a very loud *thud,* and the earth flew up and out of sight. Liv's yoke jerked between her knees, the only physical indication that the XK72 had pitched down sharply.

Redway was saying something, but Liv couldn't hear it over the alarm that now filled the entire ship with a shrill, earsplitting tone.

5

WE HAVE A SITUATION

Colonel Redway was looking at Liv as he shouted, so she assumed he was shouting something at *her*, but the sound of the alarm was so utterly all-consuming her brain could hardly process what was going on around her.

Gritting her teeth against the cacophony, Liv turned her attention to her console, but the whole thing was alive and angry, flashing lights and readouts filling quickly with endless scrolling pages of data making identification of the alarm's source far more difficult than it should have been. Finally, her attention was drawn to one indicator that was flashing in time with the sound pummeling her eardrums. She acknowledged the alert with a tap of the button next to the light, cutting it and the alarm instantly, leaving her with a ringing in her ears so intense it was nearly as painful as the alarm itself. But now, looking over at the colonel again, she could just about hear what he was yelling about.

It turned out he hadn't been yelling at her at all, but down the comms as he tried to get Artemis Control back on the line. With the alarm silenced, Redway paused, then tried again, this time without needing to shout.

"XK72 to Artemis Control, come in, please. XK72 to Artemis Control, come in, please. Do you read me, Artemis Control?"

There was nothing. As Liv's hearing cleared, she realized she couldn't hear a thing, not even a crackle or click of interference, over her earpiece. The comms channel was completely dead.

Something knocked her knee. She looked down, and saw the control yoke slowly turning, drawing an ellipse in the air. She grabbed it with one hand and reached forward with the other to make manual adjustments to the ship's lateral stabilizers.

"Axis even," she said, as she eyed the readings on her console, giving her report automatically, by instinct. "Balance zero point one and . . . holding."

"Acknowledged," said Redway, before trying to contact home base again. He gave up after just one more try, the comms channel silent. "Okay, looks like we're cut off for the moment." He leaned forward and checked his readings, giving a few switches an experimental toggle. "We have a general comms failure. No antenna power." He sat back and tapped his earpiece. "Engineering, report. What's your status? Can you tell me what the hell happened?"

"Engineering, Avery here. The . . . ah, now this is pretty interesting actually—"

"Come on, Dr. Cormack. Focus please."

"Sorry," said Avery over the comms. "Looks like the SLIP drive engaged then went out of phase almost instantly. Astrid is checking the data now."

Redway glanced at Liv, a frown on his face. Liv cut into the comms. "Data Monitoring," she said. "Mirai, what did it look like from your end?"

"Running it back now," came the flight analyst's voice. The comms clicked off, then on again in rapid succession. In the gaps between, Liv could hear Mirai typing furiously.

"Come on," said the colonel. "What have you got?"

"Looks like we tripped some kind of safety cutout," said Mirai. "The XK72's mainframe kicked in and took the SLIP drive offline a millisecond after we hit ignition." She paused, clearly parsing the complex data presented at her station before presenting it to the others. "There was power feedback. The surge blew the main antenna before the mainframe could compensate."

"Acknowledged," said Redway. He dropped his hand from his earpiece and drummed his fingers on the arm of his flight seat. "Okay," he said. He turned to look at Liv. "We don't seem to be in any danger, so no emergency. This is your show. Next step?"

Liv took a deep breath and considered. Redway was right about two things.

First, they were fine, the XK72 was (antenna aside) fine, despite the volume of the alarm.

And second, yes, this *was* her show. She'd be dammed if this stupid little incident was going to derail all the hard work of her and her team.

Liv gave Redway a nod, then opened her comms channel. "The SLIP drive can wait," she said. "We prioritize the antenna repair. Without it, it's not just the comms back to base that are down. Artemis Control won't be receiving any telemetry from us at all. They'll have us on deep space radar, but they'll have no idea what's happened. So we need to get comms back and then Artemis can advise on whether to continue with the Drop."

The comms clicked. "Aux here," said Deak. "Do you think continuing is a good idea? Shouldn't we head back to base so the whole system can be checked out?"

Redway was watching Liv, his expression hard, the earlier good humor gone. Which was understandable, to be expected even. He was doing his job, the veteran test pilot switching modes as the situation required. He was serious, but calm.

But still, the shift in his demeanor was jarring.

Deak did have a point, but Liv wasn't about to open a debate on the matter. As she opened her comms again, Redway's eyes narrowed as he awaited her decision.

"Comment noted," said Liv, "but Artemis has a lot riding on this mission. We all do."

At this, Redway seemed to relax, and he gave Liv a thumbs-up, clearly approving of her decision.

With a nod, Liv turned away from the colonel and continued with her instructions.

"We're all in one piece, so there's no reason we can't try for another Drop attempt. Once we re-establish contact with base, Artemis Control will be able to analyze the data. Ultimately, they'll be the ones who will make the call, but I'll recommend we continue. If everything is clear, I don't see them disagreeing."

"You the boss, boss," said Deak. "I'll start on the antenna. You want me to bust out the servodrone?"

"God no," said Liv, a smile appearing, despite herself. "Not unless you want to be buried under a mountain of paperwork for the next six months. If you need to go outside, you'll have to suit up."

"Point," said Deacon, a faint chuckle sounding over the thin audio of the comms. "You know how I hate all those damn forms."

"Amen to that," Avery cut in.

"Avery," said Liv, "help Deak if he needs an assist. Astrid, look at the data with Mirai, see if you can figure out what triggered the mainframe fail-safe."

"That damned computer," said Deak. "The dumbest machine I've ever tried to talk to."

Again, the aux specialist had a very good point. The ship's computer was certainly advanced, running an artificial intelligence on a quantum layer that even Liv had difficulty understanding. But that mainframe wasn't designed for the benefit of computer-human communication, it was purely for the efficient automatic running of the ship's systems, including the equally advanced SLIP drive.

Which meant, Liv knew, that getting to the bottom of the error might be difficult for them, even using Mirai's monitoring station to help sift the huge volume of data their Drop failure would have generated, even if the event itself had been almost instantaneous. What they needed—as she had said—was to get Artemis Control to figure it out, while they got on with the mission.

Avery and Astrid acknowledged her instructions, and then the comms clicked off in her ear. Liv sank back into her seat, the initial flood of adrenaline having now run its course through her body.

This wasn't quite how she had expected the test flight to go, but then again, finding and solving problems was as much the purpose of the mission as was making a successful Drop. Whether the mission was completed or aborted, either outcome would bring back a wealth of useful data and experience, and even as she thought about it, Liv began to feel that little thrill again, already looking forward to digging through the data, finding out what happened, coming up with a solution. Disappointment now gave way to anticipation.

Beside her, Redway sighed as he undid the straps of his flight seat. "Well now," he said, "ain't that a pain in the ass?"

Liv laughed, happy to see Redway's more cheerful side re-emerge. She pulled her data pad out from its slot beside her flight seat, and began rechecking her own readings and the original sequence she had run through during the countdown.

After a few minutes, it was clear that she had performed her own tasks perfectly—and if she hadn't, the computer would have told her and Redway anyway. Beside her, Redway had moved to the wall beside his position and was flicking switches amid the mass of tightly packed controls that cover the panel. He checked something on his data pad, then gave a satisfied grunt. "Well, that's something," he said.

"What have you got?"

He turned to her. "I figured out how to turn the volume down on the alarm."

Liv laughed. "Priority number one."

"But also," he continued, "I think I've found the cutout." He leaned over in his flight seat and tilted his pad toward Liv so she could see. The screen was completely filled with lines of green code. Liv tried to read some of it, but Redway began scrolling too fast with one finger. "You'll want to go down and help Data Monitoring," he said. "I can correct the code in the computer, but Mirai will need to mirror any changes I make in her own systems."

Liv nodded. That made sense. To control for variables, the equipment in Data Monitoring was completely isolated from the test vehicle's—which meant Redway was right, any change he made would need to be checked and accounted for in the other system, and, depending on the extent of the changes, Mirai might need all the help she could get in order to be ready to record the next test run.

"Agreed," said Liv. She stood and headed for the door. "You can read the line numbers over the comms and we can run the edit together."

Redway didn't answer. Liv paused at the open bulkhead that connected the flight deck to the main trunk of the XK72, but saw the colonel was now studying his data pad, brow furrowed in deep thought.

Better leave him to it, she thought.

Then she stepped over the bulkhead and headed toward the Data Monitoring module.

Liv walked down the ship's primary passageway, data pad swinging. She reached the open hatch in the floor that led down to the secondary passageway and the Data Monitoring module, and swung herself onto the ladder.

She was halfway down when she heard a heavy *thunk* from somewhere over her head. She stopped her descent and looked up, but saw only the passageway ceiling above through the circular hatch opening. As she started to climb back up, Avery's voice came through her earpiece.

"Okay, *a*, what was that, and *b*, should I be worried? I'm worried enough already. Meteorite maybe? Meteorite I can deal with. Psychologically, I mean."

Liv paused in her climb to free a hand and press the button on her earpiece. Avery's manner was sometimes difficult for others, but Liv had known him long enough to know when his chatter drifted from the excited to the concerned. He might be irritating a lot of the time, but it masked a laser-sharp focus that made him one of the best engineering troubleshooters Artemis had. "I'm checking," Liv said. "Sounded more like it came from inside."

Mirai came over the comms. "Deak's in the airlock, isn't he?"

"Negative," said Deak, cutting in. "I'm in Storage One, checking spares for the antenna."

Liv emerged through the hatchway and looked back down the passageway. The heavy bulkhead door leading to the flight deck was closed.

Frowning, she walked down toward the ship's bow, and examined the door control panel on the wall. It had two LED lights on it. Both were red, showing that not only was the door closed, but it was *locked.*

Liv touched her earpiece, opening it to all channels. "Looks like the power spike fried more than just the antenna," she said, thumbing the door control. The lights both blinked, but stayed red, and the panel emitted a low tone. She took a step back and eyed the door. "The internal bulkhead control is out. I'm locked out of the flight deck."

Nobody spoke. Not even the person Liv had expected to answer.

"Colonel, can you open the door from your side?"

There was no answer.

"Colonel Redway?"

"What's happening?" asked Deak. "You need me back up there?"

"Stand by," said Liv. She pressed her earpiece, cycling through the comms channels until she was on the one shared only by the XK72's pilot and co-pilot. "Colonel, do you read me? The flight deck door's closed. Can you open it? Josef?"

Nothing. She tried again, then cycled through the channels and tried a third time. As she spoke, she pressed the door controls, but neither Redway nor the panel responded.

Liv sighed. Despite her earlier optimism, now she knew the power spike really *had* ended the test. Not only was the antenna out, the internal door controls were fried, and the comms weren't working either—and who knew what else they'd find once they'd checked all the systems over.

Artemis were going to be *pissed.* Whoever had written the mainframe code that had triggered the SLIP drive cutoff was going to be fired. Probably out of a cannon and into the sun, Liv thought.

And she would happily volunteer to light the fuse.

But first things first. If there was a wider systems malfunction, she had to make sure they were both thorough and logical in their checks. She clicked her earpiece back to the open channel. "Liv, comms check please."

"Auxiliary, check."

"Engineering, Avery Cormack, check, check, check. And—"

"And Astrid, check."

"Data Monitoring," came Mirai's voice, "check."

Liv paced a small circle at the end of the passageway by the bulkhead, staring at her feet. Then she stopped and looked up at the closed flight deck door.

"Colonel Redway, comms check."

No reply.

"Colonel Redway, can you hear me? Come in, please."

Again, nothing. The comms *were* working, as she had just established. It was just Redway's that was out.

She tried the door control again, like the panel had somehow reactivated, the ship's mainframe making a valiant attempt to actually be helpful to the crew and reset the bulkhead release. But as before, nothing happened.

Liv turned as she heard booted feet behind her, and saw Deak and Astrid come jogging down the passageway, their footfalls in perfect synch. "What's happening?" asked Astrid, looking first at Liv, then at the door.

"I wish I knew," said Liv. "The door's locked and this panel is unresponsive."

Deak rolled his shoulder, then pounded the door with a meaty fist. The panel was heavy and thick and the sound he made was dull and hardly carried at all.

"Colonel Redway, this is Deacon," he said, voice raised in an attempt to make it heard on the other side. "Can you open the door? We're locked out from this side."

He inclined his head against the door, listening, the silent seconds ticking by. He glanced at the others. "Maybe something happened to him?"

"That sound, you mean?" asked Astrid.

Deak thumped the door again. "Colonel Redway. What's happened? Is everything okay in there? Are you hurt?"

When there was still no reply, Deak took a step back, and placed both hands flat against the door at shoulder height. Liv watched as his biceps bulged, his dark skin pushing against the tight fabric of his T-shirt.

The door remained resolutely unmoved. Deak gave up and hissed out a held breath. Meanwhile, Astrid moved forward, dropping into a crouch as she began feeling the wall panels underneath the door control. "We can bypass the electrics and manually unlock it—*ah!*" She pressed a section of wall, and a small maintenance panel popped open, revealing a mess of wires behind. "I need some tools."

"On it," said Deak. He turned to head back to Engineering just as the open comms channel clicked into life.

"Liv," came Mirai's voice. "Get down here. We have a situation."

Liv and Deak exchanged a look, but it was Astrid, still by the open maintenance panel, who answered the call.

"What do you mean, a *situation*?"

"It's Colonel Redway," said Mirai. "Just . . . get down here. Now."

"On our way," said Liv. She led the three of them down the passageway to the floor hatch.

6

THE WRONG WAY AROUND, BACK-TO-FRONT

As Liv descended the access ladder into Data Monitoring, Astrid and Deacon close behind her, Mirai spun around on her chair. "You have to see this," she said, tucking a lock of her shoulder-length black hair behind one ear.

Liv reached Mirai's position and peered at one of the array of screens that crowded around her keyboard and mouse. "What am I looking at . . . ?"

Beside her, she heard Deacon click his tongue. "What is he doing?" he asked.

The screen showed a fish-eye view of the flight deck from a position somewhere in the middle of the ceiling. The camera looked forward, toward the flight pod and seats. Colonel Redway was standing just behind his seat, in profile to the camera view. In one hand he held his data pad, which he consulted as he one-finger punched a sequence into one of the angled control panels where the wall met the ceiling.

Astrid leaned over Mirai's console, trying to get a better look. "I can't see what he's typing."

"Is he trying to open the door?" asked Deacon.

Liv peered at the screen, trying to identify which panel Redway was working on. "He might still be trying to reset the system," she said. "Maybe he doesn't even know he's cut off from the rest of us." She paused, and glanced down at Mirai's station. "Everything is recorded here, right? All ship systems?"

Mirai nodded, and pointed at the computer towers on the other side of the cabin. "Every ship function and every test parameter."

"So we can see exactly what he's doing," said Liv, "from here." She looked up at Deacon, who nodded and clicked his fingers.

"Punch it up," he said.

Mirai's fingers flew over her keyboard. The display next to the main feed blinked into life, showing a series of panels filled with code—

three down the right-hand side, and a larger one occupying the rest of the screen. The three small panels pulsed in a sequence, blocks of code appearing, followed by a flashing command prompt, then the panels refreshed and the sequence repeated. Meanwhile, the text in the larger panel grew slowly, the individual characters appearing one by one in time with Redway's typing.

Liv scanned the screen, frowning as she tried to make sense of it. She wasn't entirely sure what she was looking at, and that was the problem.

Redway wasn't actually doing what she had thought he was.

"That's not the mainframe interface," she said. "What system is he in?"

Liv glanced at the others. Deacon just shook his head, but Astrid was studying the screens intently. "I'm not sure," she murmured, almost to herself. "All the code looks the same at this level. I need to see more."

"It's the utility system, surely," said Mirai. She glanced up at Astrid, but the engineer didn't answer. Mirai returned her attention to the screen. "Door controls, or . . . wait." She leaned forward, one hand tapping the keyboard as she went down, line by line.

"What is it?" asked Liv.

Mirai shook her head and sat back, taming her loose strand of hair again. "He's in the test protocol itself. Looks like he's entering a new mission program."

"What?" Liv turned back to the two displays. The code grew, the panels pulsed with new sequences, as Redway calmly stood in the flight deck, entering the new commands from his data pad with one finger. "How is that even possible?"

"It's not," said Astrid. "The mission program was loaded at base when the XK72 entered final mission prep. I signed it off myself then locked the system. We can't get into that part of it once the mission is live."

"This doesn't make any sense," said Mirai. She tapped the keys, bringing up highlighted sections of the code feed which she studied one after another for a few moments. "He must have his own access code. Some kind of override."

As the four of them watched, more text filled the screen. This time it was long, dense, appearing in nearly complete rows as Redway completed his entry and the mystery program began to be compiled by the mainframe.

"Well," said Deacon, with a heavy sigh, "whatever it is, he sure ain't trying to get that door open."

He was right. Liv felt a cold, hard lump rise from somewhere inside her. Because there was no door fault—Redway had closed it and locked it because he didn't want to be disturbed after he'd deliberately got her out of the flight deck.

She felt the floor shift a little underneath her. She grabbed the top of Mirai's chair, knowing full well that the ship was perfectly stable and it was *her* world that was starting to move at the foundations.

Whatever was happening was now firmly outside the parameters of the mission. Any thought of another Drop attempt now left her mind, as she began to process what might actually have happened.

Because . . . what if it hadn't been an error? What if it hadn't been an accident, a breakdown, a malfunction?

What if it had been done *deliberately*, by their test pilot, a last-minute replacement that none of them really knew at all.

She could hardly bring herself to think it, and yet. She did.

On the screen, Redway kept typing and the text kept scrolling. Liv rubbed her eyes as she squinted at the screen, but soon realized it wasn't the sudden dizzying stress of her own thoughts that was making her vision go funny. She genuinely couldn't read the code. Any of it. She didn't even recognize the symbols, the lines appearing in an alphabet of characters she had never seen before.

The cabin was silent as she and others watched Redway's code grow. After a few moments, Liv glanced at her crew, and saw in their faces the same confusion—and apprehension—she felt. Deacon pursed his lips as he watched, massive arms folded tight; Mirai absent-mindedly stroked the glass paperweight by her station with two long fingers as her eyes flickered over the lines of text; Astrid stood tall, head up, neck stiff, her gaze fixed on the monitor as she scanned the code, line by line, like she could read it. Then she saw Liv looking, and seemed to relax, giving a small shake of the head to indicate it was as much a mystery to her as it was to the rest of them.

Finally, Deacon shook his head and stepped away from the console to being a slow pace around the cabin.

Liv leaned closer to Mirai. There had to be an answer. A simple one. She pointed at the screen. "The code, it must be an encryption."

The text continued to scroll, but the flow was now interrupted with blank lines followed by flashing command prompts, indicating that the computer was processing something. In the flight deck feed, Redway had now moved to the opposite wall, data pad dangling from his hand as he seemed to consult a readout, tapping buttons and flicking switches periodically, following some sequence just as mysterious as his coding.

Deacon returned to the others, and together they watched Redway in silence for another few moments. Liv knew the others were waiting for her to do . . . something. Choose an option. Come to a decision.

Lead the fucking team.

The other display above Mirai's station flashed as the main panel filled with text by itself and began to scroll, too fast now to even see individual lines, the whole thing now just a blur of green and blue and white scrawls. The mainframe had finished compiling Redway's new master program, and was now running it.

Liv took a breath. She banished the doubts from her mind, and to her surprise, this seemed to work, and she felt better—not in control of the situation, far from it in fact, but now that the surprise at Redway's actions had faded, she felt ready to deal with it. She looked down at Mirai's station, cursing to herself that she wasn't more familiar with how Data Monitoring operated. "We can't actually *do* anything from here, can we? We can't access any of the mainframe systems?" she asked.

Mirai shook her head, snatching her hand back from the paperweight like she hadn't realized she'd even been touching it. "Not directly. We can observe and record, but that's it. Data Monitoring is isolated from the ship itself by design."

"Okay." Liv touched her earpiece. "Avery, you listening?"

"I am," came Avery's voice, tight with nerves. "But I don't like anything of what I'm hearing and—"

Liv shook her head as she cut off the engineer in mid-flow. "Avery, listen. I'm sending Astrid back down. Stand by." With the comms channel still open, she turned to Astrid. "Is there any way to access or override the ship mainframe from Engineering?"

Before Astrid could answer, Avery jumped in. "Oh, well, now, actually that's a good point. A very, very good point." There was a pause, and Liv could see Avery in her mind, adjusting his glasses as he gathered his thoughts for his next breathless run of speech. "Engineering uses the XK72 mainframe, of course, like the rest of the ship, because it's designed as a fully parallel multiuser system. I mean, except for Data Monitoring, but that's a whole other story, as we've just established."

"And?" Liv prompted.

"And there are a lot of firewalls between us and the flight computers," said Avery.

At this, Astrid nodded. "We might be using the same physical hardware," she said, "but our control interfaces are completely separated. Again, by design."

Liv gave a tight grimace. "So the answer is no?"

"Ah, dah, dah, dah, dah, dah," said Avery's voice, "I didn't say that. I do actually have an idea, now that you mention it, and it might work, and it might also take a lot of time."

"Good enough for me," said Liv. She nodded at Astrid. "Go."

Astrid turned and jogged for the ladder. Liv turned back to the console, and to Mirai and Deacon who were watching her. "Okay, Astrid's on her way. What about the flight deck hatchway? Can you just access basics and open the door?"

"Well, again, the official answer is *possibly-maybe*, the unofficial Avery Cormack answer is *yes, but*. Different system but same firewalls and same problems."

Deacon hissed between his teeth. "So we have no override and no contingency?" He shook his head at Liv. "All it takes is one crewmember to lock a door and that's it, we're screwed?" He barked a laugh. "Isn't that just peachy?"

Liv turned back to the screens. Redway was studying a readout, both hands by his side, his task apparently complete.

And just what the hell *was* that task . . . and who gave it to him?

That was when the comms chimed in her ear again. She touched the control. "Avery?"

"It's Astrid," came the senior engineer's clipped tones. "Something's happening," she said.

"Where are you?"

"Back in Engineering. But we have an anomalous charge in the power combs. They're charging, safety parameter exceeded."

Mirai's eyes widened. "He's going to try the Drop again?"

"He can't be," said Liv. The combs—144 fan-like structures that studded the hull of the XK72—were an integral part of the ship's experimental engine, the equivalent of the thrusters on their conventional ion drive. On a ship that was designed to dive *through* the fabric of time and space, it was the combs that provided this transdimensional motive power.

And even as Liv uttered her words, she knew that Mirai was actually right. The comb array had one function, and one function only, and if they were being recharged, it was because they were going to Drop.

On the screen, Redway was now consulting something on his data pad. He moved to another wall panel and began typing a sequence into a recessed keyboard—Liv recognized it as the ship's modular architecture controls . . . a system which had nothing to do with the Drop.

"Ah, no, okay, this is . . . well, this is *different*, isn't it?" came Avery's voice, interrupting Liv's train of thought. "The, ah, test protocol specifies ninety-eight percent charge across the comb array. That's the maximum efficiency the system is capable of."

Astrid cut in. "Combs now at two hundred percent, and rising."

Liv blinked.

"Doesn't sound good," said Deacon.

Liv looked at him, but her gaze was unfocused as she ran options through her head. Mirai shifted a little on her seat. For the second time in just a few minutes, all of the crew was silent as they wanted for their mission lead to lead the mission.

But now, their options were limited and her decision was an easy one.

"We're taking the flight deck," Liv said. At this, Deacon nodded, his expression firm. Liv touched her earpiece. "Avery, keep working on those firewalls. Astrid, try and override the SLIP drive and take control. Deacon and I will take care of Colonel Redway."

"Acknowledged," said Avery. "But, ah, maybe you know this—I mean, I *know* you know this—but the flight deck bulkhead is blast certified. How do you plan on getting through?"

Liv glanced at Deacon. "We'll use the servodrone."

The big man nodded. "On it," he said, heading to the ladder.

"I don't know if we'll even have time for that," said Mirai. She pointed at another display, which showed a data feed she'd brought up from Engineering. "The combs are closing in on two hundred and fifty percent charge. I don't know how much longer it will be before they blow and take the SLIP drive with it."

"Astrid," said Liv, "what's your read?"

"She's right," said the engineer, the sound of fast typing coming over the comms along with her voice. "It looks like Colonel Redway has initiated some kind of runaway reaction."

"Can you shut it down?"

"Working on it."

Avery cut in. "Combs at three hundred percent and rising."

Liv swore under her breath. "Deak, what's your ETA on the drone?"

"We're not gonna make it," he said. "This stupid thing can't just be started up. Requires too much prep."

"How long?"

Deacon gave a response, but Liv lost his words underneath the sound of the ship's alarm. It might have been at a far lower volume than before, but it was unpleasant and penetrating.

"What's happening?" asked Mirai, like she expected Liv to know.

Liv cycled her comms. "Avery? Astrid?" she asked.

Avery answered. "Ah, okay, we have SLIP drive ignition. Countdown is live, thirty seconds."

"Dammit," said Liv. She raised her voice over the alarm. "Deak, get that servodrone running, now! Engineering, shut the SLIP drive down!"

"We're trying," came Astrid. "Negative response so far."

"Twenty seconds," said Avery.

Liv squeezed the top of Mirai's seat. "Is there any other way to open the bulkhead door?"

Mirai tapped at her keyboard. "Short the wall panel?" she said, pointing to her screen, which now showed a circuit schematic of the flight deck bulkhead door controls. Liv glanced over the image. She was familiar enough with the general systems of the XK72, but getting down to this kind of granular detail was more Deacon's department. Still, she could work out the control circuitry, and could see the point Mirai was indicating.

"It'll either open the door or jam it. I don't know the odds but—"

"I'll take them," said Liv. She ran for the ladder.

"Wait, you'll need tools!" Mirai jumped out of her seat and bent down to pull open a drawer underneath her console and grab a soft plastic wrap of tools. Then she headed for the ladder as Liv's booted feet disappeared through the ceiling hatch.

"Ten seconds."

In the main passage, Liv ran for the door, Mirai close behind. The two lights on the door control panel burned a steady red, locked.

There was no time. Liv knew that, but she was going to try anyway. Stopping by the door, she looked down at the control panel and reached out a hand behind her without looking, expecting Mirai to pass her the correct tool.

That was when the artificial gravity failed. Redway must have patched into a monitor and seen them, figured out what they were trying to do, and had turned the gravity off to make it as hard as possible for them, even as the final few seconds ran out.

At least . . . that's what it *felt* like. But as Liv's feet left the floor and Mirai's offered magnowrench floated just out of reach, the whole ship seemed to flip around its horizontal axis. Liv found herself still suspended in midair, but now the ceiling she was drifting toward appeared to be the floor. It didn't make any sense, but the sensation was overwhelming—things were the wrong way around, back-to-front, the XK72 now a reflected mirror world that looked and felt *wrong*. She kicked off from the wall—or was it the ceiling?—and spun around, just as her vision seemed to double, two different impressions of the passageway separating momentarily, then snapping back into place.

And then they were falling. Liv and Mirai both yelled in surprise as they were slammed into the floor, the sudden wild increase in g-force crushing their bodies against the metal grilling.

Liv tried to lift herself up, but the weight on her was total, absolute. Sprawled on the deck, she could feel every contact point on her body, the pressure and the pain growing. She tried to speak. To yell. Something. *Anything*. But it was no use. Her cheek was squeezed against rough metal. She felt a tooth slice into her tongue and her mouth was filled with the taste of pennies. Her vision curled at the edges, a creeping blackness tinged with sparks. As she struggled to focus, the double vision returned, and as she looked up, she saw Astrid running down the passageway toward them, but only in one shimmering image of the ship—the other shadowed impression of the passageway entirely empty and spinning in Liv's mind.

The fall accelerated, the XK72 and everything in it plummeting so fast the pressure finally pushed Liv's consciousness out of her body entirely.

7

CAN'T HELP YOU IF YOU PULL THAT TRIGGER

There was noise from somewhere, the sound muffled and distant, like rocks banging together underwater, and the black oblivion lifted itself from Liv's mind like a sheet being swept off old furloughed equipment back at the Artemis labs.

Everything hurt, and when she tried to move it just hurt some more, so she stopped that course of action and tried to think of another one. Lying perfectly still and breathing seemed to be a good option, so she gave it her all.

But pain was . . . good. Well, this kind of pain, anyway. It was bad and even her chest ached as she breathed, in, out, in, out, but already it was fading, to be replaced by the threat of nausea somewhere over the horizon.

But she'd take that.

It meant she was still alive.

Liv tried to move again. Her muscles obeyed, although she felt like she was made of the same heavy ceramic plating as the XK72, and the orchestra of pain that rose as she tried to get into a more upright position threatened to send her crashing into the black again. So she stopped, halfway done, and let herself sink back down again, her eyes still closed, and she breathed and breathed again. After a moment the pain and the nausea subsided, and she opened her eyes.

She was in the flight deck—had they forced the door after all?—lying awkwardly on her side. She made another attempt to sit upright only to find her arms wouldn't move how she wanted them to. Slumping against the floor, she pulled at her wrists, but they were locked together, her fingers dancing with pins and needles.

The realization that she was bound with plastic zip ties, normally used for packing equipment but now far too tight around her wrists, almost cutting off the circulation, woke her fully.

Liv jerked her head around, but the sudden pulse of adrenaline made her head throb like nothing else, the pain almost wiping her out again. She let herself lie against the floor and the thudding inside her skull abated. Clarity returned, and decided instead to stay where she was and focus on what was in front of her instead.

It was a pair of boots. She followed them up, as far as she could, but from her position could only see up to the man's chest. She saw the golden bow and arrow of the Artemis corporate logo against the dark green T-shirt, and a hand holding a gun. The gun was pointed at her.

She slumped again, and wondered just how Colonel Redway had managed to get a weapon onboard.

Just add that question to the list.

Cheek against the decking, she blinked, and then saw she wasn't the only prisoner. All the others were sitting on the floor, wrists hidden behind their backs. Deacon, Mirai, Avery. They were upright and alive and all of them were looking at her.

All? No . . . not all of them. Liv ran the list of names through her head. Titus Deacon, Mirai Ikeda, Avery Cormack. Herself. Colonel Josef Redway. That was five. One left. Astrid, that was it.

Astrid Healey was missing.

What the hell had happened?

With a grunt, Liv finally forced herself upright, pushing against the wall with her shoulder. When she was in a sitting position, she glanced along the row of prisoners beside her, but they were all quiet. Looking up, she watched as Redway stood over them all, his gun arm outstretched, the weapon tracking over them, side to side, side to side.

Liv licked her lips, and tasted blood. But she wasn't the only one sporting injuries. Redway himself had a wide gash on his forehead that looked pretty deep, the blood shiny and dark and sticky, running all the way down and soaking the shoulder of his shirt.

"Josef, what the—"

"Shut up!" Redway snapped the gun in her direction. His voice was high and tight, and she could see the tendons in his neck sticking out like steel cable as he clenched his jaw, his eyes wide. This was a far cry from his calm, almost glacial composure from earlier. For such a highly experienced military test pilot to be in such a mess . . . ?

Liv felt the nausea return.

Oh, they were in trouble, all right.

"Hey, Colonel, turn it down a degree or two, okay?"

Liv looked across at Deacon. The big man was sitting cross-legged, slightly out from the wall, his bound hands curled into fists in the small of his back. Deacon nodded his head at the others.

"You've got us covered, right? You're in charge. You the boss, boss. Okay? So just keep it together and tell us what you want us to do, okay?"

Liv watched as Redway moved over to Deacon, dropping down on his haunches so he was at eye level with the auxiliary specialist. Redway lifted the gun, a small, pale gray, blocky pistol—ceramic, 3D-printed, thought Liv, the individual tiny components easily smuggled into the ship without risk of detection and hidden—and pressed the barrel into Deacon's forehead. Deacon didn't flinch; if anything, he lifted his head a little higher, and kept looking Redway right in the eye.

"What I want you to do?" asked Redway.

"Yeah, that's right," said Deacon. "I'm thinking you need us or else we'd be dead, right? Because you're military. So was I. I know how this goes. You must have gone to a lot of trouble to get that gun in here which means you need it for a reason, right? Which means you've got something to do, and there was more than a fair chance there was something you needed *us* to do as well. Right? Something that might have needed a little persuasion."

Liv focused on the gun. They were in danger. Real physical danger. She felt cold suddenly, a solid block of ice materializing in her stomach. Then she pushed herself sideways, away from the others, as she coughed up a hot, sour liquid onto the hard metal flight deck floor. It spattered and she felt some of the drops splash back onto her face.

Clearing her throat, she sat upright and turned away from the mess. She closed her eyes, and took a breath.

"What happened?" she asked.

"*He's* what happened!"

Liv opened her eyes at Avery's outburst, and saw the engineer nodding his head toward the colonel, who was still crouched next to Deacon. Redway slowly rose, took one step over to Avery, then lowered himself in front of him. He smiled, then hit Avery across the temple with his gun. Avery cried out in pain and fear and tried to shrink back against the wall, but Redway just stood and went over to the doorway, apparently satisfied that discipline had been restored.

Liv watched Redway for a moment. The colonel leaned out in the main passageway and glanced around, like he was looking for something.

Maybe something like—

"Where's Astrid?" she asked.

"That's what I want to know," said Redway, not turning around.

Liv glanced at the others, but only Deacon seemed to be paying attention. Avery had his eyes closed, his chin dipped against his chest. Mirai, likewise, had her head inclined toward the floor. Her long black hair was loose. Liv couldn't see her face.

Liv looked back at Redway. "What do you mean?"

Redway turned. He seemed to have given up on the gun as a means of intimidation, and now used it instead to gesture in the air, punctuating his words.

"You know," he said, a wry grin appearing on his face. "This is all your fault."

Liv paused, then asked: "*My* fault?"

"Sure. Your fault." Redway pointed with the gun at Mirai. "*Her* fault." At Deacon. "*His* fault." At Avery. "*His* fault." Then back to Liv. "*Your* fault."

"I don't know what you mean." That much was true, but Liv didn't say any more. Whatever had happened, Redway had clearly been unbalanced by it, and she wasn't sure she would get anything useful out of him, nor did she want to provoke him any further. She decided to go with it—as Deacon had suggested, they all needed to *keep it together.*

Redway crossed the flight deck to Liv and put the gun in her face. With the other hand he grabbed the neck of her T-shirt and twisted it in his fist before pulling her up off the floor, dragging her face close to his.

Liv looked into his eyes. The lights of the flight deck consoles seemed to flash in their depths.

No, he wasn't broken. Concussed, quite possibly, given the cut in his forehead. But Liv knew then that his sanity was intact.

Colonel Redway wasn't mad. He was *angry.*

"So where is she?" he asked, his tone now far too calm, too measured. "Where's Astrid? I need her."

"Hey, hasn't it gotten through to you? We don't know where she is."

Redway let go of Liv, letting her crash back onto the decking, and moved over to Deacon. The colonel loomed over his prisoner, so close his boots touched Deacon's legs. Redway had his gun arm locked and the barrel pointing directly at the other man's head.

Deacon looked up at Redway. "Can't help you if you pull that trigger."

"Deak, wait!" Seated next to him, Avery jumped like he'd touched a live power outlet. He looked up at Redway, the blood from being hit by the colonel's gun spattered on one cracked lens of his glasses. "Look, ah, *sir*, what is it that you want from us, exactly?" he asked quickly, his words tumbling over each other. He stopped here and his shoulders moved, like he was trying to raise an arm to adjust his glasses like he always did, the habit nothing more than an automatic reflex now. Avery must have realized this as he did it, the way his shoulder slumped and he sighed, just a little, his hands well and truly bound behind his back.

"Look, look, look," he continued, now addressing the floor. "We have no clue what's going on, no clue at all. We don't know what you did, or what orders you were following, or who gave you those orders. And we have no idea where Astrid is, because she's clearly not here and I'm sure we'd all like to know where she is just as much as you do." He met Redway's gaze. "But like Deak said, you're in charge and you've got the gun and you call the, ah . . . well, the shots." He cleared his throat and glanced sideways at Liv. "Uh, sorry, bad choice of words, there."

Redway kept the gun aimed at Deacon, but he was staring down at Avery. He raised an eyebrow. "You finished?"

Avery cleared his throat again. "Sorry, sorry, sorry. Look, just tell us what you want and we'll try and help you. All of us."

"What I *want* is Astrid Healey," he said.

Avery shrugged as best he could with his hands bound. "Yes, but she's not here, and I am. You want an engineer? You've got an engineer. Astrid and I are both certified, Artemis first class. So you're all good. What do you need me to do?"

Redway kept his gaze locked on Avery for a moment, but Liv could see something else flicker across his face: a question, a small moment of confusion. Avery saw it too.

"What is it?" he asked.

Redway shook his head. "I don't need an engineer."

Avery blinked behind his glasses. He wrinkled his nose, clearly desperate to make an adjustment he couldn't with his hands behind his back.

"Ah, okay, so—"

"I need Astrid."

Avery immediately shot Liv a glance, his eyes wide, his lips moving to form a question Liv was already thinking. "Okay, okay, so, ah, not sure we're on the same page here," he said, looking back at the colonel. "I mean, I'm sure I'm not as good as Astrid is—"

"That is correct—"

"But I'm not half bad either!" Avery interrupted, the engineer almost bouncing on the floor in frustration.

At this, Redway paused, like he was considering Avery's words, before he turned away. "The only person I need," he said, "is Astrid." Redway looked around the flight deck like Astrid might have been hiding in there rather than the passageway outside. Liv could see his breath quickening, the pulse in his neck becoming more pronounced. His skin was slick with a dirty mix of sweat and blood.

"Maybe I'm not asking the right question," he said, still looking around, his gun arm following his gaze. He walked a small circle in front of his prisoners, peering around the walls of the flight deck. Finally he stopped and took aim again at Avery. "Where is Astrid *hiding*?"

Avery shook his head, his mouth working in silent desperation. Redway winced, like he'd just bitten down on a bad tooth, then took a step sideways to stand in front of Mirai. "Hey," said Redway. He used the barrel of the gun to part her hair, causing the young woman to flinch and jerk away, banging her back against the wall. She looked up at Redway, tears in her eyes.

"Where is she?" Redway adjusted his grip on the gun and pointed it at the center of Mirai's forehead, then turned to look at Liv. "If you don't tell me where Astrid is, I'll kill this one."

Mirai started softly sobbing. Beside her, Avery shook his head and looked at the floor. Next to Avery, Deacon was staring at Redway, the muscles at the back of his jaw bunched tight.

"The XK72 isn't that big," said Liv, lifting her chin in defiance. "Why don't you go look for her?"

Redway's snake-like grin reappeared. "Wow, and you have a PhD as well? Astrid knows this shitty tin can better than anyone. There must be a hidey-hole somewhere." He waved the gun at Liv. "You can help me find it."

"Maybe she's not here."

Redway flexed his fingers around the grip of his gun, his frustration obvious, as he turned to Deacon.

"You want to elaborate on that, Mr. Auxiliary?"

Now it was Deacon's turn to smile. He gave a half-hearted shrug. "Well she's not here, is she? That's all I know. That's all any of us know. So maybe she's not here anymore. Maybe she was sensible and stepped out of the airlock or something. Your guess is as good as mine."

Redway's mouth twitched, like the blow to his head really was clouding his perception, like he couldn't quite process what Deacon was suggesting. Frowning, the colonel looked down the line; now out of his line of sight, Deacon waggled his eyebrows at Liv and nodded toward Redway.

Liv got the message. She didn't know what Deacon was planning, but at this point, anything was worth a shot.

As Redway began to turn back around to Deacon, Liv pushed herself to her feet, her stiff leg muscles pinging in protest. "Hey! Josef! Enough of this." She half turned and held out her bound wrists. "Come on. Cut me loose and we can talk."

Redway didn't move.

"None of us want this, and I'm sure that includes you." Liv lifted her wrists higher. "You help us, we help you, and we can all get out of this together, okay?"

Redway looked like he was going to consider it, but as soon as he glanced at his boots, Deacon was on his feet. He rushed Redway from behind, wrapping his huge arms around the colonel's waist and tackling him to the ground. Redway's gun clattered to the floor; Liv ducked down and grabbed it awkwardly with her bound hands behind her back, then turned to see Deacon straddling a face-down Redway, the colonel's arms twisted behind him, his face pressed hard into the floor by the hand on the back of his head. Liv could see the line around Deacon's wrist where the zip tie had cut into his skin before he'd managed to snap it with sheer strength and a healthy dose of willpower.

"Colonel Redway," said Deacon, "I do believe I've just relieved you of duty." He gave Redway's arm a jerk and the colonel hissed in pain.

Avery was already pulling himself to his feet, a wide, toothy grin plastered across his face. "Yes, all right, nice one, nice one," he said, moving over to Liv. He stuck his right leg out at an angle, presenting his hip to her, and nodded down at it. "Ah—multitool. There's a multitool in my pocket."

Liv didn't need any further instruction. While Deacon kept his prisoner incapacitated on the floor, Liv turned her back to Avery and, craning her neck to try to look over her shoulder, fumbled with his pocket, her fingers numb. She hissed in frustration while Avery muttered encouragement, before expelling a loud "Yes!", almost directly into her ear, as she finally got the tool out. She rotated it blindly, almost dropping it, before managing to locate and flip out a pair of pliers. Avery turned and positioned his bound wrists, then gave another excited exclamation as with a sharp *snap* Liv cut through his zip tie. Now freed, Avery took the tool and cut her bonds as well as Mirai's.

"Go get me some more of these," Deacon said, nodding at the cut ends of plastic that Avery was holding. The engineer held them up in his fist, and with his other hand pointed an index finger at Deacon in acknowledgment.

"Yes, yes, yes. I'll go get some more of these," he said, then turned and jogged out of the flight deck. A second later he jogged straight back in. "*Where* do I get them?"

"Storage One," said Deacon. Avery nodded hard enough to make his glasses slide down his nose. With an adjustment, he headed off again, muttering the location to himself over and over like he could possibly forget it.

Mirai stepped up to Liv, massaging her wrists as she looked down at the two men on the floor. She swept her long hair back behind her ears and wiped her face dry. "So what do we do now?"

"We figure out what he did," said Liv. "Once we know that, we can figure out what to do to fix it."

"Fix it?" Redway's eyes rolled as he tried to look up at Liv, his mouth squashed against the floor. "You don't understand, do you? You can't fix it. There's nothing *to* fix. Only Astrid can get us out of this. Without her we're stuck."

"What do you mean, stuck?" asked Mirai.

Redway struggled a little against Deacon. The bigger man relented, moving his hand from Redway's head. He adjusted his grip on Redway's arms and rolled the colonel a little onto his side so he could speak clearly.

Redway spat blood onto the floor. "I mean we're stuck," he said. "Without Astrid, we're never going home."

The others exchanged a glance. Then Liv moved over to the pilot's position. The view out of the flight pod was just empty blackness, but that wasn't necessarily unusual. There was plenty of space that was empty, and many reasons why no stars were visible.

Liv dropped into the seat and started going over the controls. Within a few seconds, she saw that XK72 was operational—mostly. They were still cut off from Artemis Control thanks to the dead antenna, and now it looked like all of the ship's sensor arrays were out. They were *on*, feeding readings to the console, but nothing was registering.

Frowning, Liv punched the readings up into the HUD. She stood from the flight seat and leaned forward to peer at the data.

"That can't be right," said Mirai. She moved over to the flight pod and leaned on the back of the pilot's seat. "The whole sensor array must have been overloaded."

"But they're still working," said Liv. She pointed down at the flight console, where a row of LEDs all showed green. "They're showing input, but . . ." she trailed off as she looked over the console again.

"But there's nothing there?" asked Mirai softly.

Redway laughed. Liv and Mirai turned to look at him. The colonel squirmed in Deacon's grip, and Deacon responded by twisting Redway's arm a little harder, eliciting a gasp from his prisoner.

Avery ran back through the bulkhead door, carrying a small, opaque plastic bag. He came to a halt as he saw the others all staring at him. "Ah, hi." He lifted the bag. "Zip ties. What's going on?"

"Give me a couple," said Deacon.

Avery blinked behind his glasses, one lens cracked, the other still smeared with his own blood. "Oh. Yes, yes. Zip ties, zip ties." He pulled the packet open and extracted two. Leaving Deacon to secure the colonel, Avery joined the two women and looked out through the bubble. "Ah, where are we, exactly?" He waved at the view with one hand, knocking his glasses up his nose with the other. "Should we be able to see something? Where's the earth?"

Liv folded her arms. "Behind us," she said. "Maybe we just got turned over."

"Where are the stars then?" asked Mirai.

Liv and Avery exchanged a look. Then Liv stepped around the flight console, into the gap between the back of the panel and the curved front of the pod. She turned to face the flight deck and looked directly up.

It was black. Just . . . black. No stars, no planets, no light of any kind.

"There's nothing there," she said.

"Are you sure?" Avery joined her in the pod, and looked up, following Liv's gaze. "There must be something there. There has to be."

Redway laughed again. With his hands bound behind his back, he was now standing next to Deacon. Deacon pushed his shoulder, sending the man hopping sideways to regain his balance before he fell onto the deck on one knee and grunted in pain.

"Hey, Colonel Asshole, where are we?" asked Deacon. He stepped in front of Redway and pushed the man's shoulder again. Redway went with the movement, but remained on one knee. "Did we make the Drop or not?"

Redway looked him in the eye. "The Drop?"

"Yes, the Drop," said Deacon.

The corner of Redway's mouth curled up into a grin. As Liv looked at him, she felt that cold hard ball growing once again in her stomach.

"Yes, we made the Drop," said the colonel.

"So where are we?" asked Liv. Despite herself, her voice was small and quiet.

"We aren't anywhere," said Redway. "Oh, we made the Drop. We just didn't come out of it. There's nothing out there. We're stuck. The XK72 is marooned."

HE HADN'T SIGNED UP FOR THIS

Astrid," said Redway. "I wasn't lying. I need her. *We* need her."

The colonel adjusted his position on the floor, where he was sitting cross-legged, his back against the wall, wrists zip-tied behind him. It was just him and Avery now, the engineer tasked to watch the prisoner while the others got Storage 2 ready to use as a makeshift brig.

Avery sighed. He swiveled a little in the pilot's seat, Redway's ceramic pistol resting on his knee but held firmly in his hand. "Yeah, well, there's the rub," he said. He was tired, and still sore, and now in the quiet of the flight deck, both feelings threatened to overwhelm him. Then he took his glasses off—the bloodied lens at least moderately clean now—and screwed his eyes shut, finger and thumb pinching the bridge of his nose.

Screw it. Redway was on the floor and he was tied up. He could hardly do anything. Avery allowed himself to take a moment, because . . .

Because it was getting to be too much. All of it. Everything.

He hadn't signed up for this. He was an engineer—practical, hands-on, *yes,* but that wasn't what he enjoyed. He was a scientist, first and foremost, more at home developing specifications, calculating tolerances and performance parameters, translating theory into practice so ships like the XK72 and all the systems within could be built in the first place. He was smart—hell, he was quite possibly the smartest person on the entire crew, even including his immediate superior, the eminent and mysteriously absent Dr. Astrid Healey—and while he happily spent his days (and often nights) in the Artemis labs, he also knew the value of personal experience, that seeing his work *work,* as it were, provided insight he could never get from just staring at numbers on a screen.

In the end, he didn't even need to ask. He and Astrid were the primary systems engineers on the XK72 project, so taking part in the actual test flight as part of the small crew was a given. Anything went wrong, they both needed to be there, two experts on hand to save the day.

He chuckled to himself at that thought. Oh yes, save the day. He was here to show how smart he was, how incredible his systems engineering was, and now something *had* gone wrong but instead of running diagnostic checks and rebuilding those incredible systems with his own hands, everyone wowing at his expertise, he was holding a gun on their test pilot while the others got a holding cell ready.

This—whatever the hell *this* was, whatever situation they were in, wherever they supposedly were, all courtesy of Colonel Redway—was not supposed to happen.

So no, Avery Cormack had most definitely *not* signed up for this.

His thoughts returned to Astrid. She couldn't have gone, right? She was hiding, somewhere in the ship. As soon as Redway was secure, they'd start searching. Astrid was clearly hiding from the colonel, which meant she knew what was going on, what Redway had done, what had happened to the XK72. And now she was hiding from it all.

Because she knew Redway wanted her.

As Avery watched Redway, Redway grinned, then he began to laugh.

"What's so funny?" Avery asked, slipping his glasses back on and adjusting them, just so.

Redway's laugh died. "You really don't understand, Dr. Cormack. The only way to get out of here is to find Astrid. There is no other option available."

Avery pursed his lips. "I told you, I'm an engineer, just as qualified as Astrid—" *More so,* he thought, *although, okay, she knew the SLIP drive better than he did, given she'd designed the thing.* "So if you just tell me what you want me to do, I can do it."

"And like I told *you,*" said Redway, his volume rising, "I don't need an *engineer.* I need *Astrid.* We'll never get out of here without her."

Avery took his glasses off again, and immediately put them back on, a tic so automatic he didn't even know he was doing it. Redway's insistence that they needed Astrid and Astrid alone troubled him, more than he liked to admit.

Because it meant that Avery didn't know what was going on. This was a situation he couldn't simulate, couldn't diagnose, couldn't debug. It meant that he and Astrid weren't quite the team Avery thought they were, that his colleague and immediate superior not only knew something he didn't, but had deliberately kept it from him.

If Redway was telling the truth, of course. There was no particular reason why he would be lying. But nor, Avery thought, was there any particular reason why he *wouldn't*, given his position.

Avery turned away and looked around the flight deck, at the galaxy of lights that shone from the myriad control panels that covered nearly all of the walls and the angled ceiling panels close to the twin flight positions. "It's, I mean . . . Astrid and I *are* the engineers." He paused, the more he thought about it, the more puzzling Redway's insistence seemed. "There's nothing she can do that I can't. And I mean I don't even know what you think she can do that I can't do, and you don't even know us or the rest of the team that well anyway, so how do you think she can help you?"

Redway just shook his head and closed his eyes and he didn't say any more as Avery finally stopped and caught his breath, realizing that he was off again on one of his tangents. Avery knew he did it—knew that he was *known* for it—but he couldn't help it.

You can't change the color of the sky just because you don't like blue, his mother had told him, time and time again.

Avery forced himself to relax, and sat back in the seat. As he leaned back, he glanced down and noticed that Colonel Redway's data pad was back in its holder, attached to the side of the seat. Avery reached down and slid it out.

"Good luck."

Avery looked up, and saw Redway watching him again.

Gripping the gun between his knees to free both hands, Avery turned the data pad around so he was looking at the screen. He tapped the screen to wake it up; the device was locked, of course, the dialog box that appeared asking for a single passcode. Avery thumbed the screen off and stared at his own dull reflection in the now-dark screen. The data pad was both tantalizing and infuriating. Within this device were all of Redway's secrets—the access codes, the new test protocol, the adjustments to the master flight program. Sure, Liv, Mirai, and Deacon had apparently watched what he'd entered in real time from Data Monitoring, and they could roll back through the data to examine it in more detail, but the others had said the code was encrypted. The data pad would, presumably, contain the original code and protocols Redway had been tasked with entering. Accessing that would make their diagnosis of the problem far easier.

Avery knew the data pad would probably contain other things too.

Maybe . . . maybe Redway wasn't doing this alone. Of course he wasn't. He'd be following secret orders, right? And those secret orders would be on this thing. And the identity, perhaps, of those who had issued the orders in the first place. That was why Redway wasn't cooperating. He was military. He was doing what he was told to do—following orders. He couldn't risk exposing the contents of the data pad to unauthorized eyes.

And, of course, that was why Captain Jackson, their original pilot, had been replaced, right at the last minute. Colonel Redway had been parachuted in for one specific purpose and one specific purpose only.

All of that just made Avery want to crack the login even more.

He glanced at Redway, but the colonel had his eyes closed again, his chin dipped into his chest, apparently content to wait it out.

Avery tore his glasses off and rubbed one eye with a knuckle as he considered. Was he going to do this? *Could* he even pull it off? Would Redway believe him? That was key, wasn't it. If Avery was going to get some answers he had to sell what he was about to do to Redway, and sell it hard.

He took three breaths—short, sharp, hard—and put his glasses back on. He put the data pad on his lap and took the gun from between his knees. He adjusted the grip in his hand, focused on it, told himself it felt good, that he was in charge, that he had all the cards and that he could make Redway do whatever he told him to do.

Avery lifted the colonel's pistol in his hand. He'd never actually handled a gun before. He was a scientist, and while he wasn't entirely comfortable with the need for Artemis to partner with the military establishment, he accepted it, telling himself that without such partnerships and the funding it brought, he wouldn't be able to work at the bleeding edge of space engineering at all. He enjoyed his work. Loved it, even. He owed a lot to Artemis and, he acknowledged, a lot to their partners.

And besides, it wasn't like he had to work side by side with soldiers or even with military scientists, right? Back at base, they let Artemis run the show. Avery had spent several happy years working with Astrid and the others. The work was good. Exciting. They were making breakthroughs. Making history.

And now he found himself holding a gun that one of those military partners had smuggled aboard an experimental vessel on a mission that had gone very, very wrong.

He adjusted his grip. While he wasn't familiar with weapons at all, he knew enough to recognize that this one was strange. The substance of it was smooth ceramic, and it was warm. The design was all angles and edges, the interlocking lines showing how it was assembled from separate component pieces clearly visible. That was how Redway had got it onboard. The pieces of it could have been hidden in plain sight all around the flight deck and none of the others would have even noticed them.

But a gun was a gun was a gun. All you had to do was point and pull the trigger. Avery didn't need to be a soldier to understand that.

So step one, he took a breath and he pointed the gun at Redway and he ignored the way his world went fuzzy at the edges.

Because he had to really, truly *sell it*.

Resisting the urge to clear his throat, to adjust his glasses—damn, that itch on his nose was a good one, all right—Avery ground his molars and got on with it.

"Hey, Colonel."

Redway lifted his head from his chin, and opened his eyes. He looked at Avery, looked at the gun, but didn't say anything.

"Unlock this," said Avery. Keeping the gun as steady as he could in one hand—*why was the thing so damn heavy?*—he lifted the data pad with the other.

Redway didn't answer immediately. Then he said, "You going to shoot me, then?"

Now it was Avery's turn to pause. "I could."

"You could? Or you will?"

The fire Avery had tried to stoke inside himself started to go out as other emotions swam to the surface. The gun felt heavy and alien. He was alone in the flight deck with Colonel Josef Redway, a soldier, a trained killer—

Maybe that was it. Astrid wasn't missing. She was dead. Redway had killed her and then he was going to kill them all. Maybe he already had, with whatever he'd done to the XK72.

Avery's thoughts began to spin, his rational, logical self replaced by a far more basic, far more primal state of fear.

What am I doing what am I doing what am I doing what am I doing?

And . . . what *was* he doing? What *was* the plan, exactly? Get Redway to unlock his data pad, and . . . then what? Delve the secrets? Solve the mystery? Be the hero and impress the others when they got back?

Be the one who got them home?

Was that even possible? What did the data pad matter, anyway, if they needed Astrid to get home and Astrid was gone?

Avery took a deep, shuddering breath. He felt dizzy. He felt sick. He'd made a mistake. He didn't need to do anything but watch the prisoner like Liv had told him and then Redway would be locked away and they'd find Astrid and they'd get the hell out of here. Let Artemis deal with the fallout when they got back home. None of it was his problem. He was just an engineer, this was just a science project, and he knew then that there was no way he could ever fire a gun, and he knew then that Redway was all too aware of that fact.

What am I doing what am I doing what am I doing what am I doing?

"Okay," said Redway.

Avery felt the air leave his lungs. "What?" he gasped.

Redway nodded. "The data pad. I'll unlock it. You're right. Maybe if you knew what was going on, you'd understand why we need to find Astrid." He leaned forward, twisting to show his bound wrists. "You don't even need to cut me loose. I'll unlock it. Bring it over."

Avery stared at the colonel. His glasses began to fog. He ignored it. The gun was still pointed at Redway but it felt like a lead weight, and Avery's aim wavered.

It was a trick.

"Come on," said Redway.

Had to be a trick.

But Avery stood from the seat, keeping the gun up and level, his eyes on Redway. This was a way out. His mistake corrected. Redway would unlock the device willingly and Avery could forget this happened, forget the weight of the gun, the feel of the textured grip as it cut into his sweaty palm, the unpleasant warmth of the ceramic body as it took heat from his own hand and fed it back to him.

Avery moved forward, one foot in front of the other, like he was treading a tightrope. He held the pad out in front of him, but stopped just before he was in reach of Redway.

"What's the passcode?" he asked. In his ears it sounded like someone else speaking.

Redway smiled slightly, and turned his shoulders to lift his arms again. He waggled his fingers. "No code. Biometric login. You'll have to get closer."

Avery didn't move. Redway smiled again, a little wider this time. "I get it. It's a trick, and you don't trust me. But you have the gun. You're in charge now. I just need to get my fingers on the reader, okay?" Then he shuffled around on his behind, until he was facing the wall, away from the engineer. "Look, I can't even see what you're doing. I'll even close my eyes."

Still Avery didn't move. What was Redway doing? Was he going to try something? The others would be back soon. Avery knew he should just wait it out.

Or . . . he should take the opportunity. Maybe Redway was telling the truth. Maybe he needed Avery to see what was on the data pad. Maybe Avery would understand, himself.

Maybe the opportunity would be gone the minute Liv and Mirai and Deacon walked back in.

And Redway was right. Avery had the gun. The colonel couldn't even *see* him, let alone try anything.

Avery knelt down. Redway splayed his fingers enough for Avery to position the data pad in the right place. A moment later there was a soft chime and the pad's screen lit up.

Avery stepped back, and Redway shuffled back around.

"There," said the colonel. "Told you."

Avery walked backward toward the flight seat, eyes scanning the data pad, gun now hanging loosely in his other hand.

The pad's home screen showed the usual mass of icons, but they blurred in his vision as he tried to scan the screen too quickly. He stopped just as the back of his legs touched the seat behind him, and he almost fell back into it.

He turned the screen around to show the colonel. "Okay, now what?"

Redway smiled, and he nodded.

"Second page, second row, third icon. Looks like a bow and arrow."

Avery swiped and found it, the icon a stylized representation of a bow and arrow—the weapon of Artemis, the archer of myth. He touched the icon and the data pad's screen flashed, presenting him with a double-column list of files, the names of which were in some strange symbolic text that they had all seen on the computer screen when Redway had entered his own commands into the ship's mainframe. Avery scrolled down the list with a finger. There were pages and pages of indecipherable file names. Finally, he stopped and shook his head.

"So what is all this? I can't read any of it."

"Keep scrolling. You'll find it."

He kept scrolling. The others would be back soon. Maybe Redway was just playing some crazy game with him—a distraction? A chance to jump Avery when the engineer wasn't looking. Or was Redway trying to buy more time for . . . what?

Avery rubbed his face and he noticed his hand was shaking.

And then he found it. Buried in the hundreds of rows of coded file names, one in English. Avery read out the name and looked up, his eyes wide.

Redway winked. "Bingo." He shuffled on the floor, turning himself around to better face the flight seat and the engineer sitting in it. "But listen, before you open that, I have to ask the question."

Avery's forehead creased in confusion. He took his glasses off and held them in one hand, the data pad in the other. Colonel Redway's fuzzy, distant form moved on the floor again.

"Do you want in?" asked the colonel.

Avery felt that sick feeling returning. Like he wasn't here. Like this was all a bad dream. Like he could just close his eyes and everything would go away.

He tried it, just to be sure, but when he opened them again the flight deck of the XK72 was still all around him, the bound Colonel Josef Redway sitting cross-legged on the floor.

Avery put his glasses back on. Redway's face resolved, and Avery could see the expectant look on his face.

"Yes," said Avery.

Redway relaxed, then he nodded at the data pad, without saying a word.

Avery sat back, lifted the data pad, and opened the file.

And then he began to read.

9

MAYBE THIS ISN'T THE RIGHT THING TO DO

Liv stood back with her hands on her hips and surveyed their handiwork. In front of her, the entire contents of Storage 2 was stacked as neatly as possible in the middle of the passageway. Deacon maneuvered the last equipment crate into position while Mirai stepped in and pulled a soft bag down from where it was about to fall off the top of a pile, instead nestling it safely at the bottom of the heap.

It might have been overkill, clearing out the entire contents of Storage 2 rather than just making enough space for Colonel Redway to be reasonably comfortable, but when Mirai suggested it, neither Liv nor Deacon made any objection. Using the storage module was Deacon's suggestion, the aux specialist pointing out that the hatchway was far heavier—and therefore more secure—than those on the bunk modules, designed as they were to protect against potentially hazardous stowed materials. That said, they didn't want to leave anything in there that Redway might have been able to use to get out and/or use as a weapon. As a result, it had taken them far longer than Liv had expected to empty the module out, but they had also at least showed that Astrid wasn't hiding in there.

So where *was* she hiding? Liv was desperate to find her. She hoped that it would be easy, that they wouldn't have to search at all, that all they had to do was open the ship-wide comms and announce that Redway was safely locked away, and Astrid would reappear from her sanctuary.

But Liv also knew there was a very definite difference between a hope and reality.

"I think that about does it, boss," said Deacon, wiping his forehead with the stretched-out edge of his T-shirt. "Storage Two is ready for our guest."

Liv nodded, and touched her earpiece. "Avery, we're coming back. Has Redway changed his tune yet?"

Her earpiece chimed, but there was no response. Liv tapped it again, cycling the channel to the open comms that all the crew shared, so Deacon and Mirai could listen in.

"Avery, report please."

Nothing. Deacon and Mirai both froze, and looked at Liv.

"What's going on?" asked Mirai.

Liv frowned. "I don't know," she said. "Avery, respond please."

The three of them stood in silence by the pile of equipment. There was still nothing from the engineer.

Deacon clicked his teeth, then tapped his own earpiece. "Avery, this is Deak. Where are you? Come in, please."

Again, no reply. Deacon and Liv exchanged a look. Mirai just shrugged. "Comms failure?"

"Could be," said Liv, unsure of her words even as she spoke them. Already, the worst-case scenario was running through her head—Redway had gotten himself free, and Avery wasn't answering because he *couldn't*. She looked at Deacon; the expression on his face indicated the same thought had crossed his own mind.

And we should have taken the gun, Liv added to herself. *Dammit, we should have taken it.*

Deacon rolled his massive shoulders. "Flight deck, let's go."

He led the way.

The door to the flight deck was open. Deacon disappeared inside, calling Avery's name. Liv paused in the passageway and looked behind her. Mirai had fallen behind, and came jogging toward her. Liv nodded at her; then her heart leaped as someone else appeared behind the flight analyst.

Astrid!

A grin spread over Liv's face. In front of her, Mirai stopped and spun around.

The passageway was empty. Mirai turned back to Liv.

"What's up?"

Liv blinked. She'd seen Astrid, hadn't she? Or . . . someone? But there was nobody else, and even as she thought about it, the memory began to blur. It hadn't been Astrid. It was just a shape, a shadow, a movement. Maybe not even that. It was hard to tell. The passageway was a uniform charcoal gray, and as she looked, shadows seemed to crowd the corners where shadows shouldn't have been.

She was tired.

No, scratch that. She was *exhausted*.

"Nothing," said Liv quickly. Then she turned and almost walked straight into Deacon.

"They're gone," he said. Then he ducked back into the flight deck, Liv and Mirai right behind.

It was empty. No Avery, no Redway. On the floor on one side was a bunch of cut zip ties—Liv counted four, the ones that Redway had used to secure her and the others before. She looked around, but there weren't any more. Did that mean that Redway was still bound?

Mirai moved around her and dropped into the pilot's position. She leaned forward and began typing. Liv and Deacon moved to stand behind her.

Liv scanned the text that was appearing on the forward HUD. Mirai had already patched into the internal cams and was cycling through the different feeds from each part of the XK72. Engineering. Data Monitoring. The main passageway. Storage 2 (empty), Storage 1 (full), the passageway outside filled with gear. While she continued to scan, Deacon sat in the co-pilot's seat and tapped at the main comms panel.

"Avery, come in," he said, his voice now echoing through the ship interior. "Where are you? Where's the colonel?"

Images flashed on the HUD. The bunk cabin. Another passageway. Back to Engineering. Back to Data Monitoring. The ion drive module. There was nothing to see on any feed. No movement, nothing. No sign of Avery or Redway.

"Avery, report, goddammit!" Deacon shook his head, and took his finger off the comms button. "You gotta be kidding me," he said. He gestured at the display. "First Astrid disappears and now Avery and Redway? What the heck is going on?"

Liv continued to watch the feeds. Mirai had switched into one of the XK72's two escape pods now, the small circular chamber bright white in contrast to the dull gunmetal of the XK72, the safety harnesses lining the walls snapped snugly into place, factory-fresh. It was as empty as the rest of the ship proper. Then Mirai switched again, to the second pod.

"There!"

Avery and Redway appeared on the screen, Avery standing close to the camera, obscuring most of the view, with only Redway's leg visible at the side of the picture.

Deacon shook his head. "What the hell are they doing?"

Liv gripped the top of Mirai's flight seat. Whatever was going on, it wasn't good. Deacon punched the comms panel again, switching into the pod's isolated system, and Avery's voice barked from the console speaker.

"Just *nothing*, Colonel!" he yelled, the volume popping the speaker. "You lied to me. You lied to all of us!"

Then he moved away from the camera. He was holding Redway's ceramic gun by the barrel to use it as a club. Both the butt of the weapon, and his hand holding the barrel, were flecked with blood.

Mirai's hand went to her mouth. Deacon sat very still. All Liv could do was squeeze the top of the flight seat in front of her and watch the screen.

Redway was strapped into one of the pod's wall harnesses. He hung limply from the straps, legs outstretched. His face was covered with blood, the gash in his forehead having reopened. Blood also poured from his nose. His T-shirt was soaked. He hung forward a little, his hands clearly still bound behind his back.

"What's he doing?" asked Mirai, quietly. "What is Avery doing?"

Liv tapped her earpiece.

"Avery!" Her voice cracked as she fought to control her growing anger. "What's going on? What are you doing in the escape pod?"

Avery moved back into shot, this time looking directly into the camera. This close, his whole face filled the distorted fish-eye view, his glasses catching a glare from the white interior of the pod, obscuring his eyes.

"I'm getting the answers we need, Liv. The only way a bastard like Redway will understand."

Liv just shook her head. "What are you talking about?"

Deacon rose from the co-pilot's seat. "I'll stop him."

Mirai checked the console. "Starboard pod."

"On it," said Deacon, running from the flight deck.

On the screen, Avery was peering at the camera, tilting his head like he could see through the lens to the flight deck. His eyes were still obscured behind his glasses.

"He lied to us," he said. "They all did."

"Lied about what, Avery?" Liv dropped into the seat vacated by Deacon, her gaze never leaving the screen. "What did Redway say to you?"

Avery grinned. Then he laughed, the sound popping the speaker again. He stepped back from the camera, switched the gun to his other hand, then ran his blood-covered hand through his hair before adjusting his glasses, leaving a dark and sticky residue right across the lens. Sighing, he pulled his glasses off and tried to wipe them on his T-shirt, but to little effect. When he put them back on, one lens was completely smeared. Behind him, Redway slowly lifted his head—he was still conscious, but only just. Liv could see he wouldn't last too long under Avery's attention.

That Avery was even capable of such an act was a shock to her. Liv knew him as a bookish scientist, an academic who tangled his words when he got excited and who had decided to put his knowledge to practical use at Artemis.

But this? He'd snapped. Liv wondered what the hell had happened on the flight deck, wondered why she had decided it was okay to leave him alone with Redway.

"I know the truth, you see," said Avery, moving closer to Redway. He rested the grip of the ceramic gun against Redway's cheek, pushing, forcing the other man to turn his head. "The dear colonel here showed it to me, thought I would understand." Avery laughed. It was unsettling, and not altogether sane. "And wow, did I understand. Wow."

"Avery!" said Liv. "Listen to me. Drop the gun and come out of there. Come on. This is not how we do things. You of all people know that."

"No, it might not be how we do things, but it's how people like *him* do things." He poked Redway with the gun again and his sickly grin returned. "Turns out they don't much like the taste of their own medicine."

Liv stood from the seat and walked a tight circle, her hands clutching her hair. This was insane. How could things have gone so wrong? She glanced toward the bulkhead door, ignoring the way the shadows moved, willing Deacon to get a move on. At the flight controls, Mirai seemed to shrink into her seat, the small woman looking almost childlike as she watched and listened in silence.

"Okay," Liv said, coming back around and gripping the top of the copilot's seat so hard her knuckles went white. Time for a different tack. Distraction. Keep Avery talking. Until Deacon could get there. "What did you see? Avery, what did you see? What did Redway tell you? What did he do to the XK72?"

"Oh, listen, you'll like this," said Avery. "The dear colonel didn't tell me a goddamn thing. I read about it." He ducked down, his body obscuring the camera again. Liv felt her chest grow tight as she waited for whatever the hell he was going to do next, but a second later he moved back around. The gun was still in one hand, but in the other he held a data pad—Redway's.

"It's all in here. Every last bit of it. Orders. Test protocol—the *new* test protocol. All of it."

Liv narrowed her eyes as she tried to take it all in. Avery was talking so fast.

"Avery, come on, slow it down. What's on the data pad? Take me through it."

Avery stepped backward, bumping into Redway's leg and nearly tripping. As he righted himself, he kicked the offending leg, then waved the data pad at the camera.

"I actually think it's better you don't know. Actually, I mean, I really wish I didn't. It's fucked up, is what. It's all fucked up. So I think it's better you don't know. I think it's better nobody does."

"Shit!" Liv thumped the top of the seat. Mirai jumped in fright.

Avery had lost it. Time was running out.

Come on, Deak. Come on.

Right on cue, there was a thumping sound. On the display, Avery jerked his head around, and even the semiconscious Redway rolled his head toward the sound.

"Open the door, Avery!" Deacon's voice was heavily muffled on the feed from the pod, but it echoed clearly down the main comms channel. He thumped again against the closed hatch. "Come on, open it up, let's go!"

With the pod closed, Avery and Redway were completely sealed inside. Liv ran options through her head, but there was really only one. She stood back from the seat and turned around—feeling that, somehow, Avery could see her—and tapped her earpiece, switching it to the private channel between herself and Deacon.

"Use the servodrone," she said. "Cut it open."

The channel pinged in her ear. She heard Deacon let out a breath, perhaps having come to the same conclusion. "On it."

"Make it fast," said Liv.

"You think I can't hear you?"

Liv turned back around. Avery's face was once again filling the entire flight deck HUD. He tapped the camera lens, and the console speakers popped.

Liv sighed. "Just open the door and come out, Avery."

He stepped away from the camera again and looked down at the data pad in his hand. "No, I don't think so," he said. "I'm doing you a favor, trust me." He looked up at the camera. This time, when he smiled, he looked sad.

"Avery, listen to me!"

"Oh, don't get me wrong," he continued. "You'll be stuck here forever. You see, Redway was telling the truth. He needs Astrid. We all need Astrid." He lifted the data pad and waggled it in the air. "She was clever. Thought ahead. A very, very good idea." He grinned, too widely; on the flight deck, Liv could only grimace. "Really messed things up for our dear colonel here," Avery continued, "but there's really no way out without her. So, well, you and Deacon and Mirai will be stuck here forever. You've got life support and rations for a while. I don't know how long—I know it was all in the briefing manual but I never actually read the whole thing. But you'll stay alive awhile." He paused. "Or maybe you'll figure it out, or maybe Astrid will miraculously reappear and everything will be fine, and my noble sacrifice will have been a waste of time." He smiled again. "But I can't take that risk. She was right. Like I said, Astrid's clever. But she didn't do enough. Not nearly enough."

Liv tapped her earpiece again. "Deak, we need that pod opened—now!"

"I didn't finish unpacking the drone earlier," he said. "Still need a few minutes."

Liv was fairly sure that was time they didn't have. She didn't know what Avery was talking about, but she didn't like the sense of finality about it.

"Can you just take out the plasma cutter?"

There was a pause before Deacon answered. "It'll need a cable to run, but . . . yeah, that might work."

"I can still hear you," said Avery. "And I'm afraid I can't let you stop me now." He reached forward, then paused. "Maybe this isn't the right thing to do. Maybe I shouldn't do it." He adjusted his glasses, just so. "Truth is I don't know, truth is I'll never know. But I've made up my mind. No going back now." Another pause. "Good luck. You're going to need it."

The screen went blank. A moment later there was a bass drum thud and a faint, almost imperceptible vibration under Liv's feet, followed by the return of the ship's now muted alarm signal. Mirai sprang back into life, killing the alarm as she scooted forward in her seat and leaned over the console readouts.

"Oh my God," she said.

Liv leaned over her position. "What is it?"

Next to Mirai's hand, a row of four red lights flashed rapidly. She flicked switches, then returned her hands to the small console keyboard and began typing. Up on the HUD, the blank security feed was replaced by a text interface. Liv tried to follow what Mirai was doing, but it was too difficult, the text moving too fast.

"Another fault?"

Mirai stopped typing. She slumped back in her seat as, above the text display, another data readout appeared, a square outlined in green, cross-hatched in faint white, with a numbered axis listed on each side.

From the bottom of the grid, a yellow triangle icon appeared. It moved up, tracing a gentle curve as it headed for the top right corner. The triangle flashed and a small label attached itself to the underside—a string of numbers and letters, some kind of serial number identified by the XK72 mainframe. At the same time, the comms clicked on to an automatic channel, and the flight deck—the entire ship—was filled with a repeated signal designed to be the unique audio signature of the escape pod. Three short beeps, two long beeps, one short beep. A pause. Then again, and again.

Liv knew what she was looking at, knew what she was listening to, but she still asked the question aloud, as though she expected Mirai to give a different answer, her words having the power to change reality itself.

"What happened?"

"He launched the escape pod."

On the screen, the triangular icon approached the edge of the grid. Other lines appeared, the XK72 now locked on and tracking the only other object that apparently existed in the void around them. Liv glanced down at the control consoles, and saw the sensors were indeed working perfectly, all kinds of data now being returned from the rapidly receding escape pod.

And then the icon was gone, with it the audio signature. The tracking data stopped, and the sensors went dark. The escape pod had accelerated beyond their range, taking Avery and Colonel Redway and any hope of answers away from the rest of them. There was no way of chasing after them. When the escape pod's single-fire ion thruster ran out of power, the spherical lifeboat would continue to accelerate away from them, carried by its own momentum. Even if they fired up the XK72's conventional ion drive now, they'd never be able to catch up with it.

Deacon ran back into the flight deck, his skin glistening with sweat, his T-shirt damp with it. He looked at the others, chest heaving as he got his breath back, then turned on the spot and yelled at the ceiling.

Nobody spoke for quite a while after that. It felt like hours, but it was only minutes, the silence between the three remaining crew stretching out. Nobody knew what to say, nobody knew what to do. Liv felt a fatigue, deep, deep in her bones.

And then the knocking began.

10

OR MAYBE IT WAS DELIBERATE

Mirai stood from the pilot's position, and looked up at the ceiling of the flight deck because, Liv realized, that was where the sound seemed to be coming from. She followed Mirai's gaze. The knocking continued.

Deacon spoke first as he too turned his face to the ceiling. "Debris from the escape pod," he said, sounding about as certain as Liv felt. "Thing knocked a plate loose, or there's some insulation foam bouncing around out there."

Liv held her breath, waiting for the sound to repeat, but the flight deck fell silent again. Deacon was probably right, the sound was an aftereffect of the pod's launch—maybe harmless scraps hitting the hull. Maybe the release clamps that had held the pod tight in its socket had been knocked out of alignment as the pod itself blasted away, and were bumping into the hull as they repeatedly closed and opened, closed and opened, as they tried to reseat themselves. Maybe the launch had done some real damage, torn something loose, ripped the plating off the outer hull. Maybe it was just a normal, if unexpected, sound made by the XK72 itself as the ship's mainframe adjusted systems to compensate for the change in mass now that the starboard escape pod was gone.

Or maybe it was—

Knock-knock-knock . . . knock-knock-knock . . .

Or maybe it was deliberate. Intelligent.

And it was coming from *outside* the ship.

"It's Astrid," said Mirai, giving voice to Liv's own thoughts. "She was hiding *outside* all the time." She looked at the others, her expression hopeful, even happy. "We never checked the environment suit lockers. They're in Storage One."

Liv looked at Deacon, and the big man nodded, clicking the fingers of both hands as a grin drew itself across his face. "Yes, *yes*!" He shook his head and barked a laugh. "No wonder we couldn't find her. Nice, Astrid. Nice."

It made sense. Heart fluttering in her chest, Liv found herself smiling too.

They couldn't do anything for Avery and Redway, not now. But they could do something for Astrid. She tapped her earpiece, opening the main channel.

"Astrid, come in, please. We can hear you. Come in, please."

Her earpiece chimed. Liv glanced at the others, and saw they were listening in on their own comms intently.

There was no response. Deacon pursed his lips. "Still a fault?"

"Wouldn't she just use the suit comms?" asked Mirai, but Deacon shook his head.

"Not if it wasn't set up. She would have been in a hurry to get the suit on and get out onto the hull."

"Okay," said Liv. She moved to the flight seats and stood up on the pilot's position, balancing herself against the back of the seat. Stretching up, she was able to reach the bare ceiling panel where the translucent forward bubble met the XK72 main structure. She thumped her fist against it, but she quickly realized it was no good; her attempt hardly made any sound in the flight deck, let alone, she realized, on the outside of the ship. While they could hear Astrid knocking inside, sound couldn't travel in the vacuum of space—or the void outside the ship—so she would have to feel for any vibrations on the hull itself. A moment later Liv realized it was pointless anyway, trying to communicate like this. Redway was gone. Astrid was safe. She could come back in, right now.

"I'll break out another suit and go get her," said Deacon. "She might have seen the escape pod go, but if she's not on the comms she won't know what's going on." He turned to leave the flight deck, but then he stopped, mid-stride, as the knocking came again.

This time the sound didn't come from above them—it was coming from the passageway.

Deacon turned and looked at the others, his eyebrows tightly knitted in confusion. Then he spun back around as the knocking was repeated.

"Astrid?" he called.

Mirai moved past him to the door. "That's coming from *in*side." She leaned out into the passageway, hands on the bulkhead frame.

Knock-knock-knock . . . knock-knock-knock . . .

She pulled herself back in and turned to face the others. "Somewhere at the back."

Deacon's frown deepened as he looked at Liv. "Engineering? She's still down there?"

Mirai shook her head. "We saw Engineering on the surveillance cams. It was empty. There's nowhere for her to hide down there."

Knock-knock-knock . . . knock-knock-knock . . .

"Come on," said Liv. She left the flight deck at a jog, the other two following close behind.

Liv stopped at the end of the main passageway. The knocking hadn't come again. Standing by the hatch leading down to Data Monitoring, she glanced down. For a moment it looked like there was someone moving down there, the adjoining module somehow looking darker than it should have, like the lights had dimmed to minimum. Liv was about to step onto the ladder to check when the knocks came again, sudden and loud, as though Astrid had grown impatient with the others loitering by the hatch.

"Definitely Engineering," said Deacon, glancing down through the hatch. Liv watched him. Had he seen the shadows move too? "Come on."

They headed toward the stern, Deacon now leading the way, Mirai glancing around the walls, up at the ceiling, like she was expecting a panel to pop off and their lost crewmember to suddenly reappear.

Liv pondered on this as they entered the stern of the XK72.

Engineering was the largest section of the ship, and consisted of four individual modules, two large and two small, coming off a central, high-ceilinged hub. The two smaller units, port and starboard, were stores and a workshop. At the very rear were two bulkhead hatches, stacked vertically. The lower hatchway led to the SLIP drive module, the upper, accessed via a ladder, to the conventional ion drive. The lower hatchway was open, the upper closed.

Deacon led the others into the SLIP drive module.

As far as engine rooms went, the SLIP drive module was anything but conventional. The cabin was large and roomy, the five walls of the space matching the pentagonal shape of the SLIP drive itself. Liv regarded the experimental hardware, the damned thing that had gotten them into this mess in the first place. It was a solid, mirror chrome polyhedron, five-sided, occupying the center of the cabin, not connected to anything but the floor. The SLIP drive's top side was angled, each side rising up then forming a small flat top; above, the ceiling panels of the five-sided room matched the angles and themselves came to a central point above the center of the cabin. The prototype engine itself—if it could really be called an engine—was a sealed unit, with no visible joins on its metallic surface. The reason for this was simple, standard operating procedure for an Artemis test flight where the primary experimental unit—in this case, the ship's motive unit—had been designed by the company but actually fabricated by their military colleagues, who were able to draw on a greater pool of funding without the need for profit, the arrangement allowing Artemis to focus elsewhere on the project. Any experimental unit, or even a smaller part of a larger machine, was designed to be tamper-proof, allowing full, unadulterated analysis of its components and their performance once it was off-loaded after the mission back at the controlled Artemis labs and shipped back to the manufacturer for full breakdown and assessment.

The SLIP drive module was silent, save for the regular hum of the dormant ion drive above their heads. Liv, Deacon, and Mirai each moved into the cabin, stepping slowly around the SLIP drive, each of them keeping their distance for no apparent reason that Liv could think of.

But they all did it just the same.

The cabin was empty. Astrid was not here.

There were more standard control consoles around the walls. Mirai headed for one station and woke the system, then began tapping at the keyboard to start a series of system checks. Deacon, meanwhile, completed a circuit around the SLIP drive, his gaze crawling the walls and the ceiling, before he rejoined Liv's side.

"Well, she isn't here."

"Check the ion drive module."

"On it." Deacon left, and moments later Liv could hear his boots thudding on first the access ladder, and then the floor of the module directly above.

Liv moved over to where Mirai was working at the console. The other woman looked up.

"All Engineering systems are at status green," she said. Then she turned and jutted her chin at the shining object in the middle of the room. "Except the SLIP drive. There's no reading from it at all."

Live turned and looked down at the mirrored surface of the drive. "It's off? Or completely dead?"

Mirai shrugged. "That's just it, I don't know." She turned back to the console. "There are no readings from it at all. It's like it's not even connected." She raised both hands away from the keyboard in apparent defeat. "I guess this is why the colonel said he needed Astrid."

Deacon rejoined them. Liv didn't need to ask the obvious question as he shook his head and moved to Mirai's console. He looked down at the controls and rubbed his chin in thought. "Maybe Astrid did this. She . . . I dunno, did something to it."

"Sabotage?" asked Liv.

Deacon shrugged. "Sure. She sees what Redway's doing, she disconnects it so he can't use it, then she goes and hides."

Liv grimaced. He might have been right. What they needed was to find Astrid, and ask the engineer herself, and—

Knock-knock-knock . . .

There it was—as loud as anything, the heavy, hard thudding coming from directly opposite the trio at the console. The three of them turned to look. Liv scanned the room, but they were alone. Then she scanned the wall, her eyes tracing the lines of the panels that formed the entire interior structure of the XK72.

The *removable* panels.

Knock-knock-knock . . .

Before she could say anything, Deacon sprang into action. Moving across the room, he stopped at another console and opened the equipment cabinet on the wall next to it. After pulling out a large magnowrench, he then moved around to the other side of the SLIP drive and looked up at where the angled ceiling panels met the wall.

Knock-knock-knock . . .

He spun around to look at the others. Liv nodded at him and gestured at the wall.

"She's hiding in the superstructure."

"Hot damn," said Deacon. He turned back to the wall and thumped it heavily with the tool. The sound it made was not entirely dissimilar to the sound Astrid was making from the other side.

But now there was no response. Deacon looked at Liv. Liv looked at Mirai. The three of them didn't move. Liv felt herself holding her breath.

And then—

Knock-knock-knock . . .

Liv pointed at the wall. "Get her out of there!"

11

THE PERFECT PLACE TO HIDE

Liv ran her fingers through her hair and exhaled, long and slow. Her arms ached. She was hungry. She had a headache. She felt . . . empty, like she didn't have the bandwidth for anything anymore. She knew what this feeling was, and she knew how important it was for her to hold it together—not just for herself, but for the others, who were depending on her just as she was depending on them.

But for a moment—just a moment—she allowed herself to surrender to it.

She felt hopeless. They had not found Astrid, they did not know what had happened to the XK72, and it was *hopeless*.

It had taken ten full minutes to get the first wall panel off; the next four had come down more quickly. The XK72 may have been an experimental craft, but—unusual configuration of the SLIP drive module interior aside—it was built to Artemis standard, the whole vehicle modular, designed for easy maintenance and easy adaptation to a variety of missions and payloads. The internal walls, ceiling, floor were simple panels, each held in place by four magnetic bolts. Easy on, easy off, allowing infinite reconfiguration, customization. Behind the panels was a maintenance space, an envelope that surrounded the entire ship and linked each module with one continuous crawlspace.

The perfect place to hide, to lay low, to wait your chance.

That was the theory, anyway. Removing the bolts was supposed to be a straightforward task, but even using the proper tool, Deacon had found them stubbornly tight, and the plates themselves—fabricated out of a metal-ceramic alloy, like just about everything Artemis made—were actually damned heavy. After Deacon's struggle with the first panel, Liv began to have doubts that Astrid was hiding in the crawlspace. Although the engineer was older than Liv, she was far more athletic, certainly much stronger. However, Astrid was still half Deacon's size, and if he found it difficult, what chance did she have of not only taking a panel off to hide, but fixing it *back* in place afterward?

It seemed impossible, unless there was another way in, perhaps an easier access point only the engineer knew, one behind a console or even inside the back of a storage locker.

If she was even in there. Because together they'd taken off five panels, right where the knocking sound had come from, to reveal . . . nothing.

The crawlspace behind the wall was deep—Liv knew the XK72 inside out and back to front, but even she was surprised at how the gap of nearly two meters that stretched from the inner skeletal framework to the ship's outer hull felt so big. The darkness in the crawlspace didn't help with that feeling—the outer wall was covered with a hard, matte black insulation foam that completely absorbed light. Even the flashlight that Mirai had retrieved from an equipment locker to help illuminate the crawlspace didn't seem to do much. Liv had taken it from her and leaned into the gap, turning the light both forward and aft, but could see nothing but a black void in both directions; even knowing the crawlspace curved away at the rear of the ship almost immediately, Liv had been unable to see anything at all.

For a moment, as she shone the light up, it looked like there was someone crouched just above her, clinging onto the internal wall frame like a bat before darting quickly out of her beam, but it was nothing, just the angles of the shadows changing as Liv played the light around, her growing fatigue playing tricks on her.

The crawlspace, at least around the Engineering module, seemed to be empty. Astrid was most certainly not hiding *here*.

Deacon completed another circuit of the module, his fifth in as many minutes. He was staring at the floor, his hands interlocked behind his head as he paced. Liv watched him, losing herself in his constant motion, a welcome distraction from that feeling of helplessness that now, as mission lead, she tucked away in the back of her mind. Oh, she'd return to it later—that was the one thing she *did* know as a fact—but for now those emotions could sleep.

They had work to do.

Liv just wasn't entirely sure yet just what that work was.

She blinked, and found Deacon was now standing in front of her, hands on his hips. She glanced over at Mirai and saw she was watching her too.

Liv rubbed her temples, unaware of how long she had zoned out, lost in her thoughts.

"Been quiet awhile now," said Deacon, and Liv realized he was right. The knocking hadn't sounded again, not since they'd removed the panels. She nodded, but didn't say anything.

"Y'know," said Deacon, "something else comes to mind."

Liv frowned. "What do you mean?"

"I mean Avery."

At the mention of the name, Mirai almost jumped. She folded her arms tightly and looked at Deacon. "What about him?"

Liv watched as Deacon grimaced, running his tongue over his front teeth as he considered what to say. But instead of replying to Mirai, he looked at Liv again.

"Maybe it wasn't Astrid," he said. "Maybe she didn't do this. Maybe it was Avery?"

On the other side of the room, Mirai's eyes went wide. "Avery was out of his mind, you saw what he did to Colonel Redway," she said, quietly. "He was an engineer. He knew as much about the XK72 as Astrid. He could have sabotaged the mission just as easily as her." A pause. "He could have killed her."

Deacon nodded. "Killed her and dumped her body in the crawlspace?" He glanced at Liv. "Those two were alone down here."

"What about the knocking?" asked Liv. "I'll buy the fact that Avery . . . that something happened to Avery. But he seemed fine, right up until we left him to watch Redway. Now we're saying he killed Astrid, hid her body, and managed to keep it together until whatever Redway showed him finally made him lose control?"

Deacon shrugged. "He was in control until he wasn't."

"So like Liv said, who's knocking?" asked Mirai.

"Maybe he didn't kill her," said Deacon. "Maybe he just knocked her out, thought she was dead, hid her body. Now she's awake and knocking."

Mirai stood and moved to the open panels. She leaned in, looking around the crawlspace. "So why isn't she knocking now? With all the noise we were making, surely she could work out we were down here and come to us."

Deacon shrugged again. "Okay, so she was knocking and now she isn't. She could be injured. We all blacked out. Hell, I don't remember a thing about what happened. So she woke up and she knocked, and now she's out again. Hold on. Mirai, gimme that flashlight."

Mirai reached down and picked up the flashlight from where she had left it on the floor, and handed it over. Deacon took it with thanks and, stepping past Mirai, leaned into the crawlspace. He flicked the flashlight on, and shone it first one way, then the other. Liv saw him pull a face, and he turned the light off and turned back to the others.

"Well the flashlight doesn't make a lick of difference," he said, "it's damn dark in there. But listen, the crawlspace extends around the whole ship, right? Links all the separate modules of the XK72. I don't think Astrid got into it from here. She couldn't have." Deacon knocked the toe of his boot against one of the heavy wall panels that was now leaning against part of the exposed inner frame. "She can't have got these on and off by herself. There must be another access in another part of the ship."

"But the sound," said Mirai. "It was definitely coming from here."

"Not necessarily," said Liv, picking up Deacon's train of thought. "The sound could travel around the crawlspace from somewhere else."

Liv walked up to the gap in the wall and, holding her breath—as irrational as it was, she allowed herself another of those moments now, although it seemed to make her headache worse—put one foot beyond the bounds of the inner wall. Leaning into the space beyond, she turned and looked back at the other side of the module's hull.

"Deak, grab that magnowrench and try hitting here," she said, indicating the back surface of a nearby wall panel that was still firmly in place.

Liv stepped away. Deacon passed the flashlight back to Mirai, then picked up the tool from the nearby console and got into position in the crawlspace itself. Once he was sure of his footing, he swung the wrench. The impact was strong, the resulting sound a dull, metallic thud, even louder than Liv had anticipated. Deacon's hit was so hard the wrench in his hand bounced off the wall panel, sending him stumbling against the outer hull. He swore, but Liv waved him to be quiet as she listened to the continuing reverberation as it echoed from farther along the interior of the crawlspace.

She nodded, mostly to herself.

"That's quite an echo," said Mirai.

"Right." Liv poked her head back into the crawlspace. "The whole thing is a sound box. Astrid could be anywhere."

"Ugh!" Deacon spluttered, wiping a coating of black dust from his face

as he pushed himself off the outer wall of the crawlspace. As he stepped out of the gap, he turned and looked back at his handiwork. "Must have torn the insulation," he said.

Liv felt Mirai tense beside her. She glanced at her colleague, then followed her gaze as she looked back into the crawlspace.

"What is that?"

Liv frowned; then Mirai lifted her flashlight and pointed it back into the void. As she moved the light, Liv saw it. A glint, sharp and brilliant, like a star suddenly appearing in a night sky.

Deacon's wrench had chipped a triangular shard out of the insulation foam, revealing the outer hull wall behind. Surrounded by the infinitely black foam, the exposed patch shone as bright as Mirai's flashlight.

"The hell did you build this ship out of?" asked Deacon, his hands on his hips. He looked at Liv. "Is it supposed to look like that?"

Liv took the flashlight from Mirai, and, moving the beam around, examined the section of hull. She shook her head.

No, she thought. *It sure isn't supposed to look like that.*

The exposed wall was crystalline, brilliant and multifaceted. Although only a patch the size of her hand was visible, it seemed to amplify the flashlight beam, shining the light back at her with a high intensity. As Liv moved the beam, the light changed, and the exposed wall threw a multicolored prism back out into the cabin.

"I've never seen anything like it," Mirai said quietly. She moved past Liv and stepped right into the crawlspace, where she reached up and touched the exposed section, running her slender fingers over the jewel-like surface. "It feels . . . ceramic? Or like glass," she said, then she shook her head. "It's not standard material."

"Of course," said Deacon, chuckling. "Artemis makes a ship out of diamond and then they classify it in case someone important finds the bill."

The two women turned to stare at him.

"You two really are newbies," he said. "I've been on lots of missions, for Artemis and for others. This isn't the first time things are not quite what the spec sheet says." Deacon shrugged. "Look, in my experience, there are three reasons why companies lie." At this, he held out his hand, uncurling a finger to highlight each point. "To hide expenses from their investors, to hide risk from expendable employees, or to hide illegal actions by or from their partners." He paused, and uncurled a fourth finger. "Or by or from Artemis itself."

At this, Mirai spun around, her eyes wide. "Expendable employees?"

Deacon paused. Liv could almost see the thought process on his face as the aux specialist tried to figure out a way of walking back on what he'd just said. But he was taking too long. As Mirai stepped out of the crawlspace, her gaze darted between Deacon and Liv. Liv held up a hand.

"Let's not get carried away," she said, directing her comment at Mirai but casting a quick glance at Deacon. He saw it, and nodded.

"Right," he said, a sheepish expression on his face. "And look, I was talking more about the old days, back when I was military. Test flights are a complicated business, then *and* now. But things are different with Artemis. Hell, the crew of this thing are their star hires and this project is their biggest deal yet. So scratch what I said." He waved a hand. "Forget it."

Mirai seemed to shrink in on herself. Liv saw the way she had her arms wrapped around herself, like the crawlspace had sapped the heat from her body. Perhaps the damage to the insulation foam was more serious? Liv wasn't sure. The ambient temperature in the module felt normal, it was just the void behind the wall that felt cold. She'd noticed it as soon as they'd taken the first wall panel off.

"But," said Mirai, "you think Artemis has lied about the XK72."

"Hey, I'm not saying anything." Deacon pointed at the exposed wall. "But let's face some facts—this seems to be a surprise to you. But let's also take it a different way—does it matter?"

"What do you mean, does it matter?" asked Liv.

"I mean," said Deacon, "does it help us find Astrid or not?"

Mirai opened her mouth like she was going to reply, but she didn't say anything, she just looked at Liv.

Liv looked at her colleague, and found it hard to focus on her features. She concentrated, wondered if that sound she heard was Astrid knocking again or Deacon banging on the wall again or was just the thud-thud-thud of her headache. She turned back to the exposed hull, and the light from it sparked and sparkled, and each moving glint of light made the thump in her head worse.

She rubbed her temples and closed her eyes, hoping the other two wouldn't notice. But it didn't matter, because that was when she lost her grip on consciousness altogether and hit the deck with a thud all of her own.

12

WAS IT REALLY JUST THE THREE OF US NOW?

Liv woke in one of the crew bunks, now fitted out with the simple, expandable mattress someone had obviously taken from storage and laid out on the frame. She winced at the light above, and at the face of Deacon looking down at her.

"Shit," she managed to say, her voice hardly a whisper. Above her, Deacon at least cracked a wide smile.

Liv pushed herself up onto an elbow. Her head thumped and the module swam in her vision, but it settled in a couple of seconds. She went for a little more, swinging herself around so she was sitting upright.

So far, so good.

She rubbed her face, and asked, "How long was I out?"

"Ten, fifteen."

Liv looked up, her hands falling away from her face. *"Hours?"*

Deacon's smile widened. "Minutes."

"Astrid?"

Deacon shook his head, his smile quickly fading. "Not yet. Here."

Liv caught the object he tossed to her—an oblong the size and shape of a large phone, wrapped in silver foil. She turned it over and peered at the label, then looked up at Deacon.

"Strawberry shortcake?"

Deacon juggled his shoulders as he considered. "The wonders of science. But, eat. You're exhausted, dehydrated, low blood sugar. That's all. We have plenty of emergency rations. Eat. You'll feel better."

He was right. Liv's head had settled into a dull ache. She worked at the foil wrapping to expose the corner of the ration. The substance was spongy and dry, like a very stiff marshmallow, but it didn't taste too bad at all. She glanced up as she ate.

"Where's Mirai?"

"Flight deck." Deacon folded his arms and leaned against the door bulkhead. "She's going to take a look at the systems, see if she can figure out why the SLIP drive is offline." He shrugged. "Everything else looks okay. The antenna came back online, so no damage there, just no signal. But no reason why we can't Drop out of here if we can get the SLIP drive up. Wherever *here* is."

Liv paused, mid-bite. "Even if we're stuck, like Redway said?"

"Don't see why not. It's not like we need to get a bearing, or set coordinates, right? We set the program, we Drop, we go home."

"But what about his code?"

"Well," said Deacon, "we don't know what he was doing, and we don't know if whatever he did is keeping us here. So right now, maybe that doesn't matter. If Mirai hits a roadblock, we'll take a look and reassess our options."

"Okay," said Liv, nodding. She finished the last of her ration and crumpled the foil in her hands. Already she was feeling better. All she needed now was a drink, something for her head, and she could get back to work. "So while she's doing that, we can keep looking for Astrid."

At this, Deacon pushed off the wall and held up both hands. "*You* are going to rest. *I* am going to look for Astrid."

Liv stood from the bunk, then swayed on her feet as the sudden movement made her head spin. She leaned against the wall for support, then closed her eyes, and shook her head.

"Astrid could be hurt. If she's in the crawlspace, we have to get her out, as fast as we can. We need her to help Mirai with the SLIP drive."

"Absolutely right, boss, but you need to rest. We gonna do this, we might need to take shifts. But right now, all I'm saying is you take it easy for another half hour. Have some more rations. Rehydrate. Those wall panels are damned heavy, so get your strength back. I'll go back to Engineering and keep at it. You come down when you're ready."

Liv nodded, then lowered herself back onto the bunk. A half hour. Twenty minutes. Even ten. That's all she needed. Then she could get back to work. With just three crew left—*was it really just the three of us now?*—she needed to pull her weight.

"Okay," she said, running a list through her head. "Have we confirmed she's not outside, on the hull or something?"

"Confirmed," said Deacon. "Mirai checked the EVA lockers while you were out. We have three suits, all accounted for. Seals on two are intact, one is open. Maybe Astrid thought about it but ran out of time. But, she didn't take one, so she's still inside the ship."

"Okay," said Liv again. "What about comms?"

Deacon frowned. "She's never answered."

"Right, but we don't know if there is a fault, so we should check all the comms. If she's out cold, or injured and stuck, or whatever, we can try and ping her comms and maybe get a location."

Deacon clicked his fingers. "Good call. We'll get Mirai to check that now, see if anything comes up, before I get back to the wall panels." He turned to leave, then looked back at Liv and pointed a finger at her. "You, boss, get your head down and I'll see you in thirty."

"Fifteen," said Liv, forcing a smile, and she turned back around on the bunk and lay down, listening to Deacon's heavy footfalls recede. She closed her eyes, then opened them again, because she knew if she wasn't careful she would, despite everything, fall asleep. Deacon was right, she was exhausted, but they had work to do and she still had enough gas in the tank to help. If only she could get rid of the blasted headache.

She sat up again, and waited while the cabin righted itself around her. It was quicker this time, so that was good. Hydration and some painkillers and she'd be fine.

Liv pushed herself up off the bunk, and headed toward the storage units.

Liv paused by the stack of gear they'd dragged out of Storage 2, trying to take a quick tally of everything. What she was looking for were their field medical kits, either of the two that came as standard with Artemis test flights. Of course, they were in their own medical locker, which would be untouched in Storage 1.

Liv wondered if she was a little fuzzier in the head than she realized. She moved around the pile and leaned against the closed bulkhead of Storage 1 for a few seconds. She looked at the door controls and tried to focus on the switch, but that just made her head pound all the more.

She made it inside, the hatchway closing automatically behind her. The medical locker was a large red compartment on one wall. She broke the seal—Artemis would need a form filled out in triplicate—and scanned the shelves. Finding the painkillers was easy; opening the tamper-proof packaging took five times as long. She popped four pills—twice the recommended dose—and dry-swallowed them. She felt them stick in her throat, and nearly gagged.

Next step: water.

She leaned against the wall and closed her eyes and swallowed again, grimacing at the sensation as the pills finally went down. Her mouth and throat felt so dry.

Knock-knock-knock . . .

Liv froze, her heart beat a machine-gun rattle in her chest.

That sound, the same as before. Astrid, behind the wall panels, stuck in the crawlspace? Liv looked around. The sound had been so close, only . . . no, it hadn't come from the ceiling, or the wall, or even the floor.

It had come from behind her—the closed door. Someone had been knocking on the hatchway.

Liv gasped a breath, the sudden rush of adrenaline clearing her head. It was Deacon, coming to check on her, having found the bunk empty. Maybe with an update from Mirai, one he wanted to give in person rather than call over the comms and add to Liv's headache.

She turned around and—

Knock-knock-knock . . .

—hit the hatchway release. The door slid open.

There was nobody there. The passageway was empty, the contents of Storage 2 still in the haphazard pile.

"Hello?"

There was no reply. No sound of any kind over the gentle hum of the XK72.

Liv—awake and alert now—stepped into the passageway, and looked around.

She was most definitely alone.

Hearing things, now? The knocking had been the same sound as before, the sound that all three of them had heard.

But that wasn't possible. It was her imagination, the sound merely a playback from her memory, her dazed mind trying to pull itself back to the here and now.

She turned and headed toward the flight deck. And then she slowed, and looked around. Was it *darker* than normal? That wasn't her imagination, surely. She turned a small circle to look back the way she had come. There was a movement, in the window of the Storage 2's closed door.

Liv told herself it was nothing. Told herself not to worry about it. Told herself all kinds of facts and figures about the XK72 that she knew by heart so she wouldn't be able to think of anything else.

But she still held her breath as she walked back and checked Storage 2. The door slid open. The module was empty because of course it was empty.

Liv stared at the empty cabin for a while, then jumped as the comms chimed in her ear. She touched the nub.

"Liv."

"It's Deak. You up and about?"

"I am."

"Then come up to the flight deck, pronto pronto."

Deacon's voice was calm and clear, but his words served to snap Liv out of her daze.

There was work to do. Data to gather. Problems to solve. And it sounded like Deacon had just found another.

"On my way," said Liv. She glanced at the empty cabin in front of her one more time, then turned on her heel and headed down the passageway.

13

JUST A LITTLE BIT OF SABOTAGE

"What's happened?"

Deacon and Mirai turned to face Liv as she entered the flight deck. Mirai was in the pilot's position, with the aux specialist leaning on the back of her seat. As Liv walked in, she saw a stack of detached panels leaning on the port side wall, next to the black void of the revealed crawlspace.

Deacon saw Liv glancing over; he straightened and gestured to his handiwork. "Figured I'd make a few holes here and there, so Astrid knows she can get out easily if she's spooked by the noise I'm going to be making down in Engineering. I'll pull some more panels down in the main passageway, and by the airlock and storage cabins." Then he pointed to Mirai's control panel. "But we have another problem."

Liv dropped herself into the co-pilot's seat. Beside her, Mirai was studying the readouts intently, her fingers poised above the keypad.

"Mirai?" Liv asked.

Mirai tapped a few keys, throwing the readout up onto the HUD. "We have a power loss. It's slow, but steady. A constant trickle from the main grid that isn't being replenished."

Liv looked at the readings, deciphering the data. "That's impossible."

"Damn right it's impossible," said Deacon, moving closer to get a better look at the readings. "The power grid was designed to be infallible. Cosmic ray bombardment of a nanoparticle hull sublayer. That baby theoretically runs at more than one hundred percent efficiency. Even at baseline, there's a constant overcharge. We can never run out of power."

"And yet, here we are," said Mirai.

Liv leaned back in the flight seat. She could feel her headache threatening to return as she tried to parse the data readout. Deacon was right, the power system was, if not quite infallible as he claimed, then extremely *unlikely* to fail. It was entirely passive, the energy absorption a quantum reaction that required no moving parts, no operating system, not even any supervision from the ship's mainframe. Energy was absorbed, fed into the batteries via a passive control module, end of story. A brilliant piece of engineering, courtesy of Artemis, Inc.

Except.

"There aren't any cosmic rays," said Liv.

The other two looked at her. Liv leaned forward and worked her own console, bringing up another reading on the HUD. She pointed at the graphs, which were decidedly flat. "There's no sensor fault," she said. "We checked before, everything is operational. The sensors aren't showing anything because there's nothing to show."

Mirai peered at the HUD. "You're right. There's nothing. No mass. No radiation, no particles. No energy signature of any kind. There is *nothing* out there."

"No cosmic rays," said Liv, "means no power regen."

Deacon sighed heavily, running his hands over his shaved scalp. "How can there be nothing out there? Not even cosmic radiation?"

Mirai cycled through a series of readings on the HUD, all of which told the exact same story. "It fits with what Colonel Redway said. The SLIP drive was interrupted during the Drop. We're literally stuck in a void, the gap between . . . well . . ."

"Stuck in the crawlspace of the universe, and running out of power," said Deacon. "Well, that's just great."

Liv clicked her tongue as she looked over the data, searching for something, anything, that might provide a solution—or at least the start of one.

Gather data. Focus. Identify the problem. Fix it.

"How long do we have?" she asked.

Mirai checked the data. "Hard to tell. We seem to be losing power at a slightly greater rate than the ship is actually consuming it."

Deacon frowned. "How is *that* possible?"

Mirai shrugged. "I'm not sure. But then, the nanoparticle grid has never been run in a totally energy-negative space. Could be throwing the readings off." She worked her keyboard. "But at the current draw, I think we have twelve hours."

Liv felt the faint halo of dizziness threatening to return. She closed her eyes, glad she was already sitting.

"Twelve hours?" Deacon whistled. "That's not a good number."

"Avery said we had rations and life support for weeks," said Mirai, quietly. Liv glanced at her, and saw the small woman almost pushing herself back into the pilot's seat, like she wanted to disappear entirely.

"We do," said Liv, "but he didn't know about the power drain."

"Puts us a little on the clock, don't it?" said Deacon.

Liv looked over the controls, ignoring the way her heart felt like it was trying to fight its way out of her rib cage. "If we shut down as much as possible," she said, "we can run on minimum for quite a while."

At this, Mirai sat forward, quickly, her delicate fingers flying over the keyboard on the main console. "We can double it," she said. "Twenty-four, perhaps a little longer."

Liv nodded. "Do it. Power to minimum. Turn off anything we don't need. Reduce everything else as low as it will go."

"Okay," said Mirai. "It might get a little chilly."

She worked at the keyboard. Text appeared on the HUD, readings changed, and the steady background hum of the XK72 seemed to quiet down. A moment later, the lights dimmed even further than they had been—the result, Liv now realized, of an automatic compensation for the slow but steady power drain.

"A little dark too," said Deacon, looking around.

That's when Liv felt the chill. With life support powering down to minimum, the light work uniforms they were wearing weren't going to be enough, but they had nothing else save for the bulky and impractical EVA suits.

Last resort, thought Liv.

She waved at Mirai's console. "Keep the life support up a little. We need to keep warm and we've got limited options."

"Understood." As Mirai adjusted the settings, the temperature rose a little. It was cool, but bearable, and Liv thought they were about to get fairly warm as they moved around and worked, anyway.

Deacon blew out his cheeks and started to walk a tight circle around the flight deck, his hands locked behind his head. "Okay, so now we need to do something. Ping the comms, see if we can pinpoint Astrid. We see where she is, we go get her."

Liv glanced at Mirai, who nodded, clearly pleased to be given tasks to keep her mind occupied. Liv sat back and watched her, while Deacon came back to stand behind them, arms folded, muscles at the back of his jaw working as he tried very hard to be patient.

Mirai punched the controls, and then paused, hands hovering over the console. Liv glanced at her, and saw the flight analyst was slowly shaking her head.

"What is it?"

Mirai stared at the HUD. "There's no reading."

Liv felt her seat rock as Deacon grabbed the back of it.

"What?" he asked. "Where is she?"

"She's not on the ship," said Mirai, shaking her head. "Astrid isn't on the XK72."

Liv felt her seat rock again. "Well that's just BS," said Deacon. "There's another fault. Try again."

"No, the comms are working." Mirai hit a key on the console then tapped her earpiece. Liv heard the tone through her own. She looked at Deacon, and he nodded, a finger held against his. She turned back to Mirai.

"An intermittent fault, then?"

Deacon pushed off Liv's seat. "Well that's great," he said, then he sighed. "We don't have time to try and trace this bug. Okay, so nice idea, no dice, we keep looking. I'll get some more panels off." He sighed.

Liv nodded, then sank back into the co-pilot's seat, pressing herself into it as far as she could. She watched the HUD and wished for a solution to magically appear in front of her.

The XK72 was, as Redway had said, marooned—the data, or the lack of it, from the ship's sensors proved that.

Stuck, and running out of power. The crew of six now down to three. The chief engineer—the only person, said Redway, who could get them out of this—one of the missing.

So that was the problem. What was the solution?

The answer, thought Liv, was actually very simple.

They had to move.

But that conclusion led to problem two: The SLIP drive was the only method of escape, and it was offline. Related: the only engineer who could realistically get the SLIP drive back up and running, Astrid, was—

Liv rubbed her forehead, very well aware of the circular logic. But she was also very well aware of something else.

Astrid was still here. She had to be. Redway and Avery were gone, but unless Astrid had gone with them (she hadn't), then she *was* still here. People couldn't just disappear. It had been a long time since they had heard the knocking, which had been her—

It was her. It had to have been her.

—but Liv had to focus and solve the more pressing problem.

"Okay," said Liv, straightening up. "Here's the plan." She looked up at the aux specialist. "Deak, you are going to keep looking for Astrid."

At this, Deacon nodded, quickly, his face expression alive, maybe even hopeful.

"Like you said," Liv continued, "it might be an intermittent fault with the comms, so we'll ignore that for now. Start with Engineering and work your way forward. Strip the entire ship if you have to, but if Astrid's here, we're going to find her. We are going to need her."

Deacon clapped his hands. "You the boss, boss." He rolled his neck and left the flight deck at a jog.

Liv turned in her seat to Mirai. "I want you to work on the SLIP drive."

Mirai blinked. "The SLIP drive? It's offline, and I'm not sure—"

"I know," said Liv, raising her hand to cut her off. "It's offline, and it's a separate system to the XK72, but it's not entirely isolated. It's patched into the XK72 via the mainframe, which acts as the interface between the master test protocol and the SLIP drive program. Redway was able to access the master protocol, so you can too."

"Me?"

"You're not just our flight analyst, Mirai. You're our computer systems specialist too. Dig into the computer and see if you can bypass the mainframe. All we need is a reset to bring the SLIP drive back online, and we can run the test program again and complete the Drop. Maybe we're locked out, but maybe we aren't. We have to try this."

Mirai nodded. "Okay, I'll see what I can do." She settled into the pilot's seat, and looked over the controls. Then she glanced back at Liv. "And you're going to work on the power problem?"

"Yes," said Liv. She peered at the HUD. "Can you bring back the grid status?"

Mirai's fingers hit the keys, and a moment later the status readouts for the ship's passive energy absorption grid came up on the HUD.

"Looks okay," said Liv, her eyes taking in the green indicators all over the display. "No faults anywhere. Apart from the SLIP drive being offline, the XK72 is functioning perfectly." Her eyes traced the schematic of the grid's conduit matrix. There was no damage, no problem. As they had already established, there just wasn't anything for the grid to absorb.

Mirai was looking at the screen too. She pointed to a schematic on the right, a section of Engineering that ran parallel to the power grid but was totally separate from it.

"The ion drive is fully fueled," she said. "Its cells are separate from the main grid. If there was some way we could feed power from the drive into the grid, it might buy us some time." She paused. "Except that would require refitting both the drive and the grid. We'd have to take half the ship apart and, even then, we'd be out of time."

Liv rubbed her face as she thought. Mirai was right, the ion fuel cells were sitting there, at near enough to 100 percent capacity, and there was no feasible way of tapping into them.

Unless . . .

"Wait."

Mirai looked at Liv. "What?"

"That's it," said Liv, a smile growing across her face. "The ion drive. It emits ions." She turned to Mirai. "That's how it works. The drive ejects a stream of charged particles as propulsion."

"I know," said Mirai. "But that helps us how?"

Liv gestured back to the HUD. "The power grid works by absorption of energy from charged particles."

Mirai wrinkled her nose. "From cosmic rays. The ion drive exhaust is too clean. The particles ejected from the ion drive would be far too light and low energy to interact with the grid's quantum layer."

"Not if we dirty them up."

"Dirty them up?"

"Run the ion drive out of balance. That way it will emit high energy particles which can be absorbed by the grid."

Mirai looked at Liv, her expression less than impressed. "Run it out of balance? Even if you could do that, it'll be hugely inefficient. The ratio of particle sizes will be wrong. You'll burn through the fuel and the grid will only absorb a fraction of the drive output."

"But it will buy us time."

Mirai winced. "I don't know . . . I guess it would."

"Come on!" said Liv. "It's a brilliant idea."

"How will you even unbalance the drive? Everything about it is designed to keep it *in* balance."

"Oh, that's the easy part."

"So how will you do it?"

Liv sat back. "Oh, just a little bit of sabotage."

14

DEACON WAS GOING TO SAVE THEM ALL

Deacon slipped another wall panel off, wincing as the hard edges of it bit into his already sore hands, then yelling in both surprise and pain as he dropped it not on the floor of the SLIP drive module but on the top of his boot, only just catching the edge of the metal-capped toe. Pulling his foot away, he let the panel bang back against the wall, and he swore, as loud as he could. His voice echoed rather pleasingly around the tight confines of the cabin, so for the hell of it he swore again. Then he stood back and surveyed his handiwork.

In front of him, the gap in the wall was now much larger, stretching half-way around the odd-shaped room, revealing a stretch of the crawlspace beyond that was just . . . nothing. Dark. *Empty.* With the power running at minimum, the lights were dimmer than they would normally be. The SLIP drive module was full of shadows, and as Deacon blinked it seemed like those shadows were coming out of the crawlspace, filling the cabin with gathering gloom.

He swore a third time and spun on this toe, and found himself face-to-face with his own reflection in the mirrored cowling of the SLIP drive itself.

The damned thing. He aimed a kick at its base. The cap of his boot made a satisfying *thunk* against the housing, the impact vibrating up his leg. This thing, this brilliant, stupid thing, was the cause of all their problems, and . . .

Deacon stood back and rubbed his face. The air was cold, but he was hot from heaving the panels, which were now stacked all around the room. On two control consoles—now freestanding units with no wall behind them—were littered dozens of magnetic bolts.

He turned back to face the crawlspace, focusing on the outer wall of the hull. It was the insulation foam, he knew, the intensely, impossibly black, hyper-efficient surface absorbing any and all light and reflecting none, that created the illusion of a total, infinite void.

Not just light. Energy. The stuff was sucking the heat from the room, dropping the temperature even further, the air inside the crawlspace proper even colder than the air of the cabin itself, a border sharply delineating the two spaces.

Deacon shook his head as he looked into the crawlspace, and in the corner of his eye, there was a glint. He glanced toward it, where the damaged section of the insulation exposed the hull's surface beyond. The embedded jewel-like material sparkled and spun like a morning star hanging in a cold winter's sky.

Deacon frowned. It was like it was . . . watching him. Sure, it glinted now when he looked at it, but when he wasn't looking, when he had his back turned to it as he worked on the other panels, he could feel it, like it was a spotlight shining on him, like there was someone, or something, very far away, watching his every move.

Deacon tore his gaze away and, counting the wall panels he'd removed, took stock of his options.

Since he'd gotten back to work, there had been no more knocking, and while he hadn't stripped the walls of the SLIP drive module completely, it didn't seem like Astrid was in this section of the XK72.

In fact, he was starting to think—maybe *believe* was a better word—that she really wasn't anywhere at all, that the knocking probably hadn't been her, it was something else. Loose cowling. A broken hull plate. Some other system failure in the middle of all the other system failures. Sure, the mainframe said everything was fine, all systems green, but what if the mainframe had failed too? What if Astrid had vanished, maybe left behind in a universe that the XK72 was no longer present in?

It didn't make sense, of course, but Deacon wondered if that mattered here.

And all the while, the SLIP drive sat there, Deacon's mirror image working hard, the angles of the thing catching the light reflected by the exposed outer hull and shining it back—mostly at Deacon, dazzling him when he least expected it, as he huffed and puffed and shifted the heavy wall plates.

The SLIP drive. The cause of all their problems. Deacon turned back to look at it. It was a strange thing, this freestanding, trapezoidal block with a mirrored surface. Sealed, tamper-proof, able to be opened not by Artemis technicians but only by the military engineers who had built it in the first place.

The unique partnership of Artemis, Inc, and the military was something Deacon had never really thought much about, but right now he had to admit to himself it . . . bothered him. Quite a lot, actually. Okay, so it made sense—each organization, vast in their own way, had equally vast resources to draw on and some of the best people on the planet working for them, but not necessarily in the same fields, and not necessarily with the same expertise. So, divide and conquer. Artemis did what they could and farmed out the rest to their partner. The military followed the exact same logic: They did what they could and farmed out the remainder to *their* partner, Artemis. Both organizations were on an equal footing, each contracting specifics of the program to the other. Which, yes, made sense to Deacon, even if it sounded like a mountain of paperwork.

But in a situation like this, it seemed less than ideal. Because it meant that while this latest prototype, the SLIP drive, had been designed by both Artemis and military engineers, it had been built and installed by the military. Sealed to maintain absolute control conditions, the unit would then be removed after the mission and deconstructed by those same military engineers, with all data shared with Artemis.

Later.

Deacon stood with his arms folded, staring at his own reflection in the drive's housing. Less than ideal? No, right now, this arrangement was more than just a little fucked up. Sure, Artemis and the military had been cooperating like this for decades, and sure, who knew how many projects had followed this kind of joint responsibility.

Except now they had a problem, a big one, and all signs pointed to the military—to Redway, following orders Artemis knew nothing of, in a ship powered by an engine that its own crew couldn't even *open*, let alone fix.

Well, screw that.

Deacon swayed on his feet; then he blinked and rubbed his face, suddenly aware of the weight of fatigue on him, remembering how Liv had keeled over not so long ago. At this, Deacon actually found himself smiling. He was a veteran, an expert. That's why he was here. Auxiliary specialist. Someone who could do anything, solve any problem, fix any mistakes.

And Deacon knew just how good he was. That's why Artemis had lured him away from the military in the first place. They'd seen his skills, seen his potential.

The best of the best.

And yes he was tired and fed up, and not thinking right, and hearing things like a knocking on the empty space behind him where a wall plate should have been and seeing things like a person standing behind him, their reflection clear in the SLIP drive housing, when Deacon knew he was quite alone.

So yes, maybe it was a bad idea, but what else was there to do? And if he could get the thing to work, reset or reboot or whatever the hell it needed to do, then they could make the Drop and go home.

Deacon was going to open the SLIP drive.

Deacon was going to save them all.

"God. Damn. *It*."

Deacon had been at it for a solid hour, and had made precisely zero progress. The SLIP drive's mirrored shielding was completely and utterly impervious to his efforts.

But he had, at least, made some interesting discoveries.

The device *was* sealed, but the mirrored surface was not one single, continuous piece, as he had previously thought. It was made up of individual panels, each one aligned with such precision that Deacon hadn't even realized until, out of desperation, he'd done a minute, fingertip examination of the top of the SLIP drive and found the first screw, so perfectly installed he could hardly feel it under his skin.

That was when he made the second discovery: The fixings were unlike anything he'd ever seen before.

Deacon had worked on plenty of sealed prototypes, as well as most kinds of regular systems—the XK72's ion drive, for example . . . well, he could strip that down to component pieces and reassemble the whole thing with one hand tied behind his back. And as for sealed prototypes, well, even those *were* designed to be opened, if you knew how. A box was just a box, a casing just a casing.

But this thing was something else—designed to be opened like any prototype, yes, but the SLIP drive's shell had *next level* tamper-proofing.

Taking a deep, clearing breath, Deacon knelt back down close by the base of the device and ran his fingertips along the case until he felt the barely perceptible join of two panels. Peering closely along the edge, he found the screws. He got in close, closed one eye, and looked at each of the fixings.

The fabricators had gone to incredible lengths. Each and every screw was different. Deacon had found twenty-four so far; looking at the size of the SLIP drive as a whole, there would have to have been a few hundred fixings in total.

Each one, a unique design. What kind of tool did you even use to remove them? He eyed the screws running along the lowest edge. The first had a star-shaped indent. Okay, fairly standard. But the second was a crescent moon; the third, three wavy parallel lines. Then, farther along, something that looked like a trident, then a circle with a dot in the middle, then a triangle with an arrow emerged from the apex, and so on, as Deacon traced the screws along the edge of the panel.

It was . . . just plain weird. *Very* weird. But . . . okay, no, there must have been a reason behind it, some design rationale that was beyond his own engineering expertise, some new security feature he'd missed in the manuals and memos.

He stood, arching his back, rolling his shoulders to relax his sore muscles. He looked down at his reflection and thought again about the tool you would need to open the casing.

Redway had said that Astrid was needed to get them out. She was the senior engineer, Avery's boss, and had had a hand in nearly every part of the XK72 and its systems.

And, in conjunction with the military team, she was also the lead designer on the SLIP drive itself.

So . . . what if it hadn't been Redway who had shipwrecked the XK72? What if it had been *her*?

Deacon rubbed his head as he thought it over.

She knows what Redway is planning. She knows his secret orders. She sabotages the SLIP drive, stops him. Then she jumps into the crawlspace to hide. Bumps her head. Breaks a leg. Nearly bleeds out. Wakes up. Knocks. Then is out for the count again.

So maybe *she* had the tool. She opened the SLIP drive, broke it, sealed it back up so nobody would be able to fix it. It was the same tool she was using to bang against the panels from the other side.

Maybe, maybe, maybe.

Deacon stared at himself in the drive's intact casing, his eyes losing their focus in the shimmering, almost liquid surface. The rest of the cabin was perfectly reflected, the wall panels stacked in leaning piles, their magnetic bolts covering the consoles and scattered over the floor. And behind, the void of the crawlspace, a dark nothing.

And standing in the wall opening, a figure, a woman, stepping forward into the cabin was—

Deacon spun around. There was nobody there. He sighed and rubbed his eyes, annoyed at his own fatigue, his own wandering imagination, like Astrid had just been waiting there, behind the panels, waiting for an invitation to come back into the ship.

He needed to concentrate. Focus. Set a task and get on with it.

What he needed was—

He turned back around, and grinned.

What he needed was a cutter.

He looked down at the SLIP drive, and ran a hand over it. He knocked it with a knuckle, scratched it with his thumb nail. Ran his hand over it again, like a carpenter clearing dust from his workbench.

Yes. A plasma cutter would make short work of the panels. It was worth a shot, and he'd already started assembling the tool from the servodrone anyway.

Deacon clapped his hands twice. The sound reverberated loudly. He laughed, and then he gave a bow to his reflection.

And the person reflected behind him, standing in the void.

"See? There's nothing Titus Deacon can't handle. Redway dropped us into this and I'll get us out." Deacon laughed. Behind him, the reflection of Astrid didn't move, didn't speak.

Because you're not there.

Deacon whistled through his teeth. "I gotta hand it to you. This design is something else. But it's nothing I can't handle."

In the reflected room, Astrid had moved out of the crawlspace, and was standing behind Deacon, close enough to reach out and touch. She said nothing and she didn't move, but her reflected gaze met his in the drive's mirrored case.

Deacon nodded and clicked his fingers.

"Yes! That's it, Astrid, that's it exactly. I mean, sure, it's not ideal, none of this is. But sometimes, out on the field, you gotta adapt, you know? No problem. The drone's torch will slice this open like nothing at all."

He looked at her image. Still she didn't speak, but was that . . . a smile? Just a little one? A sign of approval, a signal that he was on the right track, that he was doing good?

Then Deacon pursed his lips and nodded again. "You got that right," he said. "Okay, plasma torch, plasma torch, plasma torch." He stopped suddenly; then he pointed at Astrid's reflection. "Don't you go anywhere," he said. "You're going to want to see a master at work. Show you a thing or two about how we used to do engineering work, back in the day."

Deacon laughed and punched open the door control, then stepped over the bulkhead and headed down to the storage units.

Leaving the empty module behind him.

15

SHE'S GONE LIKE YOU'RE GONE

Grunting with effort, Liv pushed herself back down the maintenance conduit, propelling herself with knees and elbows that were, by now, rubbed raw. A few moments later her feet met nothing but thin air, and with one last shove she squeezed herself backward and then dropped down onto the decking beneath the two cylindrical protrusions that formed the back of the ion drive unit.

Picking herself up, she cursed the design of this particular ship module. "Economical" was what the specs said. The ion drive might have been the primary motive unit of the XK72, but the technology was so well established and so reliable it felt like some accountant at Artemis had, once upon a time, decided that, hey now, you wouldn't need to actually, y'know, *access* it during flight, would you? The end result was a tight squeeze that brought Liv to mind of many other adjectives for the module, most of which were far more colorful than "economical."

But she's done it. Sabotaged the drive . . . and made an unexpected discovery.

Because despite the discomfort, despite the difficult access, someone else had been here before her.

Catching her breath, she examined the object in her hand—a cylinder, about as round as she could comfortably hold in one hand, blunt at one end, pointed at the other. It was metal, the dull gray of it interrupted at intervals by colored rings. There was a slot on the underside, from which ran two thick, braided cables. It had been these cables that attached the object to the ion drive, wired in to a subsystem deep inside the drive's complex machinery. Liv wasn't a drive expert, but she had enough knowledge of the XK72 to know that the object shouldn't have been in there, and that it had clearly been patched in, recently.

What it was, she didn't know, and as she looked over it again, she thought it was vaguely familiar, a bit like the core motivator of a standard runner probe. Immediately she began to doubt her own expertise . . .

maybe it *was* part of the ion drive? But that didn't explain the patch job. The ion drive was big and complicated but it was also designed along classic Artemis specs, clean and sleek and logical.

Whatever the case, it was too late now, anyway. She'd had to disconnect the object and pull it out of the way, in order to access the main drive core and make her "adjustments."

As Mirai had confirmed, the ion drive was perfectly intact, perfectly functional, the fuel cells, as the system had reported, at almost maximum capacity. Connecting those fuel cells to the grid directly was virtually impossible without dismantling the rear half of the XK72 entirely. And even if they all got into EVA suits and went outside to start stripping the hull off from the other side, reconfiguring the ship's entire drive and power systems would require so much work that they would run out of time long before the job was even halfway done.

Using the ion exhaust was their best—their *only*—option. And besides, there was no going back now, not after the adjustments she had made to the drive core, pulling the twin coils—a key component of the system—out of alignment with a few tugs on a magnowrench. The effect of her deliberate sabotage would be to unbalance the engines, causing them to fire in an inefficient and wasteful way, the resulting ion exhaust containing a greater proportion of large, high-energy particles than normal running. The passive nanoparticle grid that covered the external hull of the XK72 would capture a small fraction of this exhaust; Liv didn't have enough data to make any proper calculations, but she hoped it would be enough to at least maintain an equilibrium in the power grid, stopping the energy loss if not actively recharging the ship.

But it was while she was squeezed into the conduits around the engine core itself, firstly wrenching the patched mystery device out and then pulling on a component so deep inside the drive that she couldn't even really see it, that she realized just how inefficient her makeshift re-energization system was going to be. Maintaining an energy equilibrium wasn't what Liv wanted—she wanted to reverse the drain entirely, get the XK72 back to 100 percent operation. How—or even *if*—this was possible, Liv didn't know. But there was no time for a plan B, not now. She wasn't anywhere near a good enough engineer. She needed to run it past Deacon. He'd know.

Liv laid the mystery device in her hands down on the floor of the ion drive module, then moved to a console and brought up a systems report for one last double-triple-quadruple check.

All systems were green. The XK72 was on low power but it was, launched escape pod aside, intact, having apparently sustained no physical damage whatsoever.

That was all she could do, for now.

"Told you we need her."

Liv ignored the voice. She knew it was just in her head, her subconscious taking advantage of this momentary lapse in focus. She knew the voice didn't echo dully in the confines of the cabin.

She knew it didn't sound like Redway's voice. Redway was gone. This was all her.

"It's a good idea," said the voice, like Redway was standing right at her shoulder, the cabin so small he was literally breathing down her neck. She could feel it, soft and warm against her skin.

She closed her eyes. She let her head fall, her chin touching her chest as she did some breathing of her own.

In, out. In, out.

"And I'm sure Deacon can come up with something to help boost the re-energization rate. He's good, right? The best of the best. Artemis is lucky to have him."

Without lifting her head, Liv opened her eyes. She could see the decking, and, just at the edge of her vision, a movement, like a pair of boots quickly stepping out of her eyeline. Not Artemis-issue boots.

Military.

"It'll work," said Redway's voice. "It'll buy you enough time to pull the ship apart until you find Astrid."

She closed her eyes again.

"If she's in there, of course. But you know she isn't. She's not on the ship. She's gone. Like Avery is gone. You just have to acknowledge that fact and move on, but you're too scared to, aren't you?"

Liv sighed. "She's gone like you're gone," she whispered. She squeezed her eyes shut tighter.

There was no response.

Liv opened her eyes and looked at the floor again. Shadows moved, like there was someone else in the room with her.

"What happened?" she asked. "Did you kill her? Did Astrid get in the way and you killed her? Did you dump her outside? Or did you dump her in the crawlspace? It was only afterward that you realized what she'd done and that you needed her to fix it. But it was too late." Liv cocked her head, considering. "You weren't thinking straight. Maybe you hit your head, had a concussion, and forgot what you'd done. So you blamed us, thought we'd helped her hide from you. Is that it?"

Silence.

Liv lifted her head and turned around.

"Is that right?"

There was nobody there.

Liv's mouth was dry. She swallowed, but that just seemed to make it worse. With all that had happened, she realized she'd never had that drink.

Fatigue. Stress. Dehydration. They could do strange things to the body.

Stranger things to the mind.

Liv let out a laugh, and then her hands flew to her mouth in surprise, her eyes wide. She took a deep breath.

She was not going to give in to this. She could sleep when she was dead.

In the meantime, she had work to do. Power up the ion drive, see what happened, what needed calibrating, then find Deacon and run her plan past him.

Liv turned off the console and clambered back out of the module.

16

A COLD AS DEEP AS HER BONES

It had been hours. How many, Mirai didn't want to know. Working against a clock was not one of her strong points. Give her a *deadline,* give her a target time, date, and endpoint, whatever—sure, fine. The work will be done, and it will be done well.

Just . . . don't give her a ticking clock.

Alone in the flight deck, Mirai slumped back in the pilot's seat, and rubbed her eyes, like that would make some kind of difference. The text scrolling on the readout in front of her still didn't make any sense, no matter how hard she kicked the base of the console in front of her. She had accessed the master test protocol, but the whole thing was corrupted, overwritten by Redway, the lines of standard code intercut with the weird symbolic language he'd introduced. It was illogical, and so far had resisted all of Mirai's attempts at translation or conversion into something more standard. She didn't know what Redway had done, what instructions he'd given the XK72 mainframe before the SLIP drive slipped gears and got them stuck in nowhere, but it was encrypted like nothing she'd ever seen before.

And she'd only really scratched the surface. It was futile, she now realized, a waste of the time that they didn't have. It would be faster to give up on trying to break through the standard interface and dive into the mainframe's machine code itself—a laborious, frustrating task, Mirai knew, but working with the raw foundation of the XK72's computer system would at least let her bypass the junk on the top level.

Mirai closed her eyes. Fine. If that was the path to take, so be it. She just needed a little rest before she got started. She wasn't hungry anymore, but, holy heck, was she tired. How long had it been since all of this had started?

Her head bobbed against her chest, jerking her back awake.

Wow, okay. That wasn't good. Mirai blinked and sat more upright, and tried to focus on the text displayed on the HUD in front of her, the data blazing green, lighting up the dimly lit flight deck. Behind the HUD, she could see her own reflection in the curved window, her features lit by the data she was trying so hard to even understand.

She was not alone.

Mirai stared at the figure standing at her shoulder in the reflection, all the while aware that the figure should have been in her eyeline beside her, just, but wasn't. She didn't want to turn her head to look, in case it broke the spell, or the dream, or hallucination, whatever the hell it was.

"You're not there," said Mirai. "It's not you. It's my imagination."

In the reflection, the figure of her sister, Suki, stood unmoving, more like the image from the photograph Mirai kept next to her station in Data Monitoring than the reflection of a real person. It was two-dimensional, a flat memory dredged up and projected by her tired mind, a mind that was, she realized, probably fast asleep and dreaming anyway.

And for a moment, she let herself be carried by that dream, and in that dream she felt the joy of her sister as Mirai told her about Artemis, about the job, about the work she was going to do, about how this was what she had always wanted.

All Mirai wanted was to make Suki happy. And Suki was, more than Mirai could ever have imagined, because she knew that Mirai was going to see things she never could.

Not from a hospital bed she knew—they all knew—she would never leave.

To describe the feeling, the vast gulf of guilt that threatened to overcome Mirai as she left Sapporo to join Artemis, left her family, left her *sister*, was beyond words, beyond even the bounds of this dream. But Mirai felt it now, the lapping of a tide that ebbed and flowed but was never still.

Suki had a strength that Mirai didn't. Always had, always would. Mirai drew on that strength, turning her dream of working at Artemis into a *shared* dream, where she was working for her sister too, sharing the experience as much as she could across the miles that separated them so painfully.

And Suki was happy. She was alive and well in her sister as her sister worked, Mirai doing it for the both of them, seeing things that Suki would never see.

It had been six years since Mirai's sister died, but she lived on in her mind, always with her, in everything she did, enjoying a life shared with her sister. It was a mechanism for coping, a way of keeping the guilt in check while she honored her sister through her work.

Suki certainly wasn't standing on the flight deck.

Mirai closed her eyes—just as she did, the image of Suki moved, suddenly reaching out for her in the dark window.

Mirai nearly jumped out of the seat, her heart thudding in her chest.

The reflection was gone. Mirai stood up and looked around. There was nobody else in the flight deck. She was alone, as she always had been before she . . .

Fell asleep?

Yes. Asleep. Good. Fine. Get back to work.

Mirai rolled her neck, stretching the muscles and looked back down at the readouts on the console. Already her dream—it had been a dream, hadn't it?—was fading and she made a conscious effort to push it out of her mind, focusing her attention on the screen embedded above the small keyboard. It was set at a bad angle, and she had to concentrate and squint at the text, but that was good. The discomfort, the effort required, would keep her awake.

After a moment, she sat back in the seat, and, a little more awake now, got back to work, diving deeper into the XK72 mainframe, accessing subdirectories nobody should need to access when a mission was running, until she hit the machine code itself. This was dangerous territory, so she knew she had to be careful. Any changes—or worse, any *mistakes,* however tiny—made here, directly into the mainframe's base operation system, could have a domino effect, resulting in instant, possibly profound, maybe even fatal, effects on any one of the ship's other systems.

But Mirai wouldn't make any mistakes. She was a good programmer. That was why she was the flight analyst. Computers and the code that ran them was what she was best at. She might not be able to fly the XK72, but she could damn well pull the software apart and put it back together again. Somewhere in here was the code that linked the SLIP drive to the main ship systems. Somewhere in here was the key to bringing the SLIP drive back to life and getting them back home.

Mirai typed, and read code, searched. She followed the raw algorithmic patterns of the mainframe master code, solved equations in her head, trying to mentally simulate edits and insertions before trying them in the system itself. It wasn't easy.

And her already difficult task wasn't helped by something else she found.

The mainframe was running at more than 100 percent. That in itself wasn't an issue, and for a machine based on quantum qubits, concepts like *capacity* and *bandwidth* were a little nebulous anyway.

But as Mirai watched the system output at this deep level of the mainframe, it was like . . . it was like someone else was using the computer, carrying out some complex task or calculation beyond the standard operation of the XK72.

Mirai checked, and rechecked, and traced system usage across the whole of the ship, to every console and every part that was connected to the mainframe. All that did was confirm her first suspicion, that what she was seeing wasn't the normal operation of the ship, and that it was nothing that she or Liv or Deacon were doing somewhere else.

It was something to do with Redway's new protocol. Had to be. Something was still running, and maybe that was what was keeping the SLIP drive offline.

Mirai sifted the data and tried a dozen tricks she'd picked up to try to trace the mystery processes, but nothing made any difference. She dug deeper, diving into the raw base code of the ship's computer itself.

Then she stopped, her fingers frozen above the keyboard. "What?" she whispered to no one but herself and the shadows around her and the fading image of Suki in her mind.

She punched the readout up onto the main HUD, then sank back and shook her head.

The code—the *machine code*—was now interspersed with symbols, the indecipherable icons of Redway's secret program.

There were Greek letters, equation connectors, the symbolic grammar of physics and advanced mathematics. There were shapes that looked like the signs of the zodiac. Lines and lines of stars and circles and crescents, lines of geometric shapes and irregular icons that looked crude, hand-drawn.

They had no place here, in the heart of the mainframe's code. Mirai wasn't even sure how they were being displayed, the mainframe's registers shouldn't have been able to accept them.

Behind the wall of text and symbols, Mirai could see her reflection. And standing beside her, Suki watched, lit in pale green by the glare of the HUD, just like her sister.

Mirai ignored the image, focusing on the data. She should go and tell Liv and Deacon what she'd found. Maybe it was important, maybe it wasn't. But they'd want to know how she was getting on, and she should go and tell them, go now, stand up and leave and maybe even run and whatever you do don't look back, never look back, and don't tell them what you saw and who you saw but most certainly go find a medical kit and take something, anything, to make it all go away.

But Mirai couldn't move. She felt cold, cold to the bone and she couldn't move. There was a weight on her, the darkness of the flight deck a physical thing crowding in. She couldn't move. Couldn't turn away. Couldn't close her eyes. Couldn't *not* look at the reflection of her dead sister standing at her side.

The reflection finally moved. Suki lifted her hand, and she rested it on Mirai's shoulder.

Mirai wanted to scream, wanted to cry, wanted to do anything. But she couldn't. All she could do was sit and watch and will herself to ignore the creeping cold that was spreading from her shoulder across her body, a cold as deep as her bones, as black as the nothing outside the ship, as dark as the void of the crawlspace that surrounded the entire ship.

Meanwhile, the other user of the XK72 mainframe continued their work uninterrupted.

17

QUICK AS YOU CAN, BOSS

Liv stopped at the flight deck's bulkhead door. The module beyond was empty, but she could hear a voice from somewhere close by. It was a whispering—intense and harshly sibilant, but Liv couldn't make out what it was saying as she stepped cautiously across the threshold, one foot placed silently after the other, and looked around.

The whispering was coming from the crawlspace, the empty black void where Deacon had removed a few of the wall panels.

Liv bunched her fists, concentrating on the feeling of her fingernails cutting into the fleshy part of her palms instead of the fear—no, *panic*—that was beginning to well up from somewhere deep inside her.

"Mirai?"

As soon as she spoke, the whispering stopped. Liv took another step, then stopped, straining her senses as she tried to detect something, anything, coming from the space behind the wall.

There was nothing to see, and now nothing more to hear.

Liv took a breath and approached the gap. The closer she got to the crawlspace, the more she could feel the chill coming from it. Reaching the opening, she hesitated, just for a moment, then leaned inside.

"Mirai?"

There was a gasp; Liv jerked back and looked down, and saw a huddled form lying on the floor, curled against a still-intact portion of the flight deck's wall. The form moved and gasped again, then turned suddenly and woke with a start. Mirai looked up at Liv.

Liv dropped to a crouch beside the crawlspace opening, and reached out as Mirai blinked and struggled to sit up. "What happened? Are you okay?" Liv frowned. "Did you go to sleep in there?" She placed the back of her hand against Mirai's cheek. The young woman was freezing cold.

"I . . ." Mirai gasped for breath again, and blinked. She glanced around, like she was just realizing where she was. "I don't know."

With Liv's help, Mirai stood, and the pair stepped back into the flight deck proper. Mirai stretched, like she was just getting up from a long nap, and headed back to the pilot's seat, her back to Liv, apparently keen to return to work.

Liv watched her, chewing the inside of her cheek as she thought.

Why had Mirai been sleeping in the crawlspace?

Did it really matter? Perhaps Mirai liked the enveloping darkness, the cooler air, the way the external insulation foam seemed to deaden the air, the crawlspace offering sanctuary, comfort, or the illusion thereof.

Maybe Mirai was just plain exhausted, like she was, and Liv knew you didn't always make the most logical decisions when you were that tired.

And the whispering? Just Mirai talking in her sleep as she dreamed?

Right?

Liv moved to stand behind Mirai's seat. She looked at the reflection in the window, Mirai lit from below by the lights of the console, the indicators and LEDs looking like a smeary constellation of stars against the absolute black of the nonexistent universe outside. Behind them was the flight deck, the bulkhead door, the passageway stretching away—

Someone was coming down the passageway. Deacon. Liv turned and . . .

And there was nobody there.

"How did you get along with the ion drive?"

Liv spun back around. Mirai was looking at Liv in the reflection.

Liv took a breath and told herself to focus. "Fine," she said. "At least, I think so. But we need to boost the efficiency of the power draw from the unbalanced exhaust."

At this, Mirai nodded, and turned around in her seat properly.

"I'm sure Deacon can help there."

"Agreed," said Liv. "I need to do some calculations first." She sat down in the co-pilot's seat. She gestured at the panel in front of Mirai. "How are you doing?"

Mirai sighed. "I'm getting nowhere fast, but I actually don't think there's any point in trying to clean Redway's code out of the mainframe."

As Liv sat gingerly in the co-pilot's seat, Mirai tapped the keyboard and highlighted a panel of text on the HUD. The characters were small and dense, with strange, scrambled symbols mixed with regular letters and numbers.

Mirai shook her head. "I don't even know where to start. This is way beyond anything I've ever seen. The machine code is hexadecimal registers. There is no way that other language should even be in here—there's no character set that can display those symbols at this level of the mainframe. It's impossible."

"You're saying the mainframe is completely, what . . . bricked?"

"I really don't know," said Mirai. "There's still stuff running, including processes I can't trace. It looks like another user in the system, but it must be part of Redway's protocol. That might be what's keeping the SLIP drive offline, a deliberate block to stop us trying to fix it." She sat back and looked at Liv. "I can't find a way to bypass Redway's program in order to access the SLIP drive controls directly, to see if I could find a way to just reset the system and then initiate a Drop without using the master interface. Again, maybe that's the runaway process. But more than that, Redway's code extends down to the base layer of the mainframe's machine code. Anything I try and change down there, without knowing what it is, could be catastrophic."

Liv sighed and rubbed her face. "No mainframe, no SLIP drive. No SLIP drive, no—"

"But we have a clean backup."

Liv dropped her hands and looked at Mirai. "Of the mainframe?"

"Well . . ."

"I sense a 'but' coming."

Mirai pursed her lips and looked uncertain, but Liv gave her time—she could see the young scientist was juggling options in her head, trying to figure out how to frame something Liv had an inkling was far from the simple solution she hoped it was.

"But . . . ?" Liv prompted.

"I didn't suggest this earlier," said Mirai, "because it's . . . well, to be honest I didn't even think of it, because I didn't think there was any way whatever Redway did would reach right down into the mainframe's core systems. Everything we do on this ship, everything we program in as we follow the mission parameters, operates at the top level. The mainframe takes that and does the rest itself."

"You're saying the code entered by Redway made the mainframe rewrite itself?"

"Right," said Mirai, with a nod. "I thought it was just a matter of reprogramming, purging Redway's code. But the OS itself has been compromised." She paused. "The OS that is currently running, anyway."

Liv felt the smile growing on her face. She liked how it felt. It had been awhile.

"So we can restore from backup?"

At that, Liv saw Mirai wince.

"But," Liv continued, "the catch is . . . ?"

"It's the ship's *whole* computer system," said Mirai. "Close to ninety-nine percent of everything that's running. In some ways—in a lot of ways—the OS *is* the XK72."

"So we wipe the whole ship and restore from the backup. That'll wipe out everything Redway did, stop any running protocols. We'll be back to where we were at launch, with a clean system. We can run the mission protocol again and make the Drop." Liv paused. "Right?"

Mirai winced again. "Yes, but it's going to take awhile. There's going to be an element of trial and error as I figure out how to do it, and once I do, the mainframe will be down for a long time while it reformats and reboots. And while it's down, we'll have nothing but basic automatics, life support, things like that. Some other, simple systems. Comms, raw sensor data but no analysis or filtering."

"Okay," said Liv. "That doesn't sound so bad. We're running on system minimum already. How long is long?"

"There, I'm not entirely sure," said Mirai. "Hours, at least. Probably twenty-four."

"Twenty-four hours?" Liv frowned. "That's about as long as you said our power would last for."

"Less, at this point."

"So we have to get the ion drive working with the grid."

Mirai nodded. "That should give us enough," she said, "but yes, we absolutely have to make that work first." She leaned forward to check the console readings. "I can start working on the reboot right now, but as soon as I initiate the system wipe, there's no going back. We need to know we have the power fixed."

"Roger that," said Liv. "Do as much prep as you can now. I'll go talk to Deak." She touched her earpiece. "Deak, this is Liv. What's your status?"

The comms clicked, but there was no answer. Liv glanced at Mirai. "Do you know where Deak is?"

"SLIP drive, I thought."

Liv tried her comms again. "Deacon, come in, please."

Nothing. Liv switched over to the main ship channel on the control console in front of her. "Deacon?"

The comms clicked and the air was filled with an earsplitting whine. Mirai and Liv both grimaced as the sound increased in both pitch and volume before Liv slammed her hand down on the comms control, cutting the open link to the SLIP drive room.

Mirai dropped her hands. "What was that?"

Liv pointed at the console. "Do a system check," she said, before tapping her earpiece again to try Deacon's private channel. "Deak, what's going on?"

Mirai looked over her console, flicking switches as she cycled through the ship's reports. "Doesn't seem to be any faults anywhere," she said, peering at a readout. "Systems running at normal minimum, no change."

That was when the sound started up again. It was much fainter now as it echoed down from the rear of the XK72, rather than blasting through the open comms. Liv cocked her head, her eyes wide as she listened. The sound was industrial, like a crystal carbon saw slicing into something very hard indeed.

"What is he doing back there?" asked Mirai.

The sound stopped as suddenly as it had started. Immediately Liv tapped her earpiece again. "Deacon, come in please!"

The comms clicked. "Deak, receiving," came his voice. He huffed as he got his breath back.

"What's going on? What were you—"

"I think you need to come and see this."

Liv and Mirai looked at each other.

"Quick as you can, boss."

18

FEAR OF THE UNKNOWN

The door to the SLIP drive module was closed. Liv reached it first, but she paused at the threshold, hand reaching for the controls. Mirai came up beside her, bouncing on the balls of her feet. She didn't seem to notice Liv's hesitation, or her quick, shallow breaths.

Or her fear. Fear of the unknown. Of the dark.

Fear of what was on the other side of the door.

And then that feeling was gone and Liv felt ridiculous, but relieved, almost light-headed. She slapped the door control.

The door opened and black smoke poured out. Liv coughed, squinting into the cabin beyond as, beside her, Mirai buried her mouth and nose in the crook of her arm.

"Deacon!" Liv called out, then spluttered in the acrid cloud. "Are you okay?"

With the door open, the smoke cleared quickly. Liv coughed again, and as she waved the cloud away from her face, she found the stuff sticking to her skin and clothes. It wasn't smoke, it was dust.

"Get in here and take a look at this," came Deacon's voice. Mirai led the way through the door.

A bare-chested Deacon was standing next to the SLIP drive, his T-shirt folded and wrapped around his mouth and nose for protection. On the floor next to him was a rectangular white block about the size of a large flight case, a meter long, half as tall and wide—a power pack from the ship's servodrone, Liv realized. A long white pole was leaning against it, a thick neon-orange cable leading from it to the array of ports on the top of the power pack. An identical cable snaked from another port to the device Deacon himself was holding, a more complex tool consisting of a black metal frame surrounding a white cylindrical core, at the end of which was a circular blade about fifteen centimeters in diameter.

Liv had been right—the awful noise *had* come from a cutting tool, one of the servodrone's attachments, while the slender pole leaning on the power pack was the drone's plasma torch.

Deacon set the cutter down next to the torch and pulled his makeshift mask down as Liv looked around, taking stock of his work. One side of the SLIP drive's mirrored cowling was blackened with heavy soot, but seemed otherwise undamaged. However, the floor was covered with chunks of thick black insulating foam.

Deacon stood back and pointed into the exposed crawlspace. "Look at that."

Mirai moved closer, Liv by her side. "What is it?" asked the younger scientist.

Deacon unwrapped the T-shirt from around his neck and pulled it back on. "That's what I was wondering," he said. "You ever see something like this before?"

Liv opened her mouth to answer, but she didn't quite know what to say, so she closed it again and just shook her head.

Deacon had used the saw to slice through the insulating foam on the outer wall of the crawlspace, using the area damaged earlier as a starting point to expose more of the ship's hull.

A hull Liv knew in precise detail. A standard Artemis design, a latticework of reinforced metalwork that formed a tight skeletal structure, strengthening the outer hull. All ships were built to the same pattern, one that Artemis had developed so long ago its patent had long expired.

The XK72 was built to the same design. Liv knew, because she'd seen the designs, along with the rest of the team.

Right now, she wished she had paid more attention. It wasn't the first time she'd felt this way on this mission.

Liv had known something was wrong—they all had—when they'd seen the first patch of hull, revealed when the insulation was damaged, but now she was forced again to confront the mystery head-on.

As their earlier glimpse had suggested, instead of a regular grid-like pattern, the exposed frame was anything but. The metal beams curved, they bent at angles, they joined back up with each other, forming shapes that were regular polygons and shapes that arced and flowed, less like starship engineering and more like handmade art. In the gaps between the shapes and lines and curves were set polished colored crystals, their facets cut with precision. Liv could see now the first part that they had accidentally revealed earlier was a brilliant white diamond, set inside the apex of a triangle shape. The whole wall was studded with gems, each glittering like a star.

Liv looked at Deacon. He just nodded, and gestured to the SLIP drive behind them. "First I thought I'd try and cut through the cowling of this thing," he said. "See if maybe there was a way to force a reset manually. Tried the plasma torch, but that wouldn't even touch it. So I was going to try the saw, but . . ."

He trailed off. Liv looked over her shoulder. "But what?"

Deacon frowned. He folded his arms, tight.

Liv stood to face him. "Deak?"

He took a deep breath. "I don't know. It sounds crazy now. I mean, it *is* crazy."

"What is?"

"I thought someone was watching me." He unfolded his arms and raised his hands. "Look, I know what it sounds like, and I know it's crazy, trust me, I know. But anyway, whenever I had my back to the hull, I just . . . I don't know. It creeped me out, and I just had to . . . well, I figured if I just had a look, got it out of my system, you know, kill the distraction, then I'd be able to concentrate." He laughed, but it died quickly.

Liv frowned, but she knew better than to judge. This mission, this environment, was playing tricks on all of them. She knew that all too well. She nodded at the exposed hull. "So you cut through the insulation?"

Deacon turned back to his handiwork. "I mean, I'm kinda glad I did now. I've been an engineer for thirty years and I've never seen anything like that." He walked up to the gap in the wall panels and leaned in, but Liv noticed how he folded his arms tight again, like he wanted to make doubly sure he didn't touch anything, didn't want to put any part of himself beyond the threshold of the crawlspace again. "What the heck kind of ship has a frame like this? And what's with all these crystals? Looks like the inside of my grandpa's antique pocket watch."

He was right. The framework still did its job, reinforcing the ship's skin, but the work that had gone into the design was truly bewildering. Liv wondered if the entire ship was like this, or if it was confined, for some reason, to the SLIP drive module. The SLIP drive itself was an odd design. Perhaps the structure of the walls here, in this room, was important.

"And that's not all," said Deacon. He turned and moved back to the SLIP drive, and dropped to a crouch. "Come here and take a look at these fixings." He ran his thumb over the surface of the device, then gestured for the other two to join him. Liv peered closely at the mirrored cowling; it took her a moment, but then she saw the screws.

"That's a heck of a tamper-proof shell," said Deacon. "I don't even know what kind of multitool you'd need to open this thing. Every screw is different. And that's not all."

Liv and Mirai looked at him. Deacon stood, and pointed back into the crawlspace.

"The symbols on the screws match the ones on the hull."

Mirai stepped closer to look at the wall, shaking her head. She ran her fingers through her long black hair, and turned back to the others. "How is this even possible? These symbols, they're the same as the ones in Redway's code."

Deacon and Liv exchanged a look. Deacon didn't ask the question, but for Liv, he didn't have to.

"She's right," she said.

Deacon looked at her then looked at Mirai. "What, like they're an alphabet? A language?"

"Computer code," said Liv.

"A code we can't read," said Mirai. "At least, not without Redway's data pad."

"Which is currently who knows how far away in the escape pod," said Deacon.

Liv looked at the wall, then turned around to look at the SLIP drive. She looked at her reflected image and counted the people in the room behind her.

There were only two.

Thank goodness.

Liv turned back to face the others. "Okay, look . . ." she paused, and shook her head. Was she about to make the right decision, or not?

Go with your gut, she thought. She was mission lead for a reason.

She sighed, and continued. "Truth is, we're pushed for time here. Whatever this is—" she gestured to the exposed framework that glittered in the impossible darkness of the crawlspace—"and whatever it has to do with Redway's code, with Artemis, with the SLIP drive, with whatever, it'll have to wait. We're out of time, so Mirai is going to reboot the mainframe. That'll reset the mission from scratch and we'll be able to initiate the Drop like we were supposed to."

Deacon rubbed his chin. "And that'll get us back home, right?"

Mirai nodded. "Yes, it will."

"But," said Liv, "resetting the ship is going to take a while." She nodded at Deacon. "In the meantime, I'm going to need your help."

Deacon spread his hands. "You the boss, boss."

"I've unbalanced the ion drives, so when we fire them up—"

Deacon laughed, once, then narrowed his eyes. "Oh, you've done *what* now?"

Now it was Liv's turn to hold up her hands. "Yes, I know. But, hear me out. The drive's exhaust will be dirty—"

"Dirty as *hell*," said Deacon.

"That's the point, Deak," said Liv. "The particles will be heavy enough to interact with the power grid, energizing it just enough to stop the power drain." She paused, and raised an eyebrow. "Right?"

Deacon's expression was frozen for a moment. Liv felt her eyebrow move even higher of its own accord . . . then Deacon grinned.

"Clever. Stop the drain, buy us some time."

"Exactly," said Liv, "but I want more than that. I want to bring the power right back up."

Deacon's smile vanished, replaced by a grimace. "Difficult. The energization rate will be pretty bad. Very inefficient."

"Do you think there's a way to improve it?"

Deacon lifted a finger and waggled it in the air, but he didn't answer. Instead, he began to walk a tight circle in front of Liv and Mirai, finger still raised, gaze now on the floor.

Mirai glanced sideways at Liv. Liv nodded at her, trying to indicate that everything would be okay, before wondering whether she really believed that herself.

Deacon stopped his pacing, then turned to the other two and clicked his fingers on both hands.

"The induction combs for the SLIP drive. That might work."

Liv looked at him blankly, and Deacon's grin returned.

"We rig them up," he said.

Mirai frowned. "But the SLIP drive is offline."

"Doesn't matter," said Deacon. "There are one hundred and forty-four hyper-efficient superconductors out there, on the hull." He gestured in the air as he spoke, miming the actions for his two fellow crewmembers. "We change their alignment, we turn them into a particle capture system.

Wire them up, feed their output into the external power coupling. The grid nanolayer absorbs what it can, but the combs grab a whole lot more." He walked over to the servodrone's power pack and tools, and looked down on them, hands on his hips. "We'll need to get the servodrone itself up and running. Once I've figured out how to rig the combs, we can program the drone and leave it working."

Liv felt her smile returning again. "That'll make it a lot easier and faster."

"See, I knew you'd need me to save the day. I should ask for a raise." Deacon knelt on the decking, and began disconnecting the tools from the power pack. Liv watched him for a moment, then felt a hand on her sleeve. She turned to Mirai.

"What about Astrid?" asked Mirai, her voice barely a whisper, her eyes darting back to the crawlspace.

Liv held her breath. Nobody spoke; the only sound was Deacon getting the power pack and cables together.

"We need power," said Liv quietly. "We need power and we need to get the mainframe rebooted. Okay?"

Mirai nodded a little. Her eyes went back to the crawlspace. Then she seemed to shiver, just slightly, before nodding again. That time it looked, to Liv, that Mirai was convincing herself to go on. "I'll prep the EVA suits."

With that, Mirai turned and left. Liv watched her departing back for a moment, then sensed Deacon at her side. He had the two power cables looped over one shoulder and held a drone tool in each hand.

"We ready, boss?" He nodded toward the power pack. "Give me a hand with that?"

Liv nodded, and together they began moving the equipment out of the module.

Behind them, the stars in the outer wall glittered in a light that wasn't there, and a shadow moved in the crawlspace and then it was gone.

19

FOURTH TIME LUCKY

Liv heaved on the magnowrench a fourth time, and it was fourth time lucky, the connector plate under the induction comb finally snapped into place.

While the combs were a unique custom design, Liv was grateful that the connector modules they sat on were at least standard Artemis parts. But after a solid hour of work, Liv realized she had seriously underestimated the amount of work the rigging required, despite Deacon's detailed instructions. She knew that dragging hundreds of meters of extension cable over the hull, threading them through the comb array, and, at each comb, splicing a power relay from the cable into the base module of each comb was going to take time and effort. But what she hadn't anticipated was that to access the port under each comb, the comb itself had to be disconnected, moved to allow access, then re-seated with the fan-like structure angled a few degrees off perpendicular to maximize energization. To make a difficult job even harder, the port connectors were a tight fit, and required plenty of sweat to get the cable splice plugged in.

Shoving the comb back into position, Liv took a breath that momentarily misted the interior of her visor.

Two combs done.

One hundred and forty-two to go.

She closed her eyes and shook her head. She told herself the plan would work, because Deacon was damned good at what he did and if he said it would work, then it would work. At least they knew what to do now, and they could set the servodrone on a routine to do the bulk of the work. As an all-purpose maintenance robot, it would complete the job in a fraction of the time they could, and it would have none of the trouble the merely human crew had encountered. With Deacon inside assembling the drone, Liv had told Mirai to hit the reboot sequence on the mainframe, then don the other sealed EVA suit—there was no time to check over the one unsealed by, presumably, Astrid, but it did mean they were down to just the two—and help her out here, getting the relay splices ready to pass to her colleague.

Rebooting the mainframe before the grid was ready was a risk, but a calculated one. Every moment was precious, which was also why she'd insisted on starting on the combs before the drone was ready. Even if they could fix up only a handful of combs out of the 144, that would put them ahead.

Liv exhaled hotly again, watching her breath condense for a second on her visor before her EVA suit compensated and cleared it. She sat back on her haunches, taking a moment, her back against the body of the comb itself, careful to keep the magnetic soles of her boots in contact with the ship.

As irrational and impractical as the thought was, she almost didn't want to touch the combs—they were semicircular structures about a meter across, with twelve prongs, each of a different size, projecting out, and their brilliant silver surfaces shone in the ship's lights—but she knew the coldness that she felt through her suit as she leaned against it was nothing more than her imagination. After adjusting the tension on the safety umbilical that tethered her to the rail that ran the length of the hull, she eased herself down so she could sit properly. Her arms ached from levering the connector into place, and simply needed to rest for a few minutes. She looked up, and, not for the first time since venturing out onto the hull, considered the space in which they found themselves.

The void was a uniform black that felt like a solid mass, a heavy veil hanging over your helmet, like you could reach out and grab it in huge handfuls. That sensation was disorienting, the constant feeling that you were about to smack face-first into something you couldn't see, so Liv had kept her attention as much as possible on the ship itself, the hull well-lit by the service lights that were normally reserved for hangar work. With no external energy sources at all, let alone anything that would allow them to see, they had no option but to turn the service lights on, further draining the ship's batteries. The servodrone, of course, didn't need lights. The quicker Deacon got it up and running, the better.

The computer in Liv's EVA suit was having just as hard a time as she was. She glanced at the HUD displayed against the inside of her visor, the rows of data readouts sitting underneath the upside-down "T" shape in the center, designed to give the suit's wearer an artificial horizon to keep themselves oriented. Oxygen, good. Internal temperature, normal. Suit power, a little on the low side, but apparently good for about a hundred more hours of EVA—far longer than the XK72 had power for, at the moment.

But the external temperature, pressure, and radiation readings were blank fields, not even zero, like the suit had just bugged out. She checked the computer panel on her left wrist, but the readout there was exactly the same. The void was a perfect nothing, an *absence*. She didn't blame her suit's computer for not being able to process that information.

"How's progress?" Mirai's voice came in over the suit-to-suit comms, bringing Liv out of her reverie. As she spoke, a green icon blinked on Liv's display, indicating Mirai's location and distance at fifty meters away, just around the curve of the hull.

"I've installed two relays," said Liv, "but it wasn't easy. How are the cable splices coming?"

"They're fine, but I wonder if we might have some more compatible couplings in the stores. I might be able to make something a little better than these."

Liv nodded to herself. "Well, let's see how we go once the drone is up," she said, but then she paused as a sigh came over the comms just as Mirai's mic clicked off.

It was her imagination, again, because it had been Mirai sighing about something, and there was no way that sound had come from somewhere else entirely, not through the comms but from somewhere to her right, as though there was someone next to her on the hull, as though they had sighed and that sound had, impossibly, traveled through the void and reached Liv's ears inside her helmet and—

"If the drone threads the cable and fits the relays, it'll still be faster if I build the splices for it," said Mirai.

Liv felt her heart rate begin to go down. She nodded again, more forcefully, forcing her tired mind back to reality.

"Roger that," she said, smiling behind her visor.

And then her smile vanished, and she turned her head, looking away from the figure of Redway standing behind the comb.

She closed her eyes.

Mirai's comm clicked on again. "Liv? You okay to keep going?"

"Yes. Yes, I'm fine. We keep going until the drone is ready."

"Okay."

Liv licked her dry lips and opened her eyes. Mirai's green indicator flashed then disappeared as the comms channel closed.

Liv was alone once more. Really, truly, alone. She knew it. There was no one out here but her and Mirai and they were on opposite sides of the hull. Liv was alone. She turned her head, slowly, to check, until she could see that Redway wasn't there, because of course he wasn't. She breathed a sigh of relief, her visor momentarily misting again. When it cleared, Liv gazed out over the hull that stretched out in front of her, the silvery shapes of the SLIP drive combs reaching out into the flat black void that surrounded the ship like skeletal fingers.

Then she stood and, trying to keep her eyes low, on her feet, on the hull, she headed to the next comb as the sheer weight of the void felt like it was resting on her, pushing her down onto the skin of the XK72. It wasn't real—her movement was unimpeded, and there was no resistance. Yet part of her brain insisted on telling her she was walking underwater and another part of her was surprised at the ease of her movement, like when you reach for something you think is heavy only to find it weighs nothing at all.

"It's a bitch, isn't it?" said Redway as he walked beside her. Liv ignored him because she knew that he wasn't there and that it was her mind playing tricks. Sleep deprivation. Hunger. Thirst. The strange void reaching down into her synapses and doing stranger things.

Liv knelt by the next comb and used the magnowrench to detach its fixing and heave the weird device up to access the port beneath it. Then she reached back and grabbed the power cable, the relay splice already hanging off it. She connected the relay—it clicked into place the first time, thank goodness—then refitted the comb, pushed it askew, and spun the bolt. The whole process was still laborious and her arm muscles still sang in protest when she was done, but done it was, and in record time.

The next relay took a full half hour to fit and then Liv couldn't get the comb to lock back down. She swore the whole time behind her visor.

A laugh echoed in her ears. "Don't worry, I know the feeling," came Mirai's voice over the comms. Liv glanced up in surprise, then saw a green indicator in her HUD. She'd somehow activated her comms, although she didn't remember it. Mirai was still fifty meters away, but now somewhere in the opposite direction.

The comb locked itself back into place with a *thud* that Liv felt through her whole suit. Then she flopped down on the hull, using the comb as a backrest again, and laughed herself.

And then the laugh died in her throat, as another sound came over the comms. It wasn't from Mirai—her channel was closed. It was from somewhere else.

Another person.

Liv lifted her left hand and poked at the small buttons on her wrist computer to reset her comms channel. Her earpiece chimed, and scrolling text on her visor HUD confirmed what she'd just done.

Liv opened her comms, and held her breath.

There. Another sound on the channel between her and Mirai.

A third person, not speaking—if anything, trying to keep quiet, trying not to be noticed—but there. Breathing, very gently, very quietly.

Liv let go of her breath. She stood up, and called back to the XK72.

"Deak, are you on this channel?"

A beep, and nothing, nothing except Liv's hot and shallow breaths and the hum of her blood in her ears, and the sound of someone else breathing.

It had to be him, didn't it? He'd turned his comms on without realizing.

"Deacon, come in please."

Beep.

"Deacon, where the hell are you?"

Liv spun around, the sound of the breathing suddenly at her shoulder again. The figure of Redway loomed behind her. She yelled out and stumbled backward. As her momentum pushed her onward, she got her feet under her and ran, but her foot caught on something on the hull and she was thrown forward. For a brief, sickening moment, she lost all contact with the hull and she felt a nauseating, almost painful pang of adrenaline as she waited for the bone-jarring snag of the safety tether as it snapped her back from oblivion. She panicked, her quick breaths condensing on her visor, her view of the XK72 now clouded.

Then she hit the hull with her knees, and a split second later the chin of her helmet connected with the base of a comb. She felt a tooth slice into her tongue, her helmet's padding protecting her from the impact but not enough to stop the edges of her world from dancing with sparks. Simultaneously dizzy and nauseous, Liv struggled to swallow back the hot and bitter bile she could feel rising up her throat.

A hand grabbed her around her forearm. Liv cried out in surprise, and pulled away while still locking her own hand around the arm of the other person.

"Liv?"

Liv blinked and found herself looking at the curve of Mirai's helmet.

"Ah . . . Mirai . . . I . . . *dammit!*"

Liv fought to control her breathing. Her visor began to clear, her suit's environment controls whirring as it struggled to stabilize. A few seconds later and the hull of the XK72 resolved itself around her.

Except.

Except it looked different. Maybe she'd got turned around, maybe she'd fallen farther than she thought, somehow scooting herself around the ship in her moment of . . .

Fear? Yes, fear. She felt like she was falling, like she was drowning, like the blackness was not just heavy and dense but moving, all around her, grabbing her and twisting her and pushing her.

This part of the XK72's hull was darker than the rest, a gray that was nearly black, with the service lights all pointing away from them. But even so, there was a glint on the surface, the hull reflecting a light source from another direction.

Liv looked up. There were no stars, no suns, no anything. The void black, featureless. Yet the hull glowed, impossibly, the black metal shining toward a horizon that was—

Horizon? She was sitting on a flat plain. Smooth, endless, nothing but black metal under a black sky.

Liv's breath caught in her throat. She pulled against the arm that was holding hers, trying to get herself back onto her feet.

Then she cried out in pain. The hand gripping her below the elbow, it was—

Cold. Colder than ice, so cold her bones ached, so cold she cried out in pain again, and she turned to her rescuer and she saw—

"Liv!"

Liv blinked, looked up. Mirai was running toward her, slaloming between the irregular spacing of the combs, her safety tether sliding along the rail, magnetic boots thudding so hard on the hull Liv could feel the vibrations. Liv pushed herself up on her elbows. The hull of the XK72 wasn't black, it was a light gray, and it didn't form a flat horizon, it was curved, and the array of combs reached up all around her. She was leaning against one right now.

"Liv!" Mirai called out again. She came to a halt and knelt down, reaching out to help. Liv felt herself move, shifting backward against the comb as she recoiled instinctively from her colleague.

From what was reflected in her colleague's visor, the figure standing on the hull, watching, smiling.

And then—

"I'm fine," said Liv. Mirai grabbed her by the arm, and helped her up. Liv stood there, suddenly feeling light, feeling warm, the inescapable sensation of being free to move, like she'd surfaced from a cold, dark lake and could finally fill her lungs with air.

Mirai looked Liv up and down, her hands still supporting her. "What happened?"

Liv looked at Mirai, but now she could only see her own reflection in Mirai's visor, the hull and the combs stretching out behind her.

She took a breath, then another, and then she couldn't remember what it was she had seen.

Nothing. You saw nothing at all. You need sleep. You need food.

Liv steadied her breathing. Her visor was clear of condensation.

Everything was fine.

Everything *is* fine.

Beep.

"What's going on out there?" asked Deacon over the comms. "Everyone okay?"

Liv didn't speak. After a moment, it was Mirai who answered. "Yes, we're fine, Deak, we're fine. Liv tripped, that's all." She sighed. "This is all quite a lot of work."

"I'm sure," said Deacon. "The drone is going to be a big help."

"Where were you?" Liv snapped. In front of her, Mirai cocked her head, surprised at Liv's sudden tone. Liv ignored her. "Deacon," she said, "I called earlier but got no response."

"Hey, I've been right here, haven't moved," he said. Liv heard him clicking on something. "Internal comms showing green on all channels."

"The connection was definitely dropped," said Liv. "We were all cut off for a few seconds."

"Okay, log that as another fault to check out once we get the computer back," said Deacon. "The drone's ready to roll. How did you get on out there?"

Liv walked away and rolled her neck, her shoulders, stretching the aching muscles. It didn't help much. Her whole body was sore and crying out for rest, and a headache was thumping in from behind her eyes.

Everything is just fine. Everything is just fine.

She turned on her heel, looking out across the hull. It felt like they'd been out here forever. And . . . what exactly had happened? She caught a fleeting memory of a flat black plain, and then it was gone. Had she passed out, collapsed from fatigue?

Anyway. "I've done four combs," she said. "The drone can handle the rest."

"I still need to build the relay splices," said Mirai, "but I can do that inside while the drone does the cable. While that's happening, Liv, you and Deak can get some rest. There's nothing for us to do until the drone finishes. We can sleep in shifts for a while."

Liv nodded, thankful someone else was making a sensible decision. "Agreed."

Mirai turned her head, looking at the comb array around them. The ship's external lights caught on her visor, obscuring her face. Then when she turned back to Liv, her visor clear and free from the reflected light, something else caught Liv's eye. She could see Mirai's face clearly, but there was a white dot moving across her forehead. A moment later, she saw Mirai's eyes glance up, somewhere over Liv's shoulder.

Liv turned even as Mirai lifted a hand to point.

"What's that?"

The infinite black expanse behind them was no longer empty. At a point maybe sixty degrees from the curve of the hull, there was a light.

Mirai stepped around Liv, her gaze clearly fixed on the spot. Then she stopped and turned back around, confused. Liv moved forward to join her.

"Is that a star?" asked Mirai.

The comms beeped.

"What's happening?" asked Deacon. "Is there something out there?"

"Affirmative," said Liv. "There's something here."

The light was a solid white dot, a pinprick against the void. It didn't flicker, it didn't sparkle. Liv lifted her wrist again and tapped at the keypad, flipping her visor through every available filter, cycling from visible light to infrared, to ultraviolet, even to x-rays and microwaves, two settings normally used as shielding for high-energy welding jobs carried out during EVAs. As she moved through the spectrum, the light flared a little, the blurring edges moving, like the object was rotating.

"I can't make anything out," said Mirai. Liv switched back to the standard filter and glanced over at the scientist, and saw she was trying the same thing with her own visor. "My HUD can't get a lock on it. Whatever it is, it must be a long way off."

Liv nodded and, following Mirai's lead, brought up her HUD's target indicator, adjusting the parameters on her wrist computer. The orange box flashed in front of her eyes and floated up to the point of light, flickered green for the briefest of moments, then went back to orange and continued its lazy journey around Liv's vision. She turned the target off and stared at the point. It didn't seem to be moving, nor was it changing in size.

"You getting anything, Deak?" asked Liv.

Her earpiece beeped and Deacon's heavy breathing filled the channel. "I'm just in the flight deck now." Then she heard him drop into one of the flight seats and start tapping at a keyboard. "Nope, the sensors aren't picking up anything, except . . . hold on."

Liv and Mirai glanced at each other.

"Okay," said Deacon, "it's a faint energy signature, but it's just the light from whatever it is. I'm just registering a luminance and magnitude, that's it. I don't think the ship would see it normally, but it's the only thing out there, so there's no noise to hide the reading."

"But, what is it?" asked Mirai. "It can't just . . . *appear,* like that, can it?"

Liv could hear the tension in Mirai's voice. She looked at the light.

"It could be moving toward us," she said. "It's only just got close enough for us to see its light, or for it to be reflecting the lights from the ship."

"You think that thing is coming *toward* us?"

Liv held up her hands. "Hey, I don't know, I was just thinking out loud. We don't know anything about this place, or what might be in it, and we've got enough to do without more distractions, okay?"

Mirai looked at her, her chest heaving as her fear threatened to take hold. Liv took a step nearer and laid her hand on Mirai's shoulder.

"Mirai?"

Then Mirai nodded, and relaxed. "Yes, you're right."

"Let's get back inside," said Liv. "We'll start the drone up. Then you can get to work on the relays and Deak and I will rest."

Mirai nodded again, then turned and headed back toward the main airlock. Liv watched her. Then she turned and looked up at the strange light again.

It felt like an eye, like it was alive, but Liv knew that was her imagination, pure and simple, so she turned around and followed Mirai and ignored the feeling they were being watched.

20

EVERYTHING IS GREAT

The knocking woke her again, and this time it was loud enough for Liv to leap off her bunk. As she scrambled for the door, the knocking continued, someone hammering, hard.

"Okay, okay, *okay*!"

She rolled her neck and slapped the door control. There was a whirring, like the door had activated, but it remained closed. Liv frowned, the knocking kept going, and she tried the door control again.

The door opened this time. Beyond was a flat black metal plain under a black sky. Liv gasped in surprise, then stumbled backward, the air freezing, the chill so deep—so *malevolent*—she could feel the ache in her bones.

Then there was movement, something that caught her eye. She looked up, and there it was.

The star, shining, the single solitary point of light alone in the dark.

Then there was another movement, and she looked down. The flat metal plain had a horizon, and at that horizon there was another glow, an alien sun rising on an alien world, two black voids now separated by a cold blue glow.

Something moved in the light. Something *crawled*. Something of immense size infinitely distant, the crawling thing actually beyond the horizon, a thing as big as a city, its shadow cast as long as a light year in the alien dawn.

The cold enveloped Liv, crushing her body. She wrapped her arms around herself, but she couldn't feel them, she couldn't feel anything except the cold, hostile and dangerous.

Then she looked up and the light in the sky was spinning, a diamond turning in the night, slowly growing larger as it approached.

There was a knock on the door.

This time, Liv woke up.

Maybe it was the escape pod, that star that had appeared and which now shone in the black nothing, the life raft arcing back toward them.

Deacon had been more interested in Liv's theory than Mirai, at least. The flight analyst had reacted when Liv had voiced her thought, but not in a way that Liv liked. They were back in the flight deck, watching the light on the HUD, and when Liv spoke Mirai had jerked, her eyes blinking like she'd just fallen out of a deep sleep—a hypnic jerk, like the ones Liv had found herself experiencing more than was usual. Mirai hadn't spoken. She just wrapped her arms around herself, tight, her gaze firmly on the front view port. And then she'd left to go and rest.

"You can't exactly pilot those things," Deacon had said, watching Mirai as she walked out. Logical, as always, but Liv had been surprised at the coolness in his voice.

It was then she realized the other two were feeling exactly what she was feeling, that something bad was going to happen, that they had enough to deal with without the situation changing yet again.

Liv looked at the light, willing it to . . .

To disappear. To prove to her that it was just a figment of her imagination. Like the sounds that had woken her from her unhappy slumber, like the ghost of Redway that stood smiling at the edge of sight and was then gone as soon as she looked at him.

Like everything about this mission from hell. She wondered again if it was *all* just a dream, if she was still out cold on the decking down in the main passageway, Redway stumbling around the flight deck, wondering what had gone wrong as he had followed his secret orders. Maybe there was an Artemis rescue shuttle en route. Or maybe they really were alone, the XK72 turning end over end, floating out into the space beyond the earth's orbit, the interrupted Drop dumping them in a far-distant quadrant of the solar system, of the galaxy, all contact not just lost but utterly impossible, the test ship now nothing but a floating tomb that would spin and drift and cool until it became just a part of the universe, cold matter, insignificant, invisible, lost until the end of the universe, until the end of time.

Liv sighed. She took another bite of the crumbly blueberry-flavored ration bar (*why the fuck were they all fucking fruit flavored?*) and sat back in the flight seat. In front of her, the HUD was divided into two screens—one showed the singular white spot against the blackness, the other showed a feed from the hull, the servodrone now busy with its programmed task. This was as much as they could bring up, with nearly all of the ship's functions unavailable while the mainframe was offline.

The drone was working much faster than any of the human crew would have been able to, but even after four hours of fitful sleep, Liv had been disappointed with its progress, part of her expecting—*hoping*—that when she woke up, the job would be done and they'd be one step closer to home. Instead, she felt almost more tired than before, the wrench of waking from her nightmare sapping her energy. On the screen, the drone crawled slowly along, the boxy white bulk of its main body shining brilliantly under the hull lights which the three human crew had agreed to leave on, despite the extra power drain. Somehow it felt . . . better.

Liv looked away, forcing the half-forgotten dream about something crawling in another light out of her mind.

In the co-pilot's seat, Deacon crumpled the foil wrapper of his ration bar and tossed it onto the console. He'd eaten three of the things already. Perhaps he liked blueberries. Then he leaned forward and checked the drone's progress on a console readout. "Forty-eight combs. Ninety-four to go."

Liv did the math, and frowned at the result. "Forty-eight combs in four hours means nearly another eight hours to finish the job. That gives us just six hours before we lose power completely. Any way we can speed it up?"

Deacon pursed his lips. "We have some wiggle room. I'd rather the drone be out there making progress, however slow, than us waste a couple of hours trying to improve its work algorithm for probably little benefit."

Liv didn't say anything. She didn't need to. Deacon was right again. All they could do was leave the servodrone to do its job. In only a few hours, Liv told herself, they'd have all the power they needed, and then they just had to sit tight until the computer was back and they could do the Drop and get home.

Liv glanced at another manual readout and watched the progress bar of the computer reset, willing it to move even a pixel. It was so slow, was anything even happening? She tapped a control, and the readout changed to show CPU load—it was high, nearly one hundred percent. That was normal, she assumed. The reboot was clearly a complicated operation.

So, no problem. All systems were, in Liv's mind, anyway, green, green,

green. The drone was working (slowly but on schedule). The computer was resetting (slowly but Mirai had figured it all out). She'd gotten at least *some* sleep, and now it was Mirai's rest period.

It was all good. Great, even. *Everything is great.*

Liv told herself that, again and again and again and *again.*

And then she looked up at the feed of the single light in the sky and she told herself again that everything was fine, because maybe if she kept thinking it, she'd eventually believe it, and maybe if she believed it, she'd stop worrying about the light and the way it felt like it was watching her, the tiny glow somehow in the corner of her vision wherever she looked, reflected off the consoles and off the silver foil of Deacon's empty ration packs.

While the two of them had sat there eating, she'd turned the display off twice. But she couldn't bear *not* to see the light. Somehow, that felt even worse. So she turned it back on just a few seconds later, both times.

Liv glanced over at Deacon. He was now stretched back in the flight seat, his hands locked behind his head, his eyes closed, his chest rising and falling with the slow ease of comfortable sleep.

Liv smiled—not at the recumbent form of the aux specialist, but at her own pang of jealousy that Deacon could just go out, like *that.*

She turned back to the forward view. She leaned back, just a little. Her sore back immediately improved, so she leaned back a little more.

She watched the light, and wondered if it was really the escape pod coming home, and if Avery was alive, wondered what he'd found, wondered what Redway had done, wondered who he was working for, wondered if even Artemis knew, wondered what had happened to Astrid, wondered about the moving mass at the edge of the black metal plain and wondered about the light from the hidden sun over the perfectly straight horizon and—

Deacon laughed, quietly. Liv jerked her head up, her heart racing. She'd fallen asleep. Deacon was still in the same position, lying back, his eyes closed. Was he talking—laughing—in his sleep?

Liv felt her headache beginning to return.

"Hey."

Liv jumped again, and Deacon opened his eyes. They both turned around in their flight seats as Mirai stepped over the bulkhead and into the flight deck. She was still wearing the bright orange jumpsuit that was the inner lining of her EVA suit, the top half folded down and tied around her waist.

"Mirai," said Liv. "You should be resting."

"Can't sleep," said Mirai. "Every time I drop off, I have a nightmare and wake up." She offered a weak smile. "I swear, it's more exhausting lying there trying to sleep. I may as well be doing something."

Deacon laughed again and stood from his seat, gesturing for Mirai to take his spot. "I'll go get you something to eat," he said. He patted her on the shoulder as he passed and headed out of the flight deck. "I hope you like boysenberry."

Mirai thanked him and sat in the co-pilot's position. Liv watched her as she glanced over the displays, her gaze holding for a moment on the view of the light on the HUD.

"So," said Liv brightly, trying to distract Mirai . . . and trying to distract herself

was it the pod was it Avery was it Redway were they out there could they reach them

by gesturing at the control panel in front of her. "Everything is running like it should be." She ran through an update, Mirai nodding as she took it in.

Then Liv looked past Mirai, into the dark corner of the flight deck, where the form of Redway stood, his face hidden in the shadow.

Liv returned her attention on the console, focusing on the readings, reciting numbers in her head.

There's no one there. There's no one there.

"It's a great plan," said Redway's voice, perhaps inside Liv's head, perhaps not.

Beside her, Mirai sat back in the seat. "It's a great plan," she said.

Liv shot Mirai a look. Mirai straightened immediately. "What's the matter?"

Redway's eyes glittered in the shadows.

"Nothing," said Liv.

"It'll work," said Redway, "and soon enough, we'll be flying home."

Mirai smiled. "It'll work, and soon enough, we'll be flying home."

Liv stood from her seat, and rushed to the door.

"Liv?"

She stopped at the bulkhead, not sure if it was Mirai who had called her name, or Redway.

Or both.

"I'm going to check the ion drive," said Liv, turning her head to look over her shoulder, but not far enough to actually look at Mirai. Or Redway.

Heavy footsteps sounded from the passageway. Liv looked back around as Deacon approached, an opened box of ration bars in one hand and a refilled water bottle in the other. She brushed past him. He stopped and turned.

"Hey, Liv, what's up?"

She didn't pause.

"Nothing," she said, but what she really meant was *everything.*

21

IF YOU DON'T LISTEN TO ME, IT'LL BE TOO LATE, FOR EVERYONE

Mirai felt like she'd been watching the screen for hours, but according to the chronometer on the panel in front of her—one of the few basic but independent systems still available to them while the computer rebooted—it had only been forty minutes since Deacon had delivered her food and drink and left her to it in the flight deck. He wanted to look at the SLIP drive again. Why, Mirai didn't ask.

On the feed from the hull, the servodrone continued its work. It looked painfully slow, the complex robot crawling from comb to comb, its multi-articulated arms moving in smooth balletic motion as it completed the task Mirai and Liv had programmed it for.

And it was driving her crazy. But she also knew it was working far faster than she, or Liv, or Deacon ever could, so for the moment, there was nothing for them to do but wait.

Mirai was tired, there was no doubt about it, but she didn't want to sleep, because with sleep came the dreams and the vision of an endless black metal plain under a black metal sky. Being awake was far preferable to that.

Even if being awake meant having to be with *her*.

In the corner of her eye, she could see her.

Suki stood in the shadowed corner of the flight deck, her face vanished in the darkness save for the glitter of her eyes. How long she had been there, Mirai didn't know. Maybe she was always there, always with the sister who got lucky and was still alive, and it was only now that Mirai could see her. Maybe it was an . . . omen? That Mirai was soon to join her sister, that they would finally be together again?

But Mirai didn't believe in omens. What she did believe in was how even the healthiest minds could be affected by stress, and fear, and fatigue. Some people coped better than others. Mirai had always put herself in that category—solid, stoic, scientific—but maybe she didn't know herself as well as she thought she did.

So she ignored Suki, and kept her eyes on the progress of the drone. It was repetitive. Monotonous. Like watching . . . well, it was like watching a slow robot fix something slowly. She reached forward and adjusted the HUD's brightness, kicking it up until she couldn't see her own reflection in the curved expanse of the window behind the HUD.

So she didn't have to look at the reflection of Suki who was now standing right at her shoulder.

She wasn't there. She wasn't real. Mirai knew that, so she ignored her. She leaned into her fatigue, allowing herself to yawn, long and loud, and she stretched, stretched until her muscles ached, because that meant that she was alive and that Suki's ghost was her mind playing tricks on her as the weight of the void pressed down on them all.

Mirai enjoyed being on her own. The ship was quiet. The lights were down low to save power. It was calm, and restful. She liked the dark, she wasn't scared of it.

Right? *Right.*

She yawned again and settled back. Just a few more hours and they'd have power. A few after that, the computer would be back and then the real work could begin.

"You know how this will end, don't you?"

Mirai cleared her throat and listened to the way it echoed around the empty flight deck, unlike Suki's voice in her head which was dull and flat, because it wasn't a *sound* at all, because she wasn't there and Mirai was alone on the flight deck.

She rolled her neck and focused on the HUD feed, narrowing her eyes against the brightness of the display as she concentrated on the movements of the servodrone.

"You know it as well as I do," said Suki's voice, the lilt of her Japanese so familiar, the Hokkaido accent strong, just like Mirai remembered, just like her own. "You know that there is no way out. This plan won't work. It was never going to work. This place is the last that you will show me."

Mirai yawned again, although it was a little more forced this time. "The thing about voices in your head," she said, addressing nobody but the silent video feed of the working drone, "is that they can't be trusted. They're just your subconscious, screaming into the void, digging up all the shit it can because that's the way we are built. Like when you stand on the edge of . . . I don't know, a tall building, or a bridge, and somewhere at the back of your mind a voice tells you to jump. We can't help it. It's the way our brains are built." Mirai grinned. "The human mind is a miracle, very clever and very dumb at the same time." She shrugged. "Take pattern recognition, for example. Whether it's the shape of a face in the clouds or the voice of your sister in your ear, it's the same thing."

Then she glanced away from the glare of the HUD, and out of the corner of her eye, she saw Suki squeezing her hands in front of her, like she always did when she was worried or . . .

Or afraid. Like she was a lot in those last days.

Mirai looked away. "So I know that you're not there," she said, "even though I can see you and I can hear you. You're a ghost, an echo from my own memory, amplified by whatever this place is that we're in."

Then she stopped, and cocked her head. "Actually, maybe that's it? This place. It's a true void. No matter, no energy, nothing. It's *empty*. So maybe that's the problem. The ship is matter and it is energy, and so are we, the crew. So what happens when you put it into a negative space? Perhaps that matter and energy start leaking out. So, okay, take it a step further. Thoughts are energy, right? So consciousness is energy. And if that energy is leaking out, then we start to see things and hear things. What we dream internally can be projected, externally. It's logical." She paused again. "And, actually, that's pretty interesting, right?"

On the screen, the drone fixed another relay and moved to the next comb.

Mirai looked at Suki's reflection. "Right?"

"You don't really believe that," said Suki. "What were you just saying about pattern recognition? Seeing things that aren't there?"

Mirai shook her head. "Haven't you been listening to a word I've said? Listen, you want to pick a fight with your own subconscious, you'll lose every time."

"I'm here and you know it."

"Uh-huh."

"And so is that."

"So is what?"

"Look at the comms."

Mirai adjusted herself in the seat. Then she sighed, and looked down at the console in front of her. Just for a moment.

Just for a second.

"I told you," said Suki.

As she spoke, the light on the external comms channel flashed, indicating a signal. It was faint, and distant, but it was there.

"If you don't listen to me, it'll be too late, for everyone."

The light flickered again, then died. Then, a few seconds later, it came back.

Mirai frowned and opened the channel. There was a faint beep, and then a haze of white noise filled the flight deck as she listened in. When the light flashed again, there was a tiny variation in the static. The light died again, but when it came back, the pulsing sound was much louder, the source much closer.

It was communication. Signals being passed back and forth, between something close by, and something far away.

Mirai adjusted the channel, trying to clear the interference, but nothing seemed to work. The signals became clearer, louder, but it was still just pulses of noise against a background roar. She was puzzled, unable to figure out what the noise was. There was nothing in the void, so even an empty channel should have been clear and silent. Then she realized the background was interference from the ship's systems.

The next burst of sound was loud enough to make Mirai jump. She reached for the controls, turning down the gain. The signal continued for a few seconds, then cut. The reply—because that's what it was, it was a reply—came ten seconds later, and was faint, but clear.

"What . . . ?" Mirai muttered to herself. She leaned over the console, trying to get a fix on the signals, but the sensors showed nothing, except for the servodrone now outside, working on the hull.

Mirai looked up. On the camera feed, the servodrone had stopped work and was standing up on three of its legs, its curved white back pointed toward the camera. It had unfolded its other tool arms, and was holding them all up as it faced away from the ship.

Toward the single point of light, the solitary star hanging in the dead night of the void.

Mirai shook her head. "What on Earth . . . ?"

"I told you to listen," said Suki. That was when her hand grabbed her shoulder. Mirai wanted to scream in terror, but her breath left her lungs as the infinite cold cut through her shoulder like a blade, making the joint pulse in nauseating agony. Mirai couldn't move. On the HUD the servodrone continued to communicate with the star, while in the reflection,

Suki's hand gripped her shoulder, her body just an outline in the shadows behind the flight seat, her eyes glittering in the dark.

This wasn't real. Suki wasn't here. Mirai was alone. Mirai *knew* she was alone. There were only three of them left on the XK72.

The comms light flashed, brightly this time, and the white noise chatter from the drone increased in both frequency and volume.

Finally, Mirai found her voice. She cried out, and pushed herself up in the seat.

As soon as she was on her feet, the pain vanished, the cold in her bones gone, the flight deck silent. She spun around. She was alone, like she always had been. She turned back to the HUD. The servodrone was folded down onto the hull, like it had been before, the heavy-duty power cable firmly held in two of its tool arms.

Mirai fell back into the seat. Rubbing her forehead, she ran a systems check on both the XK72 and the drone through the manual systems that were still available to them. Both came back green, and then a flashing indicator told her the drone was awaiting command.

That was a surprise—it hadn't finished the job, had it? Mirai punched up the servodrone's UI on the console, directly accessing its log. Mirai skimmed the long table of data, and saw that the running program had been interrupted by an external user. The drone had paused, awaiting confirmation to either continue or abort.

"External user?" Mirai dug deeper into the interrupt, trying to determine what had caused the drone to stop. The log itself wasn't particularly informative—"external user" could mean any number of things. It could even have been something as simple as failure of the last cable fitting. The program Deacon had fed into the drone was quick and dirty, and while the drone was perfectly capable of solving its own problems, it was possible, maybe even likely, that it had encountered some problem with the fitting and was awaiting a new instruction.

Scrolling through more logs, Mirai eventually found the right timestamp. Opening the "external user" file, she was confronted by a screen that made her stomach flip.

It was Redway's symbolic code. Pages and pages and pages of it. Mirai sank back in her seat, shaking her head as the HUD display continued to scroll by, the bizarre text apparently without end.

Was the code somewhere else in the ship, external to the mainframe

OS? Or was it in the servodrone's computer, having spread to it from the XK72 like a virus?

Or had it received the code from somewhere else? That chatter, that noise—was it a real transmission that had lit the comms channel up? But a transmission from where? There was nothing out there but the drone—

And the light.

Shifting forward to the edge of her seat, Mirai hesitated before bringing the comms record up. She wanted to solve this mystery, but a part of her wanted to find nothing at all, just an empty log file, nothing recorded by the drone because there had been no transmission and the white noise had just been a bug in the system.

She hit the key, then closed her eyes as the flight deck was filled once again with the roar of white noise. A few seconds later came the faint pulsing sound, and then the louder popping and clicking as the drone returned communication.

Mirai killed the feed and sat back.

It couldn't be. It was the drone. It was bugged. It was their own fault, the routine they had programmed messy and incomplete. All she had to do was tell the drone to keep going. A single command, easy.

That was when she realized the rush of white noise hadn't stopped. Mirai opened her eyes and stared at the console. The recording log was off, but the comms channel was open.

The drone was transmitting again.

Mirai reached forward to cut the channel, but stopped as the light on the console flared brightly, punctuated by a burst of static as loud as a gunshot, followed by a clear and loud beep as the external comms channel cleared and the drone signaled to the flight deck.

HE. IS. COMING.

Beep.

Mirai froze, her hands over the comm controls. She looked up at the HUD. The drone had turned again, but now seemed to be looking directly into the hull camera, the three red LEDs on its beetle-like head staring right down the barrel.

The comms light pulsed in time with its harsh synthesized monotone.

HE. IS. COMING.

Beep.

HE. IS. COMING.

Beep.

HE. IS. COMING.

Beep.

Mirai heard the roar of an ocean in her ears, and she felt the abyssal cold of deep black water in her bones. Her shoulder burned as Suki's dead fingers squeezed and squeezed and squeezed.

WHO. IS. THIS. WHO. IS. COMING.

Beep.

WHO. IS. THIS. WHO. IS. COMING.

Beep.

WHO. IS. THIS. WHO. IS. COMING.

Beep.

And then an alarm sounded—a proximity alert, the XK72 detecting a mass out in the supposedly empty void.

Something *was* coming.

On the other half of the HUD display, the spinning star in the black sky had grown larger.

Much, *much* larger.

22

IT'S HEADING FOR US

Liv met Deacon in the central passageway as he came pounding down it from the SLIP drive module, the alarm echoing down every section of the XK72.

"Now what?" asked Deacon, not pausing as he led the way to the flight deck.

Liv followed him inside. There, Mirai was sitting in the pilot's position, hunched over the main console. The display on the HUD now showed only the hull feed of the strange light. It was bigger than it had been before—much, much bigger—and now looked like a glowing white diamond, rotating as it approached.

Liv dropped into the co-pilot's seat. She scanned the readouts, but with the mainframe still rebooting, the data they showed were limited. She reached forward and silenced the alarm, then looked at Mirai. "Do we know how close it is?"

Deacon grabbed the back of her seat, rocking it a little as he leaned forward to stare at the display. "And do we know *what* it is?"

"We only have very basic sensor readings," said Mirai. "All I can tell you is that it has mass and is just twenty thousand meters away, closing slowly." She looked up at the display. "It'll be here in ten minutes, bearing directly."

—Was it the pod was it Avery was it Redway were they out there could they reach them—

"What?" Deacon blew out a long breath. He looked at Liv. "Whatever it is, it's going to hit us. We need to fire the ion drive up and move out of the way."

Liv looked over the controls. With the mainframe out of action, was it even possible to manually pilot the XK72? She knew the answer was a yes, *but*. She thought back to her own handiwork in the drive core.

Was that about to become yet another huge problem?

"Liv?"

She turned and saw Mirai was looking at her, waiting, like Deacon, for an answer. She turned back to her controls.

"We can try," she said. She pulled the control yoke out with one hand, but it was heavy, the movement stiff without the computer to guide it.

Liv started to get a very bad feeling about what was going to happen in a little under ten minutes.

—Was it the pod was it Avery was it Redway were they out there could they reach them—

She turned to Mirai. "I'm going to try and push the ship around manually, but it's going to be difficult. When I give the word, fire the ion drive, but you'll need to keep your hand on the governor—*there*—because there's no computer to control the output and it'll be totally out of balance to start with. Too much drive and we'll get into a spin. Okay?"

Mirai nodded. "Confirmed," she said, readying her hands over the controls. Liv sat back and glanced up at the HUD. The object was getting larger even as she watched.

She checked the readings, but they still told her almost nothing. Something with mass, with density, with speed. Coming in fast.

She paused. No, it wasn't coming in fast. It was coming in *slow*. Even as she watched the basic sensor reading, she could see the object was slowing on its approach.

"What are we waiting for?" asked Deacon. "Let's go."

"Ready and waiting," said Mirai.

Liv didn't answer. She was still looking at the display. The slowing speed, the way the thing was rotating . . .

"It's artificial."

—Was it the pod was it the pod was it the pod was it the pod was it the—

"It is the pod?" asked Deacon. He looked at the others. "It *is* the pod. But it can't be. Can it?" He pointed at the screen. "You can't fly an escape pod."

"It's heading for us," said Liv. "Deliberately."

Mirai looked over the readings on the console in front of her. "And it's slowing down."

Deacon moved around to the side of her seat, and crouched down so they were at the same eye level. He looked at the HUD, then looked down at the controls.

"Try the comms."

Liv nodded and reached across the console. Just before she hit the control, Mirai almost leaped from the pilot's seat, diving across the console to bat Liv's hand away.

"No, don't!"

Too late. Liv had already hit the button. Instantly, the flight deck was filled with the roar of white noise, behind which was a distinctive repeated pattern of beeps.

Liv felt the muscles at the back of her jaw tighten as she squeezed her molars together. She looked at the others. Both Mirai and Deacon were silent, their eyes wide.

The signal continued. Three short beeps, two long beeps, one short beep. A pause. Then repeated.

"The escape pod," said Liv. She looked up at the gently spinning diamond of light on the HUD. "Avery and Redway are . . . coming back."

Why, then, am I so afraid?

23

THERE WAS NO ANSWER

Deacon and Mirai stood side by side outside the starboard escape pod hatchway, Liv behind them. Aside from the ceramic gun Redway had smuggled in—a gun now in Avery's possession—there were no weapons aboard the XK72. The fact that Avery was armed came very clearly to the front of Liv's mind; it must have done for Deacon too, as he had gone back down to Engineering and grabbed the largest available magnowrench from an equipment locker before Liv had even finished voicing her concern. Mirai, meanwhile, clutched one of their field medical kits to her chest. None of them had any idea of what they would find in the pod, or whether Avery or Colonel Redway were even still alive. The ID signal continued to be broadcast by the pod, right up until it had come in for an automated dock, but there had been no response to their attempt to contact the occupants over the standard comms. Either the channel was offline, or neither of the occupants were able to respond.

How the pod had come back to the XK72 was perhaps not quite so mysterious—nor as frightening—as Liv had thought, as she waited for the final docking clamps to show green on the panel beside the pod's hatch. The pod was designed to home in on a friendly target, if one was available. So as they waited, Mirai had suggested that it had simply looped on a long elliptical path after launch, before the automatics locked on to the XK72 and the pod guided itself back into its port.

Simple.

Right?

Liv rolled her neck. In front of her, Deacon flexed his huge shoulders, the contours of his muscles rolling underneath his T-shirt. He rocked a little from side to side, adjusting his grip on the wrench. Beside him, Mirai was perfectly still.

There was a soft chime, and the wall panel indicator changed to green. Liv wasted no time and gave the order . . . while allowing herself a microsecond of fear, uncertainty, and doubt, regretting that she so easily gave the command to do what she was perfectly capable of doing herself, except she didn't want to.

"Open it."

Mirai sprang into life, stepping forward to press the wall control before immediately stepping to let Deacon stand in front, the wrench now held out in front of him.

There was a hiss as the pod hatch irised open. Immediately, Liv knew something wasn't right. In front of her, Deacon swore.

The inside of the pod was immaculate, the white surfaces factory-fresh, the brightness standing in sharp contrast to the dull gunmetal gray of the XK72, the lights of which had been on low for hours now. Liv winced at the sudden glare and blinked away the purple afterimages that danced in front of her eyes.

Avery was sitting against the pod wall, strapped into the safety harness. Liv couldn't tell if he was dead or alive—the harness kept him upright, but his head lolled against his chest and his arms and legs dangled loosely. The blood they had seen splattered on his shirt and hands during his last communication before ejecting the pod had now congealed into a thick black coating. To Liv, it seemed like it was too much blood . . . and none of it, not a single spec, had tarnished the gleaming white interior of the pod. The thought, however, didn't linger very long in her mind. There was another very pressing question to ask.

And it was Deacon who asked it.

"Where the hell is Redway?"

Engineer Avery Cormack was alone in the pod.

Of Colonel Josef Redway, there was no sign.

It was . . . impossible. Liv felt her temples begin to throb as she tried to understand what she was looking at. Mirai, shaking, dropped the medical kit and turned on her heel, nearly a complete circle, before stopping to face Liv, her mouth downturned in what Liv recognized as deep, deep fear.

Redway was gone. Redway was *gone.*

Deacon kept silent, and moved forward slowly on the balls of his feet, keeping the magnowrench ready as he approached Avery. He stepped across the threshold and into the pod, then crabbed sideways, keeping his front to the engineer while glancing around. But there was nowhere to hide. The pod was small and the whole of the inside was in clear view from the XK72's passageway anyway. Redway was not in the pod, and, as there was no airlock, there was no way he could have exited it without depressurizing the small cabin.

Deacon turned his attention to Avery, peering at the engineer, his face twisted into a hard frown. As Liv watched, she could see Avery's chest rise and fall, very slightly.

"He's alive," she said, stooping to pick up the medical kit from where Mirai had dropped it, before joining Deacon in the pod. He stood to one side, still on alert, while Liv sat on the padded seating next to Avery's harness and checked the pulse on his wrist. His heart rate was slow, but it was regular, and it felt strong. Lowering his arm, she looked over his chest, then gently took hold of his chin and tilted his head back. Avery didn't respond to her touch, and when she pulled back one of his closed eyelids—realizing now that his glasses had fallen off—the eye itself was rolled back in its socket.

Mirai found her voice. "Is he hurt?"

Liv sighed. "I don't know. I don't think so. None of this blood is his. He's just unconscious."

Deacon hefted the wrench and used it to point at Avery. "The gun, Liv. Grab the gun."

Liv nodded, and quickly reached around Avery's middle, feeling along his waistband. After a moment she froze, then repeated the action.

"Liv?" asked Deacon.

All Liv could do was sit back and shake her head. "It's not here," she said, then she glanced around. "I can't see it."

The interior of the pod was immaculate; the gun was nowhere in sight.

"I don't see the data pad either," said Mirai, who was still standing on the other side of the hatchway, inside the XK72, as she looked around the pod.

Deacon's jaw was set as he moved closer to Avery, holding the bulky end of the magnowrench just a few millimeters from the engineer's face. "What the ever-loving fuck did he do?"

"We can ask him when he wakes up." Liv looked at Mirai. "Go get a bunk set up. We'll bring him inside."

Mirai nodded. She turned and ran down the passageway.

Liv stood from the pod's padded seating and got to work on the straps holding Avery in. "Come on, help me get him out of this."

Deacon laid the wrench down on the seat, then knelt on the other side of Avery and undid that set of straps. As the harness was released, the engineer toppled forward, his head rolling. Deacon caught him, then hoisted him over his shoulder in a fireman's lift. Maneuvering carefully in the tight confines of the escape pod, Deacon got Avery through the hatch; then he headed down the passageway toward the bunk modules.

Liv watched him go. Then she turned and sat back down in the pod. The pod was very small, and it was very empty. There was nowhere for Redway to hide, and, as she looked around, she realized Avery's glasses were also missing. In fact, the slack harness used by Avery was the only sign that anyone had ever been in there. The other harnesses, enough for eight people, were neatly folded in place. The entire escape pod was spotless and gleaming. And while Liv couldn't exactly remember how badly Avery had beaten Redway, surely there would be *some* signs of their fight, wouldn't there?

Liv frowned. It wasn't just that. She didn't remember the pod looking *this* good, although she knew that was likely just her imagination, having become used to the dark and dim interior of the XK72 for so long.

But still, the feeling didn't leave her. She pressed her hand into the seat beside her, as though testing the firmness of the padding was going to set her mind at rest. Then she did a slow circuit, checking the pod's consoles. The controls were simple, designed to be operated by untrained, and possibly injured, occupants. Liv flicked a few switches experimentally, but nothing changed and nothing happened. She wasn't entirely sure what she was expecting, anyway.

On the other side of the pod, opposite the hatch, was a small circular porthole. With the void beyond an infinite blackness, the porthole was nothing but a black mirror. All Liv could see in it was her own dull reflection surrounded by the sharp white of the pod interior. A few lights on the wall panels winked at her.

So, where was Redway? Perhaps the void *wasn't* empty. Had the pod docked with another ship, or been picked up, or even landed somewhere? But that didn't make sense—Redway would have had to have gotten out alone, taking the gun and the data pad and, for some reason, Avery's glasses, and relaunched the pod with Avery still inside. But was the alternative any more or less logical, that Redway had disappeared into thin air? The pod had no airlock, no way to open the hatch while it was in flight without the explosive decompression killing both Redway and Avery and leaving very clear evidence of what had happened.

Liv sat back down. Of course, Redway wasn't the only impossible disappearance on this mission, and the feeling that came with that thought was . . . confusing. It was relief, perhaps, that Astrid had disappeared too, that she wasn't stuck in the crawlspace and they hadn't abandoned their search for her because she wasn't there to be found anyway.

She looked around, slowly, taking in every detail. Everything clean and sharp. No blood. No data pad. No glasses. No gun.

Shaking her head, Liv turned back to the controls. If the pod was in full working order, as it seemed to be, its flight would be fully logged. Not only that, the internal camera feed—the one Avery had used to communicate their final moments to the flight deck—would have recorded the entire journey.

Liv nodded to herself. Okay, that was something. With the pod's system now relinked to the XK72, she could review the log and security feed from the flight deck, and then when—Liv refused to think of it as an *if*—Avery regained consciousness, he could tell them what he'd learned from Redway, about the mission, about his sabotage. About their fight.

Liv turned on her heel, and then caught movement in the corner of her eye. She turned again, only to see her reflection in the porthole. She waited a moment, letting her heart rate settle, letting the thundering in her head fade away.

"Are you in here, Redway?" she asked, and she surprised herself by asking it out aloud. Her voice echoed dully in the small pod.

There was no answer. The pod was empty, and Liv was alone.

24

FIVE. TEN. FIFTEEN. NOTHING.

On her way to the flight deck, Liv stopped at the bunk room. Deacon was leaning in the hatchway, arms folded, watching as Mirai cleaned the blood from Avery's face with wipes from the medical kit as the engineer lay, unconscious, on the bed. Deacon and Liv nodded at each other in acknowledgment, then Liv moved over to stand by the bunk and looked down at their patient.

"No change?" asked Liv.

Mirai shook her head. Avery's T-shirt had been removed, his bare chest shining from where Mirai had already cleaned up the blood. His eyes were closed, and there was no movement behind the lids. His chest rose and fell slowly and evenly. It was like he was just asleep.

"He doesn't seem to be injured," said Mirai, finishing up. "None of this blood is his."

"No, it's Redway's," said Deacon. "We saw Avery beating on him before he punched the eject."

Mirai laid the back of one hand on Avery's face. "He's very cold too." She looked up at the others. "Maybe the pod's environmental control malfunctioned."

Liv nodded at Mirai. "Okay, let's get him warm. Anything else we can do?"

"I don't think so. None of us have any more than basic first aid training, and we don't have anything aboard except the standard field medical kits. We can't do anything except keep him comfortable until we get back home."

With a huff, Deacon pushed himself off the bulkhead and moved to one of the storage lockers in the cabin, from which he pulled out a blanket, still sealed in its plastic wrapper. After tearing it open, he held the blanket up by one edge and let it unfold itself before handing it to Mirai. She took it, straightened it up, then tucked it in around Avery.

Liv moved to Deacon's side. "Thoughts?"

Deacon breathed in, long and hard, through his nose, before exhaling just as dramatically. Then he shook his head. "I don't know." He looked at Liv, his expression finally softening. "Either he'll regain consciousness and tell us what happened, or . . ."

Liv nodded. She knew what he meant. Avery would either come out of it or he wouldn't, and there was nothing they could do to help him.

"And anyway," Deacon continued, "Astrid is gone, and we thought Redway and Avery were gone too. At least we got one back, right?" He sniffed. "Meanwhile, we got work to do, boss."

Deacon was right—and just as he spoke, an alert chimed in Liv's earpiece. She reflexively touched it, then saw the other two do the same.

Mirai rose from Avery's bunk. "The drone's finished," she said, her voice almost a whisper, and when she looked at Liv, she looked afraid.

Understandable, thought Liv. With the induction combs linked up, it was time to see if their master plan was going to work. If it didn't, they were back at square one, on a ship losing power in a void that made recharging the grid impossible.

"That was fast," said Deacon. "I thought the servodrone had hours to go?"

Liv frowned. "It must have sped up as it learned the routine. But you're right, we need to check the work. If we're happy, we can fire the ion drive and start to draw power. It might take us awhile to get it right, but we should be able to switch back to system normal." She paused, and wrinkled her nose.

"What is it?" asked Deacon.

"I was going to check the escape pod's log and camera feed, see if that could tell us where they went and what happened to Redway."

"We have time," said Mirai. "If we get the power working, we're going to have a few hours before the computer comes back online. We can take the time and review the data."

"True," said Liv. Then she turned to Deacon, but he was already nodding.

"I'll check the drone's logs and look over the combs, make sure it's done what we wanted."

"Shouldn't someone watch Avery?" asked Mirai.

Deacon pursed his lips. "I can look at the log from here, if someone else wants to check the combs?"

"Mirai and I can do that," said Liv. "Let us know as soon as Avery comes around."

"Oh, don't worry, I will."

Liv cocked her head as she thought back to Avery's fight with Redway, the surprising amount of strength he must have summoned to overpower a trained soldier. She looked back down at the unconscious engineer. "We have anything we could restrain him with?"

"We have plenty of power cable," said Mirai. "Meters and meters spare."

Deacon clicked his fingers at her. "Good thinking," he said. Then he looked at Liv. "Leave him with me."

Liv nodded. "Okay, let's go."

She turned and left the cabin, Mirai following close behind.

Liv dropped herself into the co-pilot's chair, exhaling heavily after a solid hour of work outside the ship. It was perhaps an unnecessary extra task, but given how quickly the servodrone had completed the last set of combs, Liv was determined to use the extra time available to check the grid and make sure the robot had done what it was supposed to.

Going out onto the hull, things looked very different, the entire surface now crisscrossed with thick power cables. The servodrone, having completed its task, had parked itself right by the airlock, giving both Liv and Mirai a fright as they turned to see it. Mirai then immediately ordered the drone to move away—right over to the opposite side of the hull, completely out of sight.

But the machine had done its job, and done it well. Liv didn't know why the second half of the task had taken far less time, but everything looked good after their manual check, so she wasn't going to complain.

"Now or never," said Liv, as she leaned over the controls and gave a sideways glance at Mirai, sitting in the pilot's seat. Mirai was staring straight ahead, clearly exhausted, but she gave a small nod.

Liv looked down at the ion drive controls and flicked two switches, setting it to manual, thankful that the standard drive was so basic as to not require mainframe oversight. Between the two switches was a small push lever. Liv flexed the fingers of her right hand, then set the nub of the lever into the center of her open palm. She held her breath, and gave the lever the slightest of touches.

There was no sound, no vibration, nothing at all to indicate she'd done anything at all. But Liv watched the manual readout on the console. All they needed to do was set the drive to the barest minimum, so it was just ticking over. With her little handiwork in the core of the drive, the unbalanced engine would begin spitting dirty exhaust, and the lower the output, the better they could control the power draw.

There. A tiny light, a square LED buried in the console, went blue as the ion drive engaged. Liv counted the seconds, willing the power grid indicator to change from the steady trickle loss first to something stable, then to an increase.

Five. Ten. Fifteen. Nothing.

Liv nudged the lever again, moving it not more than a couple of millimeters.

The power indicator flickered, then came on as a steady green light.

They'd done it. It was working. The power grid was absorbing the dirty exhaust.

The XK72 was slowly starting to recharge.

Liv took her hand from the lever and slumped back. "Well done, Mirai."

Mirai didn't answer. Liv turned to look at her, and saw she'd fallen asleep. She reached over and nudged the flight analyst.

"Hey, we're all good."

Mirai blinked and sat up, looking first over the controls, then at Liv, a faint smile on her face.

"So far, so good," she whispered.

"You need to get some rest," said Liv. "We'll need you when the mainframe comes back online." She glanced down at the console. "You've got four hours."

Mirai nodded and slowly lifted herself out of the flight seat. Liv watched her disappear down the passageway; then she turned back and sank deeper into the co-pilot's seat. She was tired too, but didn't feel the need to crash like Mirai.

But still, the seat was quite comfortable, and the orange inner lining of the EVA suit she was still in provided a little extra warmth and padding. Liv soon found her eyes closing; then she snapped herself forward and sat up straight. Okay, so perhaps she was a little more tired than she realized, but she could rest later.

Liv stood and did a circuit of the flight deck—staying on the other side of the cabin from the gap in the wall and the crawlspace beyond—stretching her arms above her head. Then she stopped by the bulkhead door and tapped her earpiece. It was time for an update from Deacon.

Nothing happened, not even the standard tone indicating an open channel.

Liv sighed, unable and unwilling to find the energy to try to troubleshoot a faulty personal comms right now. Pulling the earpiece out—with some satisfaction—she walked back over to the flight console and dropped the bud next to the keyboard, then punched the main comms.

"Deak, this is Liv. Any change with Avery?"

Beep.

There was no reply. Liv frowned, but at least the ship-wide system was operational. Perhaps the personal comms had gone down? She tried again.

"Deacon, come in, please. Your private comms might be out—use the main panel."

Beep.

Nothing.

The ship-wide comms were integrated into the panels beside each door control. Deacon must have been near one, surely.

"Deacon?"

Or was the ship-wide system down as well? Liv glanced down at the comms panel, but the status indicator was green. She reached forward and switched it off then back on. The light went off, then came back on.

"Deacon, come in, please?"

Nothing. Liv grit her teeth, unwilling to troubleshoot yet another fault which, she knew, would show as no fault at all. Maybe if she just hit the console with a wrench—

Then the main speaker popped and the comms beeped again, but the tone was faint and distorted, hazed with white noise.

Okay, that was better than nothing, but there clearly *was* a fault somewhere.

Just . . . great.

Liv sat down, and began cycling through the comms channels, trying to trace the fault as best she could without a computer to help her. She punched up a signal readout on the small console display, and when she clicked through another channel, the data line on the readout suddenly spiked, indicating the channel was in use. As she pushed up the gain, the flight deck was filled with the harsh roar of white noise.

Wincing, Liv turned the volume down, then looked over the controls, trying to see where the signal was coming from. As she worked, tuning the controls as she chased the transmission, the white noise began to resolve into a clicking, pulsing sound. The readout began to home in on the source.

It was the servodrone, waiting out on the other side of the hull.

And then, a louder sound, grinding and mechanical and buzzing.

Liv turned the volume up a little. The new sound was still coming from the servodrone. The robot must have developed a fault, or some system was shorting or overloading, causing huge interference over its command channel. Liv tapped the keyboard, but without the main ship computer, she only had limited access to the drone's system from inside the ship. To investigate further, she'd have to go outside and access the drone's maintenance terminal.

Then there was an electrical buzz, a burst so loud Liv gasped in surprise. She scrambled for the controls, switching from the drone's command channel back to the ship-wide comms.

"Liv?"

She jumped in her seat and looked around. She was still alone in the flight deck.

"Liv, it's Deak," came the voice, which Liv now realized was coming through the main speakers. "Where are you?"

Liv hit the comms button. "I'm in the flight deck. I think there's a fault with the comms."

"Okay, but you should get down here," said Deacon.

"What's happened?"

"Avery is awake."

25

I JUST DON'T REMEMBER A THING

I really wish I could tell you what happened, but honestly, I just don't know. I just don't remember a thing."

Avery slapped the edge of his bunk by his hip, rattling the makeshift binder of heavy-duty power cable that linked his wrist to the bunk's side rail. The engineer shook his head and sighed, and played his tongue along the edge of his teeth, clearly thinking things over as he lifted his wrist and looked at the restraint. He was sitting up and seemed unhurt, although according to Deacon, he had complained of being cold. Deacon had given him a fresh T-shirt, and he had two extra blankets wrapped tightly around his legs, the edges pulled up to his chin with his free hand.

Liv and Deacon stood next to the bunk. Mirai remained in the doorway, her arms folded tightly. She looked deeply uncomfortable and utterly exhausted. Liv wondered how much rest she'd been able to get, if any.

Liv had arrived to find the two men in conversation. Avery seemed subdued and quiet, a marked difference from his old mile-a-minute chatterbox demeanor. But that was fair enough, Liv thought, considering what he had been through.

Which was . . . what, exactly?

Because he didn't remember a thing. Or at least, that's what he said. Was he telling the truth . . . or was he playing games? As Liv listened to him and Deacon go back and forth, she had to admit she didn't quite know what to think. All she knew was that he didn't seem to be himself.

"Okay," said Deacon, "let's back it up, try again, see if we can knock anything loose, okay?"

At least, Liv thought, Deacon's earlier—and quite understandable—anger had seemed to have evaporated.

Avery sighed again and nodded. Then he lay back a little, getting himself comfortable with the pillow between his neck and corner of the bunk. He closed his eyes, blew out a slow breath, then adjusted his shoulders again.

It looked like he was trying very hard to cooperate. Liv wanted to ask Deacon if Avery had mentioned his glasses yet, or asked for a spare pair, but the fact that he still wasn't wearing any probably answered that question.

"Okay," said Avery. "I can do this." He blew out his cheeks and shook his head, like he was psyching himself up for some major task.

Deacon and Liv exchanged a look, and Deacon gestured for her to try. She nodded, and took a step closer to the bunk. She looked down at Avery. His eyes were moving rapidly behind his closed lids.

"So, you remember the accident, Avery?" she asked.

Avery nodded. "Yes, that I do. Colonel Redway had locked himself in the flight deck. Astrid and I were down in Engineering trying to override the computer to get the door open, but we couldn't do it. The induction combs began charging up, going way beyond their design threshold. The SLIP drive kicked in and then—" At this, Avery opened his eyes. "Boom. Lights out."

"Okay," said Liv, "what happened when you woke up? Do you remember anything after that point?"

His forehead creased in concentration.

"You were the first one awake," said Deacon. "You were already tied up on the flight deck when I came around."

Avery closed his eyes again. After a few moments he sighed and slumped back against the pillow.

"Sorry, it's all hazy after that. I remember . . . pieces. Images. Feelings. I don't remember waking up, but I remember us all in the flight deck, and Redway was angry, yelling." He frowned, and opened his eyes to look at Deacon. "Then you got free, and then we had Redway tied up."

Deacon raised an eyebrow. "And then?"

"I'm not sure," said Avery. "I remember Redway told me something. We went to the escape pod . . ." He froze, then looked at Liv. "The data pad. Redway's data pad. He showed me what was on it. It was in the escape pod. I remember reading something on it."

"We've looked," said Deacon. "The pad's not there. It disappeared along with Redway."

"And your glasses," said Liv.

And the gun, she thought.

At this, the corner of Avery's mouth flickered, almost like he was about to smile. Then he shook his head and said, "I'm sorry, I just can't remember." He sighed. "I know this isn't much help. Have you looked at the pod's computer yet? Everything will be in the log, plus there's the feed from the internal camera. You'll find the answers you're looking for there."

Liv felt her eyes narrow. There was something about the way he framed that statement. People didn't talk like that.

People with nothing to hide, that is.

"We haven't yet," said Mirai, from the doorway. Liv and Deacon both turned to her. "The mainframe is being rebooted," she continued. "The XK72 is running on nominal systems. We can't access anything else for another few hours." She looked at Liv. "Sorry, turns out we do need the mainframe for that after all. We're locked out of the pod's system until it comes back online."

Liv felt her heart rate kick up. First, the fact that they couldn't check the pod's systems now was irritating, more than it should have been, Liv knew. But second, Liv was even more irritated by Mirai giving out the information so readily.

Because for some reason, she didn't really want Avery to know all the details. She watched him, but Avery didn't react much to the news. He just nodded in acknowledgment, then looked at Liv again, a weak smile on his face.

Liv sighed. Okay. Maybe it was time to give him the benefit of the doubt. She had no idea what he'd been through. He might have had a brain injury. Amnesia—true amnesia—was a strange but also rare thing. There was more than a good chance that his memory would return. Avery was conscious and showed no signs of any other impairment, physical or mental. What he needed was time to rest and recover.

Liv's jaw muscles tightened, her back teeth grinding once more. Yes, that was all well and good. But . . . there was something about him. Maybe he'd been affected by his experience. Or maybe there was something else. Sure, he seemed to be his old self . . . except for the way he sometimes spoke, the way he sometimes looked at them.

Or maybe it was nothing but Liv's stress and fatigue.

"Don't worry, we'll get there, we'll get there," said Deacon. He turned to Liv. "I think we should leave it there and just let him rest. The harder he tries to remember things, the further those memories might sink. It's best to just leave it alone and let it all come back in its own time."

Liv nodded, and was about to say something else when Mirai cut in.

"We should all rest."

Liv and Deacon turned to her. She wasn't looking at them, or Avery, but at the floor.

"There's nothing we can do until the computer is back up. We have power now. We're exhausted and hungry. So how about we eat and get some rest and then when the mainframe is back up and the XK72 is running to protocol, we do the Drop and get the hell out of here."

And then she turned and walked away.

"Wow, is the flight analyst okay?" asked Avery.

The . . . *flight analyst*? At this, Liv raised an eyebrow, but it was Deacon who replied.

"Mirai's fine, she's just tired." He knocked the side of Avery's bunk. "Hey, you hungry? I can bring you a ration pack."

"Oh, I'm not hungry," said Avery. "Just thirsty." He lifted his hand, pulling the binder cable tight. "Any chance you can take this thing off?"

Deacon and Liv looked at each other. Deacon gave a noncommittal shrug. "I'll need to get a tool to undo it," he said, but Liv gently touched his elbow.

"I think we should leave it on, for the time being at least." She smiled at Avery. "We don't know what caused your amnesia—it would be good for you to rest, get some sleep, but we don't want you to wake up in a confused state and injure yourself accidentally."

Deacon nodded at her, then turned to Avery. "Actually, that's a good point."

"Oh hey," said Avery, "makes sense to me. We wouldn't want any more accidents to happen."

Then he lay back again, closed his eyes, pulling the blankets up to his chin. "Any chance we can turn the heating up? It's cold as hell in here."

"I'll see what I can do," said Deacon. He and Liv exchanged another look, then together they left the module.

As they headed together down the passage, Liv nudged Deacon's elbow again and led him around the corner to the next hatch bulkhead.

"What do you think?" she whispered.

Deacon pursed his lips, and glanced back the way they had come.

"He's back and he's in one piece," he said. "I'll take that as a win."

Liv folded her arms, tight. "You think he's okay? You don't think he's . . ."

"Off?"

Liv nodded.

"Well, he's in shock," said Deacon, rubbing his scalp with both hands. "But he seems okay. We don't know what happened to him in the pod. I was expecting worse, frankly. So yeah, he's off." He paused. "Why? You think something else is wrong?"

Liv grimaced. "I'm not sure."

"I mean, I get it. He attacked Redway. Beat him up pretty bad. So I say we keep the restraint on. Okay, maybe he has amnesia, maybe he's messing with us. But he can't do anything tied to the bunk. We can keep him comfortable and we can get home."

Liv looked at him, but she didn't answer.

"Liv?"

Finally, she nodded. Deacon was right. That was the most they could do. It was the most they *needed* to do.

"I'll see about the temperature," said Deacon. "We should have enough power now. I'm starting to feel the cold myself."

With that, he headed off. Liv watched him; then she turned and looked back down the passageway toward the bunk cabin. Something caught her eye—some movement in the shadows—but then it was gone, if it had ever been there.

26

WHO. IS. THIS. WHO. IS. COMING. HERE.

Avery lay on his bed, eyes open, a faint smile on his lips. He listened. He did not move. He did not breathe. The ship was silent save the usual background hum of large and complex systems running automatically to keep the occupants alive. Avery had heard nothing else for more than an hour now. The crew were resting.

He sat up. He pushed the blankets off. He swung his legs over the side of the bed, and went to stand. Immediately he was jerked back as the restraint on his wrist pulled tight against the rail.

He sat back on the edge of the bed, examining the makeshift binding around his wrist, the fingers of his other hand playing over the bolt that held it closed. It was fairly ingenious, built out of a power coupling Deacon had pulled out of the Engineering stores, strong and secure. Avery lifted his hand, tugged at the heavy-duty power cable, pulling it tight against the bunk rail, then relaxing, repeating this over and over.

Then he pulled the cable tight, and moved his other hand toward the cuff—close, but not touching. Avery's smile widened just a fraction, and then—

He stood from the bed, and, both arms swinging freely, walked out of the room. Behind him, the binder sat on his bed, the cuff still closed, unopened, bolt in place, the power cable unbroken.

Outside, in the main passageway, Avery cocked his head and closed his eyes as he listened to the XK72 humming quietly on minimal operation. With power restored, Deacon had reset the environment controls, but with him and Liv and Mirai resting, the ship had cycled into night mode, the lighting low and purple, designed to be relaxing for tired crew.

He turned in a circle, eyes still closed, face turned to the ceiling.

Then he jerked his head around, his nostrils flaring as he caught the scent.

He opened his eyes and headed down the passageway.

Mirai rubbed her face with her hands, trying to get some warmth back into her skin. Dammit, why was it so cold? Deacon had said he'd warmed things up, but this low-power night mode just seemed to drag everything back to where it had been before: too cold, and too dark.

She still hadn't been able to sleep. Lying in her bunk, her mind spinning with thoughts she didn't want, her vision flashing with things she didn't want to see and which, she knew, weren't even there. So she'd gotten up, and headed down into the Data Monitoring module. The computers there, separate from the ship's mainframe, were still fully operational, so she thought she could at least do . . . something. Topmost in her mind was reviewing the footage from the escape pod, if she could perhaps find a way to bypass the XK72's main system and import the data directly to her station. Except . . .

Except she couldn't bring herself to try it. She didn't want to see what had happened. Let Liv do it. Deacon do it. The three of them do it.

Just . . . not her. Not now.

Not alone.

Instead she picked something more straightforward, something less . . . important. Less terrifying.

Redway's code. She decided to run another pass over it. Whether she cracked it or not, it was immaterial now, the exercise just busywork to pass the time. Once the mainframe rebooted and they made the Drop and got home, it was a problem for Artemis.

On her way, she went to Engineering and picked up a magnowrench, the largest one she could find. She'd swung it a few times, experimentally, feeling both ridiculous and comforted at the same time. That wrench now sat on the console next to her keyboard.

Mirai pulled the blanket she'd dragged from her bunk tighter around herself and tapped at the keys, running another decryption algorithm on Redway's messed up symbolic code. Within just a few minutes, her natural curiosity had turned what was supposed to be a simple distraction into something far more consuming. Because . . . what if she *could* crack it, co-opting the sheer computer power of the Data Monitoring module? They'd find out just what Redway had done. Maybe even why. The others would be pleased. Artemis would be pleased.

Maybe Suki would be pleased too.

And she *was* making progress. The data regurgitated by the new decryption attempt was mostly garbage, but Mirai had found a tiny fraction of it was starting to come back as recognizable commands, consisting of settings and parameters for the ship's systems. Mirai wasn't an engineer and couldn't make sense of much of it, but she knew enough to recognize Artemis code when she saw it.

"Well, hello there, Mirai Ikeda."

Mirai jumped in her seat and turned toward the voice.

Avery stood at the base of the access ladder that led up into the main passageway. Mirai hadn't heard him come down, but she saw that he was barefoot. When he took a step toward her, he was completely silent. He didn't even seem to be breathing.

Mirai shrank back into her chair, the blanket pulled tight around her body with both arms, a protective cocoon. "You should be resting." She glanced at his hands. "Who took off the binder? Was it Deacon?"

Avery smiled, then held up the wrist that had been bound and looked at it.

"Oh, yes," he said, "he did. Deacon did." He dropped his arm, then shrugged as he began to walk toward her. "Well, no use keeping me locked up, is there? There's nothing wrong with me, and there's work to be done." He stopped by Mirai's station, and cast his gaze over the bank of computer displays. "What are you doing, Mirai?"

She looked at his face, his eyes lit in the reflected glow of the computer displays. The corner of his lip was curled up in a slight smile. It wasn't an expression she recognized from him. He still wasn't wearing his glasses—perhaps he hadn't brought a spare pair on the mission. Not that it seemed to be bothering him. He seemed to be reading the computer displays well enough.

For a brief moment she didn't think it was him—thought that the man standing by her station, the man who looked like Avery Cormack and sounded like Avery Cormack, wasn't the engineer at all.

And then the moment passed. When he glanced at her, Mirai looked away. She pulled her chair back close to the console and focused on the screens, her hands ready at the keyboard to continue her work.

"You really need to go and rest," she said, still not looking at him, but feeling his gaze on her like a spotlight. She tapped at the keyboard, deliberately trying to lose herself in the pages of code, but unable to focus on a single line of it. "I'll call Deak. He can take you back—"

As she spoke, her right hand groped the empty space next to the keyboard. With a start, she turned to look at Avery.

"Oh, are you looking for this?"

He lifted his hand, holding the magnowrench aloft.

Mirai's heart thudded in her chest. There was no way he could have picked it up off the console. Mirai was sitting between him and the space next to her keyboard where it had been lying. Maybe it was a different tool? Maybe hers was somewhere else, on the floor; maybe she'd left it somewhere else in the room.

Avery laughed quietly as Mirai looked around, ducking her head down to check underneath the console, her gaze scanning the floor for the missing item. "Oh, no, this is yours," he said, as though reading her mind. He turned it over in his hand, then held the grip end out to Mirai. "It's a good idea. You don't know what might be walking around the ship, right? Especially in the dark. So you have to take care of yourself. Don't worry, I get it. Good thinking, Mirai."

Mirai blinked at Avery. He grinned, and wiggled the wrench at her. Mirai took it, instinctively drawing it in to press against her chest. The metal tool was ice cold, cold enough that her hand began to hurt, cold enough that she could feel the chill penetrating even the doubled folds of her blanket.

She ignored both, and kept her eyes on Avery. "Thank you," she said, her voice barely audible even to herself.

Avery gave a theatrical bow, arms spread wide. "My pleasure, Mirai Ikeda." Then he cocked his head. "Mirai Ikeda? Japan. Hokkaido. Sapporo, right? Nice place." He gestured at the photo pinned to the side of one of the monitors. "The lovely Mirai, the lovely Suki. Quite a pair."

The pain in Mirai's hand was growing as she squeezed the cold metal of the magnowrench, one thought clear in her mind.

There was something wrong with Avery. She knew amnesia wasn't just a loss of memory. A blow to the head could result in lots of things. Personality changes. Behavioral issues.

But then there was what he had done to Redway, *before*.

The chatty scientist, excited about the mission, thrilled to be part of it, had beat a trained soldier to a bloody pulp.

So maybe something *wasn't* wrong with him. Maybe this is what he was. A monster, who had just been good and clever enough to hide his true nature.

Mirai adjusted her grip on the wrench, no matter how cold it felt, no matter how much her arm ached. "Avery, listen to me," she said, putting as much as she could into keeping her voice loud and level. "You need to go back to your bunk and get some rest. You might think you're fine, but you're not. You'll feel a whole lot better once you've slept. There's nothing to do right now, and the computer won't be back online for a few hours yet. Come. I'll take you back."

Avery smiled. The two of them stood facing each other, silence spreading between them.

Then Avery lifted his hands in apparent surrender. "Hey, no problem, maybe you're right." As Mirai moved toward him, he backed away and shook his head. "It's okay. I'm good. I can manage. And, yeah, now you mention it, a lie down sounds pretty good." He gestured toward Mirai's station. "You just get on with your work there. You must be getting pretty close to cracking the colonel's code. So, please, carry on. I apologize for the interruption."

He turned and headed to the ladder, then paused.

"You're right, by the way."

"Right about what?"

"Oh," said Avery, glancing back over his shoulder, his face cast in a shadow that made him look like someone else entirely. "Most things."

He resumed his walk, and stepped onto the ladder. Mirai watched him as he ascended. Once he was gone, she fell back into her seat and focused on her breathing to calm herself.

She needed to talk to Liv and Deacon. They were both sleeping—but this was important.

Deacon. She'd wake him, rationalizing that his strength would be needed if Avery's demeanor went south. She spun her chair around, and was about to patch her comm through to Deacon's bunk when she saw the channel lights were silently flashing in what was obviously a repeated signal.

Mirai's thoughts raced. Was it Deacon? Liv? Had Avery attacked them when he'd gotten free from his bunk—and all this while, one or the other of them had been trying to warn her, punching a sequence into the comms in the hope that she'd see it and take action while Avery harassed her in the Data Monitoring module?

She clicked the main comms channel on. The cabin was instantly filled with a white noise roar, punctuated by a staccato clicking, an electric buzz that was a crude approximation of human speech generated by a machine that couldn't talk. Wincing against the aural onslaught, Mirai turned down the gain. The signal cleared, and the buzzing was now understandable.

HERE.

Beep.

HERE.

Beep.

HERE.

Beep.

HERE.

Beep.

Then the white noise rose again. Mirai turned everything down, but nothing made any difference. When she turned the comms channel off, the sound just continued, so loud it was like a physical force, like the strange pressure she'd experienced out on the hull of the XK72.

Mirai screwed her eyes shut, her hands pressed against the sides of her head. She had to tell the others, had to reach them, warn them, do *something.*

Then she slid off her chair and toppled sideways to the floor. Her body jerked on the floor, curling into a fetal position, her hands wrapped over her head. She lay there, shaking, unable to think, unable to hear anything except the roaring that filled the room and the grinding voice of the servodrone as it repeated its warning over, and over, and over again.

HERE.

Beep.

HERE.

Beep.

HERE.

Beep.

HERE.

Beep.

WHO. IS. THIS. WHO. IS. COMING.

Beep.

HERE.

Beep.

HERE.

Beep.

HERE.

Beep.

HERE.

Beep.

27

YOU DIDN'T ANSWER MY QUESTION

Knock, knock!"

Deacon looked up from his position down on the floor behind the SLIP drive as Avery appeared in the hatchway. The engineer was smiling, and barefoot, and absolutely not tied to his bunk.

"What are you doing?" Deacon stood, swinging another of the servodrone's spare cutting attachments to rest on the decking, Avery's interruption as infuriating as it was surprising.

Infuriating because Deacon hadn't been able to sleep, his mind too preoccupied with a mystery that did nothing but grow and grow and grow.

Infuriating because he had to get the SLIP drive open. *Had* to. He was a master engineer. If he could just get the damn cover off, he could see what he was working with, figure it out, get it up and running.

Get the hell out of here. Get back home. Bypass the mainframe entirely, kick-start the Drop himself, without needing to wait for the computer to come back online.

So he'd broken out another of the drone's plasma cutting arms, dragged a smaller spare drone power pack out of storage, hooked them up, and had got to work. Progress had been . . . well, nonexistent, but he was damned if he was going to let a piece of machinery break him.

Deacon looked Avery up and down. "Who released you from your bunk?"

Avery frowned, like he didn't understand the question. Then his face broke into a grin and he raised both hands, turning his wrists in front of him as he looked at them.

"Oh! Yeah, it was Liv." He dropped his hands. "Liv! It was Liv. Y'know, we have a lot of work to do and there's nothing the matter with me, so I thought, y'know, I can get back to work, lend a hand, get this place fixed up. Y'know. Liv agreed."

Deacon lifted his chin. "So where is she?"

Avery frowned. "Who?"

"Liv."

Avery didn't answer. Instead, he narrowed his eyes, like he didn't quite follow what Deacon was saying. Now it was Deacon's turn to frown. Whatever had happened to Avery in the escape pod, he must have had a serious blow to the head and was now suffering from a concussion. He shouldn't have been wandering around the ship like this. He was a hazard, both to himself and to the others.

Maybe he had been before, given what he'd done to Redway.

Avery's gaze fell to the SLIP drive, and he moved closer, both hands outstretched toward its mirrored surface, his grin growing wider the closer he got.

"Avery!"

His head snapped around at Deacon's voice, his smile gone.

"You didn't answer my question."

Avery's lips moved, like he was running the earlier part of their conversation through his head. After a few moments, he simply said, "Who?"

"Okay, you need to get back to your bunk and rest." Deacon leaned the plasma torch against the side of the SLIP drive—the damn thing still didn't have a mark on it, despite his best efforts—and moved toward Avery. "I'll take you back there and then you and me and Liv and Mirai can have a talk about how you need to stay put, okay?"

Avery tilted his head at Deacon—it reminded Deacon of his old dog—then he turned to the SLIP drive again.

"How's it going with this thing?" he asked, completely ignoring Deacon's instructions. "I'm guessing you haven't managed to open it yet, have you?" He laughed. "No, I guess not. I'd know about it if you had. We all would."

Deacon shook his head. "What's that supposed to mean?" He sighed and made to grab Avery by the arm. "Come on. Time to leave."

Avery sidestepped the big man. Deacon shook his head—he was sure he'd taken hold of his arm, but Avery was now standing a meter away from him and was peering at his own reflection in the top of the SLIP drive's cowling.

What the hell had Liv been thinking, releasing Avery, when he was clearly sick, injured, deranged, whatever? Head injury. Oxygen starvation in the pod, perhaps? Could be. Could well be.

"It's a fascinating design, this thing, isn't it, Titus?"

"That is *enough*, Avery," said Deacon. "We're going, even if I have to carry you." He rushed forward, ready to pick the much smaller man up and hoist him over his shoulder—and then he stumbled and fell, hitting the deck on his knees as his arms swept through nothing but thin air.

Deacon recovered, blinked, and pushed himself to his feet, only to see Avery now standing on the opposite side of the SLIP drive.

It was impossible. Deacon clenched his fists, and watched Avery as Avery watched his own reflection.

Then Deacon took a deep breath, and he let it out, slowly, through his nose. "Okay," he said. It was time for a different tactic. "Listen. Let's get you back to your bunk. I'll call the others, we can have a talk, see what we can do, okay?" He spread his hands. "So maybe you can help with something, huh? We can probably set you up with a terminal or something, and you can patch into the system, help Mirai with the computer."

Deacon stepped slowly around the SLIP drive, toward the engineer. Still Avery wasn't paying him any attention, his gaze fixed on his reflection. As Deacon approached, he glanced at the SLIP drive. He saw Avery's face there, but for a moment, he wasn't sure *who* it was.

Deacon gestured toward the mirror casing. "And once I get the cover off, we'll be able to dig into this thing and see if we can fix it. I could use your help with that, when you're feeling up to it."

Still Avery stared at the housing. He lifted his arms toward it again. To Deacon, it looked like he was about to conduct an orchestra, or give the SLIP drive a hug.

Now.

Deacon made a grab for Avery's arm again. His hand swept through nothing but air, his knuckles knocking painfully on the SLIP drive. He gasped and retracted his hand to his chest.

"Son of a—!" He looked up. Avery was once again on the other side of the room. "Avery, I don't know what the hell you're doing or . . . *how* you're doing it, but listen—"

"Y'know, Titus, there's something weird about this room, isn't there? Titus?"

Avery looked up. Deacon jerked his head back. It almost felt like the other man was standing right in front of him, his face too close, nose to nose. But the SLIP drive stood between them.

Then Avery smiled and turned on his heel to face the gap in the SLIP drive room's wall. He lifted his arms wide as he walked toward the crawlspace, and the weird patterned lattice that was exposed from beneath the black insulation.

"I mean," he continued, "I've seen some strange things in my time, and I know that Artemis operates at the bleeding edge of technology and engineering. That's why you're here, right? This whole ship is proof of that." He pointed at the wall, and glanced over his shoulder at Deacon. "But this? This is pretty fucked up, am I right? I mean, have you *seen* this? Really looked at it?" He turned back. "It's wild. Just look at it. All these stars and moons and symbols, and gemstones? I mean. None of it is structural either. It can't be. Look. Some of these support frames don't even connect to each other. The superstructure of the outer hull should be regular, reinforced with these crossbeams. This is more like art, am I right? Dark art at that."

Avery glanced over his shoulder again. "That's not to say it's not functional, of course. Everything has a purpose."

Deacon licked his lips. "Avery," he said, his voice almost a whisper. "What is going on?"

Avery turned to face Deacon, his mouth curled into the cruel smile again.

"And that's only a part of it," he said, as he began to make his way back around the SLIP drive. Deacon started walking backward, keeping the same distance between them.

"This is only a fraction of the hull," said Avery. "Imagine if the *whole* of it was like that? Can you imagine that? That they built the ship's skeleton to a design none of you had ever seen, keeping that a secret from the very crew who were going to pilot it?" He paused. "Can you imagine what kind of *power* there must be, here, with all of us?"

The pair continued their slow dance around the SLIP drive.

"And you haven't even looked at the floor, have you?" Avery pointed down between his bare feet. "You were all too busy with the walls, looking for poor Astrid." He chuckled. "Floors are difficult, I'll grant you that. Taking off wall panels is one thing, but you have to leave yourself something to stand on. But have you even *looked* at them in here?"

He stopped. He nodded at Deacon, like he was expecting him to do what he was saying.

Deacon glanced down. The floor was the same dark gray as the rest of the ship's interior. The floor panels were smooth, but not shiny. Like the wall panels, the joins between them were perfect, but clearly visible, with bolts at each corner, allowing a magnowrench to easily detach them from the frame underneath.

Then Deacon saw it. The SLIP drive room was pentagonal, apparently designed to follow the lines of the SLIP drive itself. To achieve these angles on the floor, the plates were custom-cut, aligned to fit for maximum strength but also maximum efficiency. In a room with five sides, the floor plates were not rectangular, as they normally had been, but triangular. There was a geometry to them, the way the panels were arranged, the way their borders aligned and intersected.

Deacon took a step back toward the wall, so he could get a better look at the floor. Yes, there was a pattern there, the floor panels forming their own shape, drawn by the lines between them.

Deacon frowned. Actually . . . he wouldn't have done the floor like that. Yes, you'd have to cut the panels, and you'd want to space them properly, get them aligned, keep wastage to a minimum. But there seemed to be too many panels, too many joins, too many lines. True enough, they all came together to form a regular pattern, indicating a conscious design, but it wasn't entirely logical.

Deacon glanced up at Avery. He was still smiling. Deacon sniffed and shrugged, making a show of not falling for his distraction. He didn't know what Avery's game was, but he wanted no part of it.

"Yeah, so what? This room is an odd shape. The floor panels are custom-cut. Big deal."

Avery laughed. Deacon did not.

"Avery," said Deacon, "you and me are going back to your bunk and I'm going to damn well tie you to it myself with a half kilometer of heavy-duty cable."

"See, this room, it's like this for a reason," said Avery, looking around, ignoring Deacon. "Everything has a purpose, a function. You might call it the SLIP drive module. And that's perfectly true. It's a module. This whole ship is made out of them. But this *shape*. This design. It's not *just* a module. You're all doing it a disservice. No, it's more like a . . . oh, I don't know, a . . . *lens,* right? A focal point, everything aligned around this magic box just so. The walls and the floor and this thing right in the middle of it all."

"I've had enough of this."

"I quite agree, Titus." Avery stepped up to the SLIP drive and put both hands on it as he leaned across. "Now, do you want me to open it for you or not?"

Deacon blinked. "What? It's sealed, and nothing will cut through it. We need the tool that Astrid had."

Avery glanced down at the mirrored casing. He ran his fingers along the infinitely fine lines where the strange screws were almost invisibly embedded.

"No, we don't," he said. He walked around the SLIP drive, hands trailing across the surface. Then he stopped and bent down to look at the angled sides. "I think you actually did more damage than you think." He stood up and looked down at the drive. "I guess I should thank you for that. That's what brought me here. That's what let me in."

Deacon grimaced, like he'd bitten into something sour and rotten. Any thought of getting Avery back to the bunk had left his mind. The SLIP drive was what he was interested in. And if Avery knew something about it . . . ?

"What are you talking about?"

"Here," said Avery, motioning for Deacon to join him as he crouched by the side of the SLIP drive. "Come and take a look."

Avery shuffled to one side, and Deacon cautiously bent down next to him. They were on the side of the SLIP drive facing the door—Deacon took one quick glance over his shoulder, eying the exit, thinking he should go, now, get Liv and get Mirai and get Avery back to his bunk. There had to be something in the medical kits that they could use to knock him out and maybe even keep him under until they were back on Earth.

Then Avery hissed between his teeth, and Deacon snapped his head back around, his attention drawn back to the mystery of the SLIP drive.

Avery placed his hands on the mirrored cover, feeling again the join between the panels that formed the casing. He ran his fingertips over the screws, pausing like he was feeling each unique symbol, reading them like a blind man reading braille, before moving on to the next one.

"Oh, that's clever," he said, "clever, clever, clever. But it's not enough. Not anymore. See? The drone's cutter did do something."

Avery tapped the seam, then pulled his hand away as Deacon leaned forward to get a better look. He was right—at the join, there was a mark. Deacon ran his thumb over it. It was a cut, not deep, hardly a scratch, but it was something. He turned to Avery, only to find the engineer grinning right in his face.

"That's all I needed," said Avery. "Oh sure, it doesn't look like much, but it's enough. More than enough." The smile dropped away. "Thank you."

Before Deacon could reply, Avery placed both palms on the SLIP drive, on either side of the panel seam and the mark from the plasma cutter. He pushed, and the housing moved under his hands, the shining metal sliding apart—not along the panel joins, but like the metal itself was liquid, the structure just separating as Avery pushed the panels out of the way.

A red light shone out from the interior. Deacon jerked back, his skin intensely cold where the light hit it. Avery continued to push the panels apart. Then he stood and, grabbing the edge of the SLIP drive, pulled up. Now the panels separated along the joins, and the entire top of the casing swung upward on a recessed hinge.

The temperature dropped and kept dropping as the red light flooded the room. Deacon stood and wrapped his arms around himself as he squinted into the light pouring out from inside. He hadn't known what to expect. This was a new engine, the technology so experimental—so advanced—that it was kept a secret from the crew itself.

But an engine was an engine. Deacon knew that. He'd seen them all. Thirty years a military engineer, a drive system specialist. Even if a piece of machinery was unlike anything he'd seen before, give him time, he could figure it out. Titus Deacon could talk to machines, and machines listened.

But this was . . . he didn't know what it was. As his eyes adjusted to the glare, he could see something inside. "What am I looking at?" he asked. The thing inside was moving, floating in the red light.

It was a cube, perhaps fifty centimeters along each edge, and it was the source of the light. The glowing cube rotated in space, apparently floating free of any connections. Some kind of superconducting magnet, perhaps. That, thought Deacon, explained the cold, and also explained why it had to be a totally sealed system. A device like that could only operate under a set of extremely specific conditions.

Then he blinked, and looked again, and the cube—

No, it was—

It was a shining trapezohedron, a brilliant multifaceted jewel, shining scarlet, the angled faces of the thing throwing the light all around the drive room as it spun on its axis. The trapezohedron—

No, it was—

It was a *dodecahedron,* the twelve pentagonal sides matching the pentagonal shape of the engine block and the five sides of the drive room. It spun, floating free, shining bright. The dodecahedron—

No, it was—

Deacon staggered back, pushing the heels of his hands into his eye sockets. The light, the shining, shining light, he couldn't get it out of his mind. The light was red, the room was red, and when he closed his eyes he saw a red light, and he pushed and pushed with his hands until it felt like he was pushing his eyeballs out the back of his head, but the red light didn't fade, didn't diminish, and all the while he felt cold, the cold of the bottom of the sea, the cold of the abyssal depths of empty space.

"The fuck is that thing?" Deacon gasped. He dropped his hands and shook his head, then opened his eyes, but just a little. Through the crack of his eyelids he could see the thing—object—shape—floating in the red light, changing shape between the beats of his heart, between the time it took for what his eyes received to be transmitted to the optical cortex in his brain. The object shifted without moving, changed without changing, rearranging itself from one configuration to the next, as though it had never been the previous shape and would stay in its current form for eternity until suddenly it was something else. A pyramid. A cube. An icosahedron. A stellated . . . something. A shape that defied mathematics, the angles impossible, a horror in Euclidean geometry.

But while the object's shape continued to change, one thing remained the same.

The red light. The shining, shining red light.

"It's beautiful, isn't it?" asked Avery.

Deacon risked a sideways glance, his eyes aching in their sockets. Avery stood right by the open cover, head tilted as he looked at the object dancing at the center. Then he turned to Deacon and held out a hand.

"Come, look closer. Look into the light."

Deacon felt his legs move, his feet shuffling on the floor, even though he didn't really want to move, didn't really want to see. Everything was red, everything was cold, everything hurt.

But Avery reached out a hand and Deacon watched his own arm raise itself, his own hand reaching out. Avery took his hand, and Deacon felt a searing cold, a cold so deep it made his bones ache, travel from his hand, up his arm, to his shoulder. A cold so deep it burned like the hottest fire.

Avery smiled in the shining light, pulling Deacon closer.

"Look into the light, Titus. Tell me what you see."

Deacon grit his teeth against the cold, against the pain, against the light. But he couldn't take his eyes off the object. It changed shape, and changed again, and again, and then—

And then he saw what was inside it.

Blackness, the endless black gulf of chaos, a void of primal dark suspended in a blinding red light.

As he watched, the blackness seemed to grow. Then, in that blackness, he saw stars. First just one, then another, then another. As each appeared, the next appeared faster, until the black void was filled with stars. Millions and millions of stars.

As Deacon watched, the stars wheeled, forming crescents, bands of light, spirals. They formed clusters and galaxies, and then the view zoomed out, those galaxies becoming themselves pinpricks of light, stars within another galaxy, and then another, and another. The view wheeled again, and now it showed the infinite universe as a single layer, stacked on top of another, on top of another, on top of another.

Deacon tried to turn away, but he couldn't. So he screamed instead, rooted to the spot, lost in another world of red light and black nothing and spinning stars and infinite universes in an infinite stack that pushed all and every thought from his mind.

Avery grabbed Deacon by the shoulders, and moved him without resistance until Deacon was staring blindly into Avery's face.

All Deacon could see was red light and all he could feel was black cold.

"I know, I know," said the thing that looked like Avery Cormack but that Deacon knew was just something that had borrowed his form and come back in the escape pod. "It's beautiful, isn't it? It's beautiful because it's the truth." The red glow in Deacon's vision began to fade, and now he could see Avery grinning. "Don't you feel you could just reach right in there and pull yourself in? You're lucky, Titus Deacon. There are not many who have seen the true nature of reality, the infinite dimensions that make everything." He looked over Deacon's shoulder at the SLIP drive, his face bleached red by the light. "I'm going to need your help, Titus."

He pushed Deacon and Deacon stumbled back, half-doubled over, until he hit the wall. He stayed here, muscles rigid, paralyzed, staring, as Avery moved around the SLIP drive.

"It's okay," said Avery. "It's okay. It's okay."

Then he took a step toward Deacon with an arm outstretched, and smiled, and Deacon found he couldn't move a single inch, a single muscle, a single blink of an eye. He stared at Avery's hand as it got closer and closer, moving so slowly, so very, very slowly.

Then the SLIP drive room shimmered in his vision, and split into two hazy, overlapping images that danced in front of his eyes, both the same, and yet completely different, two component parts of a whole. In one version of the SLIP drive room, Avery was standing in front of him, hand outstretched.

In the other, it was someone else.

Deacon yelled as one hand grabbed his shoulder and one hand grabbed the side of his head. He felt a searing burning cold on his face, and he tried to bat the hand away. He felt something move, something in his ear go *pop*, and then the cold was gone and the double image spun and snapped and he closed his eyes.

There was another *pop*. Deacon felt a wave of pressure across his whole body, and then it was still and quiet and his skin crawled like he was covered in ants.

He felt the other hand let go of his shoulder.

He opened his eyes.

The red light was gone.

In the SLIP drive room, the thing that looked like Avery but wasn't him lowered its hand. It stood very still for a long time, then it lifted its face and sniffed the air.

Its meal was gone. Taken from it. But, no matter. There were other sources of energy aboard the ship. It lifted its hand and curled it. In its palm sat Deacon's comms earpiece.

The thing that looked like Avery but wasn't him closed its fist around it, and then it wasn't there, and the room was empty, the SLIP drive sealed shut, the red light gone.

28

LIV SAT BACK AND LISTENED TO THE NOISE

Liv jerked away, then hissed in pain as something small and hard dug itself into her back. In a daze, she arched her body and reached behind, pulling out the clasp of the flight harness.

She had fallen asleep in the pilot's position. She sat up and looked around, not remembering being in the flight deck, not remembering sitting down. She'd been with Avery and Deacon at Avery's bunk, and then she'd—

Liv yawned, and rubbed her face. And then nothing, because she didn't remember. That was what fatigue did. Not just tiredness, this was pure exhaustion, the textbook definition of. Physically, mentally, she was spent.

So yeah. She'd wandered into the flight deck, and sat down, and fallen into a deep slumber.

That was fine. If she needed sleep, who was she to argue?

The flight consoles were mostly dead, and the lighting in the flight deck was at minimum, which meant the mainframe was still rebooting. Liv checked the system chronometer, but it didn't tell her anything useful—she didn't know when she'd fallen asleep, and she realized now that she hadn't checked when the system restore had started. It was a long process, but the progress bar on the console was so very close to the end.

Liv raised a finger to her ear. Then she remembered she'd taken her comms out, the earpiece now sitting on the console in front of her. Fair enough. She leaned forward and activated the ship-wide system. The speaker popped and crackled as she depressed the call button.

Liv gave it another try. This time the comms beeped like it was supposed to, and the line was crystal clear.

"Mirai, this is Liv. How's it going down there? Any progress?"

Beep.

There was no reply. Liv tried again.

"Mirai, you awake?"

Beep.

Nothing.

Oh well, thought Liv. She could hardly blame her.

She adjusted the control and pressed the button again.

"Deak, you copy?"

Beep—and silence.

Deacon too, huh? Or . . .

Then she remembered the fault, remembered trying to trace it and failing in her task.

Here we go again.

Liv leaned over the console and switched comms channels. The lights on the panel flicked green again, so . . . maybe it was back up? She picked up her earpiece and put in back in place. As she pressed the button on the console, her earpiece chimed.

Oh, okay, so, that *was* working now. She switched channels again, going from ship-wide to personal. Perhaps Deacon or Mirai had left their earpieces in and could hear her, if the comms had fixed themselves.

"Mirai, come in please."

Beep.

A moment later, the flight deck was filled with a harsh hiss of white noise. Wincing, Liv turned the volume down.

There went that theory. The comms were still up and down. Liv began to cycle through the channels, switching rapidly between them. Sometimes that cleared glitches, but not this time. The static fuzz continued, the comms console lighting up as a signal came through. Scanning the channels again, Liv watched the readings as the signal came and went, along with the noise, the comms status light flashing in time with the interference.

There. The signal locked on strong, allowing Liv to isolate the source of the interference. It was coming from outside the ship, but very close—the servodrone, parked out on the far side of the hull.

Liv sat back and listened to the noise on the drone's command channel. She really was going to have to suit up again and go outside to turn the machine off manually. She watched the signal light pulse in time with a clicking sound that was buried in the rush of static.

And then she sat up. That other sound, a harsh, sibilant buzzing that almost sounded like—

Sounded like *words*?

Liv turned the volume up.

HE. IS. HERE.

SCKRHSSHHHHVRSHHHHHKKRRRRSSSHHH

THEY. ARE. COMING.

VRSHHHHHKKRSCKRHSSHHHHHRRRSSSHHH

HE. IS. HERE.

HKKRSCKRHSSHHHHHRRRTKKKK

THEY. ARE. COMING.

FSWHHHZZZZZKKKSHHHHHH

Liv sprang out of the seat and killed the comms, then reached over to another control, activating the external camera on the ship's hull.

Liv gasped.

The drone was still there, out on the hull, but it was not alone. Standing next to it was—

Avery.

He was barefoot, dressed in just his Artemis T-shirt and pants, and standing facing away from the camera.

It was impossible. He was out there, no EVA suit, no magnetic boots. The ship might have been stuck in a weird void, but outside was just as hard a vacuum as regular space—if anything, the environment was even more hostile, if that was possible.

Liv stared at the display. For a second, she was unsure of what she was even seeing—was this a dream? A nightmare? A hallucination conjured by her sleep-deprived brain?

And then she snapped to her senses. No, this was real.

This was happening.

Avery turned his head slightly toward the drone, like he was listening

but sound can't travel in a vacuum Avery can't stand in the void this is a dream this is a dream this is a

and Liv turned the comms back up, then toggled another manual tuning control up on the readout. She repeatedly stabbed the button to adjust the setting, and eventually the signal cleared with a regular comms tone.

Beep.

YES.

Beep.

WHO. ARE. THESE. WHO. ARE. COMING.

Beep.

YES.

Beep.

YES.

Beep.

That was when she saw something else. There was Avery, standing on the hull. There was the drone next to him, the pair surrounded by the infinite black nothing in which the XK72 floated.

And then, a light appeared—another star in the infinite, featureless void. It was faint, more or less at the same angle they'd first seen the returning escape pod. It grew brighter, and it sparkled, even though there was no atmosphere to make it sparkle.

And then . . . another appeared, next to the first. It began to grow and sparkle too.

And then another.

And another.

And another.

As Liv watched, the flat blackness outside the ship slowly became populated with stars. After just a few minutes, it was like a night sky viewed from anywhere in normal space.

Liv lowered herself back into the pilot's seat—slowly—unable to take her eyes off the display. She flipped the comms again, ready to call Deacon and Mirai, but when she pressed the call button all she got was an earsplitting burst of static. She tried another channel, got the same, and the same again when she tried a third. Leaning over the comms readout, Liv could see the signal from the drone had now flooded the entire comms system, jamming every channel.

Liv tore out her earpiece and swore, loudly. On the display, the star-spangled sky grew brighter as the stars themselves grew slowly, inexorably, larger, like they were coming toward the XK72. Neither the drone nor Avery had moved.

Liv leaped from the chair and raced out of the flight deck.

She had to find the others.

Fast.

29

WE NEED TO GET OUT OF HERE. WE NEED TO MOVE.

Liv skidded to a halt at the bulkhead hatch that separated the SLIP drive module from the rest of the ship.

The cabin beyond was empty. Another plasma cutting arm from the servodrone's cache of parts was lying on the floor by the wall, its power cable snaking to a smaller auxiliary power pack that sat against an intact portion of wall. The mirrored housing of the SLIP drive had another sooty smudge on it, but the shining pentagonal block was still perfectly sealed.

Liv took a step forward into the cabin, glanced around, then turned to hit the ship-wide comms on the panel next to the door control.

"Deacon, come in please. Where are you? We have a situation."

Beep.

There was no response, but at least the ship-wide comms was holding out after Liv had switched channels.

"Deacon, come in, please."

Beep.

Where the hell was he?

Liv turned, ready to head to the bunks, when the ship-wide comms chimed.

"Ah . . . Liv?"

It was Mirai. She sounded . . . weak? Tired?

Or injured.

Liv froze on the spot, scanning the passageway ahead of her, as though she expected the flight analyst to appear from around the next bulkhead.

"Mirai! Where are you? Are you okay?"

"Liv, there's something . . ."

"Mirai?"

Mirai sighed, long and hard, like she was fighting against pain, physical or, perhaps, mental.

"I think there's something in the ship," she said.

Liv stared at the comms panel—but not in disbelief. She didn't know where Mirai was, but one thing was perfectly clear.

She knew. Just like Liv did.

Avery it's not Avery it's not Avery it's not Avery it's not

Liv closed her eyes, concentrating on the here and the now. "Where are you?"

"Data Monitoring."

"I'm coming down."

She released the comms button.

Beep.

Liv found Mirai collapsed on the floor of the lower module, trying to pull herself up into her chair. Liv dropped down the last few rungs of the access ladder and helped Mirai to her feet, then settled her back into the seat, Mirai conscious but almost a deadweight.

"Mirai, what happened?" asked Liv. She carefully took Mirai's head in her hands and coaxed her to look up into her face. Mirai didn't resist, but she winced when she saw Liv, her eyelids fluttering like she was staring into a bright light. "Did he attack you?"

Mirai frowned, and closed her eyes tight. Liv dropped her hands, allowing Mirai to turn away from her again.

"I . . . I . . . I'm not sure, I'm not sure." Mirai's voice was a whisper, punctuated by shallow, almost difficult breaths, like she was coming around from a heavy daze. "I'm not sure," she said again. "I'm not sure."

Then she paused, her breathing slowing, her eyes opening. She looked up at Liv.

"It's not Avery."

Liv didn't answer. Instead, she slowly, carefully, considered what Mirai had said, trying to understand it, trying to parse it, willing it not to be true but knowing it was and that Mirai was right and that Liv knew it as well.

And then Liv nodded. When she spoke, she didn't really hear her own voice. It felt like she was watching from a distance, like she was merely an observer to her own actions, another version of herself screaming at the nightmare that she now found herself trapped in.

"It's not Avery," was what she said.

At this, Mirai grabbed Liv's wrists and squeezed, hard. "He came down here. But . . ." She trailed off, and shook her head again, like she was trying to clear her thoughts. She blinked, rapidly, then rubbed her eyes with the heels of both hands, and didn't speak again.

Liv stood back. When Mirai looked up at her, Liv nodded vaguely over her shoulder. "He's—*it's*—outside, now. On the hull, with the servodrone."

Mirai's expression flickered. "What?"

"Here, look."

Liv moved around Mirai's chair and brought up the surveillance feed from the hull on one of the computer displays.

There, on the hull, stood Avery—the thing that looked like Avery—unprotected, apparently impervious to the void. Next to him was the servodrone. Both were facing away from the camera, watching the sky as it filled with more and more stars.

No, not stars, thought Liv. *Lights.* Lights that were growing in size as well as number as they approached the ship.

"He's not wearing a suit," Mirai said under her breath, leaning forward to stare at the screen.

"I guess it doesn't need one," said Liv, and as she said it, she felt the tight coil of panic begin to wind tighter and tighter inside her.

It. Doesn't. Need. One.

She paused then, and closed her eyes, fighting against the lightheadedness that came with her fear, willing that fear to abate, telling herself she didn't have time to give in to it, not now.

It worked, and she opened her eyes. She tapped at the keyboard again. The small readout was filled with a page of text, which she scanned quickly. It was as she thought. She pointed at the screen. "According to the running log, no external hatchways have been opened either."

Mirai worked her jaw up and down, trying to find the words. She turned back to Liv. "When he came down here, he took me by surprise. I thought I was just too busy to notice, but it didn't seem like the hatchway here was opened, or that he'd come down the ladder. He just—"

"Appeared?"

The two women looked at each other, Mirai searching Liv's face, looking for acceptance, belief in her story, belief in what she saw. On Liv's part, she knew her crewmate was telling the truth.

Then Mirai turned back to the screen. "Those lights," she said, her voice remarkably level and calm. "That's how the escape pod first appeared."

Liv nodded. "Whatever they are, they're coming toward us. Only it's not just one this time. It's hundreds. Thousands."

"Where's Deacon?"

"I don't know," said Liv. "He must be somewhere." Even as she said it, a terrible thought occurred to her.

Because Deacon couldn't have disappeared.

Just like Astrid

or Avery or Redway or the escape pod or or or

couldn't have.

Liv tapped the controls and opened the ship's internal comms channel again, but before she could even call for Deacon, the cabin was filled with the white noise roar, punctuated by the harsh electronic buzzing of the servodrone, the robot's attempt at human speech now a garbled mess of junk signal.

Liv killed the channel.

"He's not on the ship, is he?" said Mirai, quietly, giving voice to Liv's own nightmare. "Like Astrid."

Liv stared at Mirai, but it took her a moment to find an answer, and that answer was entirely the truth and it was simply: "I don't know."

In silence, the two women turned and watched the image on the display. Avery and the drone hadn't moved, and around them, the black sky was scattered with lights, all of them white, many of them far larger than they had been even a few minutes ago.

"We need to get out of here," said Mirai, not taking her eyes from the screen. "Whatever is happening, we need to get out of here. We need to *move.*"

As if on cue, there was a very loud, very sharp double chime that echoed around the monitoring station. Immediately the ever-present background hum of the ship altered in pitch.

The XK72 mainframe was back online.

Liv and Mirai looked at each other.

That was when the room lurched, the floor tilting to an angle sharp enough to throw Liv to the floor. Recovering, she looked up to see Mirai still in her seat, clutching the station in front of her.

"What's happening?" called Liv.

Mirai scanned her console, but shook her head.

"I don't know," she said, tapping some controls. "The Data Monitoring module is separated from the primary systems. The computer has rebooted. Everything is back up, but that's about all I can tell from here."

Then the ship lurched again. Liv quickly scrambled to her feet, and anchored herself to the back of Mirai's chair in case it happened again.

"We're moving," said Liv, looking at the console over Mirai's shoulder. Lights flashed, and a readout spun with new data. "That feels like a broken stabilizer."

Mirai nodded and then, seeming to realize something, looked up. "The ion drive. The mainframe will be trying to balance it, but it can't."

Liv made for the access ladder. "I'll get to the flight deck and shut off the drive. If the computer has been reset to preflight conditions, we can engage the SLIP drive and make the Drop now."

"Understood," said Mirai. She slid off her seat, and was about to follow Liv when she stopped. "Wait," she said. "Look."

Liv turned from the ladder to see Mirai pointing at the main display. The feed from outside still showed the drone on the hull, and around it, the points of light were now wheeling in the blackness of void as the ship swayed on its axis. Of Avery, there was no sign.

"Where is he?"

"Shit," said Liv. "Come on."

She led the way up the ladder, Mirai close behind.

30

SHE THOUGHT SHE PREFERRED THE SHADOWED HALF-LIGHT OF BEFORE

As Liv came up into the main passageway and rushed toward the flight deck, Mirai right behind her, she slowed as she saw someone moving in the multicolored light thrown by the control consoles in the cabin beyond. The shape was just a shadow, but it was big, cast long by the console lights, moving like someone was pacing up and down.

Avery. Or whoever—*whatever*—it was that was pretending to be him.

Liv stopped, but then the movement was gone and the shadow with it. Then the ship lurched again. Liv wheeled her arms to keep her balance as Mirai grabbed hold of her arm, then the floor returned to level.

There was no time to waste. Liv led the way quickly down the passage, arms out for balance in case the whole thing tipped again. She paused in the doorway, holding onto the bulkhead, but for now the XK72 remained stable.

There was nobody in the flight deck. The main display still showed the view of outside, the servodrone standing on the arc of the hull, the black void filling with impossible lights.

Liv crossed the cabin just as the ship dipped again, propelling her toward the pilot's station. She grabbed hold of the seat and swung herself into it. A moment later, Mirai followed, strapping herself into the copilot's seat before checking over the systems in front of her.

Liv snapped the main display off, and they both looked up. The view through the curved bubble of the ship's nose was now unimpeded, and they could see the growing star field outside with their own eyes.

Liv hit a control and the ship shuddered. Mirai jerked in her seat, and Liv heard her take a deep breath.

"It's okay," said Liv. "We can do this. We're almost there." She returned her attention to the control she had just engaged—it should have cut the ion drive. She tried it again, but all it did was make the ship roll, the panel in front of her lighting up in red before the ship stabilized once again.

"Manual override isn't working." Liv paused, sitting back a little. "I must have damaged the drive more than I thought."

Mirai nodded and rubbed her face, just as the ship tilted forward again. Mirai was held fast by the seat straps but Liv had to throw her hands out in front of her to stop her smacking headfirst into the control console. Lesson learned, she quickly fitted her own straps and got to work.

"Okay, so we're locked out and the mainframe is looping through an emergency procedure," said Mirai, reading off the console display to her right. "It's pulsing the ion drive to get it back into phase."

As if to underline Mirai's assessment, the ship rocked again. Liv watched the control console, taking note of the readings and indicators that flashed in time with the cycling of the ion drive by the XK72 mainframe. It was registering a fault—Liv's handiwork in the drive core, a fault that couldn't be corrected. Instead, the computer was stuck, sensing both the imbalance in the drive core and a corresponding surge in the power grid, cutting the drive so balance was restored and the surge dropped, then cycling it again in an infinite and futile loop. And with the master control unresponsive, there didn't seem to be an obvious way of overriding it.

Unless—

Liv frowned, and checked the readings again. She gestured to her small screen. "The induction combs are registering as overloaded. We're locked in a positive feedback loop. The more the computer cycles the drive, the more the combs overload, and the power surge makes the mainframe cut the drive again." Liv paused, and ran her tongue around her teeth as she thought things over. "We'll need to disconnect them."

Mirai turned in her seat to face Liv. There was a long pause before she spoke, the disbelief evidenced in her expression. "*Disconnect* them? It took us hours to rig that up, and that was with the servodrone doing most of the work."

The ship swung forward again. Liv listened to the whine of the ion drive coming from the back of the XK72 as the ship's computer made another of the infinite attempts to rebalance the engines.

"We have to interrupt the drive," she said, glancing over the controls. "Or we won't be able to make the Drop. The mainframe won't let us."

"And we're back to square one," said Mirai. She pulled against her straps as she balanced on the edge of her seat. "But disconnecting the combs with the drone and Avery still out there? There's no way we'd be able to get even a few couplings off before they come for us."

Liv didn't reply. Mirai was right. They had to clear the combs, but they wouldn't stand a chance out there. Then Liv slapped the console with the flat of her fingers.

Of course, that was it.

She looked at Mirai. "We don't need to disconnect them, physically, I mean. We can just cut them off from the power grid. That'll clear the overload."

Mirai's eyes went wide. "You want to disconnect the whole power grid?"

"No, just the combs. Do you think it can be done?"

Mirai turned back to the outside view, just as the ship's nose dipped again. Then she glanced back at Liv. "I don't know. Maybe?" She paused. "The nanoparticle array has a control box to feed absorbed power into the ship. Turning that off would have the same effect as disconnecting all the combs."

Liv nodded. "Good work. We kill the control box, it'll disconnect the nanoparticle array. The combs will still be absorbing the ion exhaust, but the power won't go anywhere."

"But," said Mirai, "the control box is by the airlock—*outside*."

Liv pointed at the screen. "The drone is on the other side of the hull. We can get out, disconnect it, and get back inside before it can make it over to the airlock."

"What about Avery?"

Liv didn't answer. She could feel Mirai next to her, the younger woman holding her breath.

"Well, we don't know, do we?" Liv finally said. It was as good as she could come up with, and she knew it wasn't enough.

Now it was Mirai's turn to pause. Liv glanced at her, and saw her staring ahead, nodding, perhaps more to herself than to Liv.

Then Mirai took a breath. "It only needs one person," she said. "I'll do it. You're the pilot. As soon as the control box is disconnected, you can stabilize the ion drive and prep the Drop." She blew out her cheeks, paused, then hit the release on her seat straps. "I'll get suited up." She went to stand, then paused. "We might be tight for time, though. Disconnecting the control box might take a little while. They'll know I'm out there as soon as I step out of the airlock."

Liv shook her head. "You don't need to disconnect it. Take the plasma cutter from the SLIP drive module and plug it into the external power output by the airlock. All you need to do is slice the box through. That'll take it offline."

"It'll also disable the ship. We wouldn't be able to make a repair ourselves."

"We won't need to. As soon as the ship stabilizes, we Drop." Liv gestured to a readout on the console. "We've got enough power now, and we won't be staying here any longer than necessary."

Mirai nodded and stood. "I'll be as fast as I can."

"I'll be ready."

As Mirai got up and left, Liv focused her attention on the controls, and began running through the standard pre-mission flight prep—or as much of it as she could with the mainframe preoccupied with its error loop.

That was when something moved, in the corner of her vision. Mirai, perhaps, forgetting something?

Or Avery?

Liv spun around, but there was nobody there. Turning back around, she looked into the viewing bubble. All she could see was her own face, a ghostly reflection lit from beneath by the flight controls in front of her, the strange star-lights outside now larger still. The flight deck behind her was—

Was not empty. In the reflected world, Liv was not alone. Colonel Redway now sat in the co-pilot's position, watching her. Liv could actually *see* the other seat out of the corner of her eye, and she knew there was nobody physically there.

The ship lurched, Liv moving with the motion. She couldn't tell whether Redway's image was affected by the movement or not. He certainly didn't show any signs of trying to keep his balance.

Liv felt dizzy. "What's going on?" she demanded of the mirror world.

Redway's image didn't move. He was looking at her, his expression one of complete indifference.

"What did you *do*?" asked Liv. Her eyes felt hot, tears pricking at the corners. "Who were you working for? Did Artemis know? *Tell me what you did!*"

Redway blinked, and in the reflected world he leaned forward. His mouth moved, like he was saying something, but it wasn't words, it was bursts of static, and buried in that static, the electric buzz of the servodrone's attempted emulation of words. On the console in front of Liv, the comms light blinked rapidly, in time with the sound. She glanced down at the light, shaking her head.

Redway kept talking. He looked agitated. He waved his arms. He was shouting. He pointed at Liv, pointed somewhere else, but all Liv could do was sit there, and shake her head, and listen to the distorted staccato roar of nothing.

The XK72 bucked again, the sudden movement throwing Liv forward. As her seat straps cut into her shoulders, she looked up. Redway was gone.

Liv pushed herself back into the seat and pulled on the straps to tighten them.

Enough.

Enough.

She punched up the main display and cycled through the feeds, stopping when she saw Mirai in the inner airlock chamber, checking the helmet seal on her EVA suit, the long white wand of the drone's plasma cutter leaning against one wall, a coil of fat orange cable on the floor.

Liv opened the comms. "That was fast."

Mirai straightened up and grabbed the plasma cutter. "I'm going out. Get ready to clear the drive error as soon as the control box is out. You don't need to wait for me to confirm, you should start getting a whole load of alerts that the nanoparticle array is disconnected."

"Copy," said Liv, watching as Mirai opened the outer airlock. She felt her whole tired, exhausted body tense. She forced herself to breathe, to relax, and it seemed to work.

"Be careful," she said as Mirai stepped outside, but when she released the comms button, all she got was static.

Mirai hesitated on the threshold of the outer airlock door, one foot in, one foot out. It was bright outside, which she hadn't expected. The whole hull was now evenly and flatly illuminated by the growing number of lights that punctuated the blackness all around her.

She thought she preferred the shadowed half-light of before, when they'd been out rigging the power relays under the uneven glare of the maintenance lights.

Stepping out on the hull itself was always slightly unnerving, the upright doorway instantly becoming a large rectangular hatch beneath her feet, but as she moved now she felt the pressing need to look behind her, like there was somebody right there, ready and waiting.

Like Avery.

She turned, and saw nothing. She was alone on this section of the hull. If Avery was still outside, he wasn't in view. Nor was the servodrone.

Mirai took a breath. She was afraid, there was no point in pretending otherwise. But she didn't need to be out here long. She rolled her neck inside her helmet. Liv would be watching her, waiting for her to get the hell on with it. The comms light in Mirai's helmet HUD flickered, like Liv was trying to get through, but Mirai knew if she opened the channel it would be nothing but white noise.

Time to get to work. Forgoing the safety tether for speed, Mirai uncoiled the plasma cutter's own cable, and fitted it to the power outlet by the airlock hatch. She hefted the cutting wand in her gloved hands, getting it comfortable in her grip.

The power grid control box was only a couple of meters away, a slightly raised pod a meter long with a featureless cover, underneath which Mirai knew were a series of ports and other controls, linking the nanoparticle array under the hull skin with the ship's power system, and also allowing the XK72 to couple with a ground-based power source back in its Artemis hangar. Trying to disconnect the box manually, following proper procedure, would take ten, fifteen minutes.

But only ten, fifteen seconds to slice through it with the plasma cutter.

Mirai swung the tool and crossed the short space toward her target. Planting both heavy magnetic boots astride the control box, she considered the best place to cut when she saw a flash of white in her peripheral vision.

Mirai looked up, then spun around, almost tripping over the cutter's cable. Inside her helmet, the comms channel burst into life, the indicator light flashing brighter than ever, in time with the rhythmic buzzing that was buried in the roar of white noise that filled her helmet.

The servodrone took a step forward, cutting Mirai off from the airlock, its white bodywork flaring again in her vision. As Mirai watched, it rotated the segments of its insect-like chassis until it reconfigured itself into something more bipedal. Then it opened its four tool arms wide, forming an "X" as the three LED lights that indicated its primary optical unit was focused on her.

Mirai gasped, her breath momentarily fogging her visor before the suit's internal environment control whirred to life and cleared it.

Beep.

"Liv? Can you hear me?"

WHO. ARE. THESE. WHO. ARE. COMING.

Beep.

The drone's optics shifted, the three lights turning into spinning jewels as it refocused on Mirai. She took a step backward. The servodrone didn't move. It seemed to be assessing the situation.

Beep.

The machine's grinding circuits forced the words it couldn't speak out across the open comms channel, its voice an alien vibration that drilled into Mirai's skull.

WHO. ARE. THESE. WHO. ARE. COMING.

Beep.

The machine fell silent, the static rush dying in Mirai's ears. It didn't move. And neither did she.

Was it . . . was it waiting for some kind of response?

Mirai tightened her grip on the plasma cutter that hung from her right hand. It was a powerful device, and could make short work of the control box. But the drone to which the tool actually belonged was far larger and far tougher.

Would she be able to even damage it before it killed her?

"What do you want?" asked Mirai, slowly and quietly.

She moved her fingers over the cutter's controls.

Beep.

Silence reigned.

Mirai glanced down. The control box. She would cut into that first, get the job done. If she was fast, she could do it, let Liv get on with her task, and then she could worry about the drone.

She breathed in, breathed out, slowly, calmly.

Beep.

HE. IS. HERE.

Beep.

WHO. ARE. THESE. WHO. ARE. COMING.

Beep.

HE. IS. HERE.

Beep.

The drone shuddered, and it took a heavy, unstable step forward.

Mirai felt the hairs on the back of her neck stand up, her whole skin—her whole *body*—crawling with fear as she processed the drone's mechanized words.

Then, her gloved index finger finding the recessed manual control on the plasma cutter, she activated it. The long pole kicked in her grip, the glowing tip an incandescent, fuzzy ball of energy.

"What do you want?"

Beep.

The drone shot forward, pushing itself off the hull as it leaped toward Mirai. Surprised at its sudden burst of speed, Mirai cried out. She stumbled backward, and reached behind with her free hand, pushing herself off the side of the control box even as she swung herself around and stabbed the plasma cutter forward, sweeping the tip across its cover.

But the angle of her attack was wrong. The plasma cutter melted a hole in the top of the box, then embedded itself in the casing. A huge shower of white sparks erupted silently into the void. Then, as the tool jarred in her hand, Mirai slipped and fell sideways onto the hull.

She was lucky. Her fall took her out of the drone's path enough that the huge machine just clipped her shoulder. She felt something crack—whether it was the ceramic reinforcing plate on her EVA suit, or her shoulder joint itself, she couldn't tell—and was swung around in an arc as she kept hold of the plasma cutter. Her back slammed into the hull and immediately her HUD was filled with a series of red warnings.

Righting herself, Mirai spared the drone only a glance as she pulled herself up and then ran to the control box, taking the plasma cutter in both hands as she fought to free it from the half-melted casing. She grunted with effort, her breath loud in her ears, her helmet fogging once more. Then the sound of static grew again, drowning everything out, a sound so loud she realized she was screaming with effort and she couldn't even hear it.

As Mirai wrenched the plasma cutter, the business end of it carved through the innards of the control before Mirai flew backward, propelled by her own momentum and the force of the box itself exploding. As she fell, she saw the white carapace of the servodrone looming over her, the four tool arms reaching forward, pincer-like claws at the end of each ready to grab and quarter her if they got within reach.

Mirai yelled again and swung the cutter in both hands like a broadsword. The tip hit the drone under one of its arms, sending blue jags of electrical discharge shorting across the side of the machine. The drone jerked backward, three arms flailing to grab the cutter as the fourth shook, useless as the damaged joint motor fried. All the while, the grinding voice of the drone barked across Mirai's comms, the broken speech degenerating into computerized, angry buzzing.

Mirai pushed on with the tool, trying to angle the cutting torch to sever the drone's arm completely. She succeeded, the arm falling away in a starburst of sparks. The plasma tool skittered across the drone's chest, burning a sooty smear across the white plating, before the drone was finally able to catch the improvised weapon in two of its other claws. It lifted it up; Mirai yelped as she was hoisted off her feet. Then she fell back against the hull as the drone snapped the plasma cutter in two, leaving Mirai holding a splintered shard in her hand.

She could feel the heat through her glove already. The drone had broken the cutter and ruptured the power line that ran down the length of it. The jagged end of the fragment in Mirai's hand spat blue-and-white fire, the stream of free energy so powerful Mirai had to push against it just to hold the fragment level.

The drone's optics fixed on her, and it tossed the dead part of the tool away. Its three remaining arms spun in their sockets as it reconfigured the tools for closer combat. Mirai was pinned beneath the drone, with nowhere to go.

She thrust the flaming, broken end of the cutter at the drone. It swerved out of the way, then swung an opposite arm, the clamp-like tool on the end closing painfully around Mirai's upper left arm. Mirai screamed as the drone lifted her again, another pincer grabbing her right leg, just above the ankle.

The pain nearly made Mirai pass out. She blinked the tears and sweat from her eyes, and kicked out with her free leg just as she stabbed again with the flaming torch.

She hit the drone at the junction between the machine's waist and the heavy plating that protected its legs. The cutter met a little resistance at first. Then the unleashed energy burned through the casing and the plasma stream hit the drone's main power conduit. Sliced clean through, the drone's fuel cell immediately leaked into the machine's interior. A second later, it caught, and the cell itself exploded.

Mirai passed out, the plasma torch slipping out of her hand as the drone was blown to pieces, the burning debris scattering across the hull and out toward the gathering lights.

With nothing to stop her, her arm and leg still held by the now-dead drone's tool hands, Mirai was thrown off the hull and into the void, carried by the shock wave.

31

THEN LIV FEINTED TO THE LEFT

On the flight deck, Liv had her eyes fixed on the controls. The mainframe was still cycling the ion drive, trying to clear an error that it didn't know didn't exist, but with some determined effort and lateral thinking, she had at least been able to wrestle the unresponsive controls enough to suppress the violent swings of the ship into little more than periodic, uncomfortable shudders. The light on the comms panel flashed incessantly, but Liv had the main channel off. It was pointless trying to keep in touch with Mirai as she worked on the hull, the roar of interference from the servodrone flooding the entire communications system.

She glanced up at the main feed, but the angle was wrong, and she could only see the far edge of the power grid control module. Mirai was working out of sight on the other side, but the more direct camera feed from the airlock wasn't any better, the view obscured by the flaring star-like lights.

There was no sign of Avery or the servodrone. Not good. On another screen, the internal feeds cycled automatically. Liv didn't know where Deacon was, but she hoped he would appear (reappear?) somewhere.

That was when she saw it. A silent shower of sparks, filling the main feed, cascading in a fan-like arc right across the screen. There was a chime from the console. Casting her eyes briefly downward, Liv saw the data readout screen on the main panel change, the endless scrolling text of the looped error replaced with a status report and a new alert: a fault with the power grid. The timbre of the ship's hum altered as the mainframe finally gave up on the ion drive, and now patiently—and dumbly—awaited a new command, satisfied the power surge was under control.

Liv let out a breath, and felt herself sink back into the seat. Mirai had done it. With the control box blown, the power grid was separated from the induction combs on the hull. With no overload registering, the ion drive was uncoupled and able to be manually deactivated.

They were ready to go.

There was another flash on the screen, bright enough to make Liv blink and look back up.

The servodrone had found Mirai.

Liv felt her heart kick into high gear as she now saw the small woman struggling against the ridiculous bulk of the robot. Liv could only see them at the edge of the picture, and then there was a third flash of light. Liv's jaw dropped open as she saw Mirai tumble *away* from the XK72, her brilliant orange environment suit flaring in the void, surrounded by a scintillating cloud of debris from the explosion.

Liv reached forward, activating the comms. "Mirai! *Mirai!*" Her screaming voice echoed around the flight deck, but when she released the button she was met yet again with the raw sound of nothing, as loud as an old-fashioned rocket engine.

Liv killed the comms and went to stand, only to be stopped short by the seat straps. She looked down, trying and failing to release the mechanism with her shaking hands, her mind racing.

It's going to be okay it's going to be okay it's going to be okay it's going to be okay.

Mirai could survive for several hours in the environment suit, she told herself. The XK72 was operational, she told herself. I am a qualified pilot, she told herself, and with careful nursing of the sabotaged ion drive, she could go and pick Mirai up. Unlike the powered launch of the escape pod, Mirai's tumble was low velocity. Liv could reach her, bring her in, and then they could go home together. Already the mainframe had picked up Mirai's mass, and was alerting the ship's crew—now numbering just one—with a proximity alert.

It's going to be okay it's going to be okay it's going to be okay it's going to be okay.

She could do this.

She *would* do this.

Finally, Liv managed to operate the strap release, freeing her from the seat. She stood, and, looking up at the curve of controls that arced over the flight positions, began the standard process to take full and proper manual control of the ship, with some necessary adjustments that would allow her to compensate for the damaged ion drive.

But, as fast as she worked, already the proximity alert had begun to change, the frequency of chimes becoming less and less as the ship's sensors struggled to keep a lock on Mirai.

There was no time, no time, no time.

"Knock, knock!"

Liv spun around.

Avery stepped out of the crawlspace on Liv's right. Across the flight deck, straight ahead of her, was the main bulkhead door, beyond which she could see the passageway and the next hatch, leading to the EVA suits, to the airlock, to Mirai.

But there was no way she could make it. Avery was closer to the door than she was.

"Feels good, right?" Avery smiled. "You're back in control of the ship, finally."

Liv lifted her chin and clenched both fists. "Get out of my way."

She almost called him—*it*—Avery, but she bit down on her tongue. It hurt, and Liv focused on the sensation, using it to clear her mind.

"It's too late," said the thing that wasn't Avery. "You know that. You can't save her. She's gone. Like the others. You just have to accept that."

Liv took a step forward, then froze as the thing lifted a hand and tossed something small at her. She caught it reflexively, then opened her palm to see what it was.

It was a comms earpiece.

"Clever Deacon," said the thing. "He got away. But you won't be so lucky."

Liv squeezed her hand shut. She really was on her own now.

"I don't know what you are," she whispered, "but I told you to get out of my way."

Not-Avery smiled, and lifted both hands, turning them in the air as he looked them over.

"You know who I am, Liv. I'm Avery Cormack. I'm your engineer."

"If you're my engineer," said Liv, "then I'm your mission lead, and this is your mission lead telling you to get the fuck out of my way."

The thing dropped its hands. "It won't work, Liv. You can't save her. You can't save any of them. And soon enough we won't be alone anymore."

Liv breathed, hot and heavy, through her flaring nostrils. She had to get to Mirai. She took a step forward, toward the door, but the thing moved sideways, now directly blocking her path.

"Okay, fine," said Liv. She backed off. Not-Avery didn't move, but a strange look passed over its face, one Liv hadn't seen before.

The thing that had taken Avery Cormack's form was . . . *uncertain.*

Then Liv feinted to the left.

Not-Avery went with it, but it was already moving in the wrong direction as Liv ran to the hole in the wall, leaped over the frame, and dived into the crawlspace.

32

SPIRALING AROUND CONCENTRIC CIRCLES

As soon as she entered the crawlspace, Liv felt dizzy. She ducked, instinctively, as the weird pressure she had felt outside the ship returned, like a heavy blanket was draped over her. It was almost like an active, alive thing—when she straightened up, and raised her head, she could feel it pushing back against her.

That wasn't the only unpleasant sensation. She immediately felt a strong sense of presence, and she twisted her head around, unable to resist, but she was quite alone in the dark of the ship's inner skin. In front of her, the crawlspace ran straight ahead and then curved out of sight, leading down the whole length of the ship, linking the individual modules of the XK72 with a single continuous conduit.

There was a noise behind her. Liv turned to see the black silhouette of the thing that looked like Avery Cormack step through the opening in the flight deck wall, backlit by the relative brightness of the cabin beyond. As it moved toward her, it snarled—an animal noise, something old and primitive, and edged with the same kind of alien static that filled every comms channel on the ship.

Liv didn't waste any more time. She turned, and ran, almost blindly into the dark ahead of her. She held her arms out, hoping to use the inner and outer walls for guidance once it had gotten too dark, but after a few seconds she was enveloped in blackness and may as well have had her eyes closed.

Liv ran. The crawlspace was relatively wide, but as she gained speed she found herself bouncing between the inner and outer walls, both as cold as ice. The heavy foam coating the outer wall was harder than she expected, and even in her desperation she wondered again about what was behind it, whether the strange jewel-encrusted lattice of the SLIP drive module extended around the whole of the XK72.

All she had to do was keep going. She knew she would, eventually, come to another wall section Deacon said he had removed. With any luck, it would be one near the airlock. She just had to put enough distance between her and the thing behind her so she could get in and lock it out, giving her the time to put the EVA suit on and go help Mirai. She didn't know how, not now, but she didn't know what else to do.

She had to try.

Behind her, she heard the thing in pursuit, its footfalls thudding in an even rhythm, growing louder, echoing oddly despite the deadening effect of the insulating foam. It sounded like it was moving on all fours.

It snarled again, the sound so loud, almost in Liv's ear, that she gasped in surprise and pushed on. Her left shoulder bumped into the inner wall, and running her hands blindly along it, she felt the familiar cables and ducting that were right where she expected them to be.

That was when she fell, tripping on a bulkhead. She flew forward, and raised her arms in front of her face, but it was her knees that connected with the floor first. The impact jarred her whole body; a second later, a deep, searing pain exploded in both kneecaps. She tumbled sideways, her face protected by her arms, but not the back of her head, which hit the outer wall. She yelled out in pain, the blow cushioned by the foam but still heavy. Rolling onto her back, she gritted her teeth against the shock of the fall, and as the initial starburst of pain began to subside, she pushed herself backward with the heels of both hands, readying herself to twist and resume her flight.

Behind her, a light appeared in the dark, and then another, and then another. Wide-eyed, Liv fought to right herself as the lights got closer. Reflecting dully off the panels of the inner wall, the illumination now showed her pursuer.

Liv got up, but stumbled again, as she tried to process what she was looking at. It still looked like Avery—well, it was wearing the Artemis T-shirt, anyway—but its head was nothing but a gaping maw of teeth, spiraling around concentric circles that seemed to go on forever, surrounded by a multitude of thin, writhing tentacles, covered in suckers that themselves had rings of razor-like teeth. It pulled itself forward with arms that looked human but were too long, able to reach both the inner wall and the outer. As it came closer, the tentacles stretched out, adhering themselves to the walls, floor, ceiling, where they remained plastered and twitching. New tentacles sprouted from the maw, taking their place. In a few seconds, the whole of the crawlspace Liv had just run down was cut off by a mass of seething green-blue flesh.

The thing looked at her, its glowing white eyes now the only light source, a dozen spots scattered somewhere on the head behind the tentacles that Liv was grateful she couldn't see.

Liv pushed herself back, scooting along the floor, legs kicking out as she tried to gain traction while keeping the flailing tentacles at a distance. She made slow progress on the smooth floor, tentacles lapping at her boot and lower legs, leaving behind a reddish oily trail like they were bleeding.

Liv yelled out, partly in fear but mostly with the effort of trying to desperately scramble away. She couldn't hear her own voice. It was drowned out by the white static roar that emanated from the slavering mouth that the creature stretched toward her.

She wasn't going to make it. She was too slow, her senses too numbed by an adrenaline hangover and a palpable sense of dread as dense as the void of the crawlspace. She began to slow in her backward crawl, unable to take her eyes from the shining lights in the dark.

The thing, sensing its prey was now much closer, lunged forward, the tentacles slapping both sides of the crawlspace as it used them to pull itself closer, the serrated teeth of each sucker cutting into insulating foam and metal wall plate alike. As soon as one set of tentacles had latched on to the surfaces, spreading out like the red oil they were leaking, almost like they were absorbing into the contact surface, a fresh set of tentacles sprouted and repeated the action, the sound a sickening, wet squelch.

Then there was a crack; it sounded like a gunshot in the enclosed space, muffled by the sound-insulating properties of the black foam. Liv, braced for the tentacles' embrace, glanced instinctively toward the sound, which had come from the outer wall, somewhere underneath the last writhing tentacled mass that clung to it. The sound came again, louder this time, and Liv could see the foam cracking. The thing pulled again, and more of the foam gave way.

Liv finally got to her feet and turned to run as the whole outer wall split, the insulating foam shattering as the tentacles pulled it from the wall. Liv had a glimpse of the framework beneath, the illogical, secret, *impossible* framework behind it

yes, it's here it's around the whole ship

the crystals and gems reflecting the white light from the creature's eyes back in a myriad of sparkling colors.

The creature roared again, the sound nothing but pure white noise. As

Liv pushed off on her toes, a sprinter's last attempt to beat the gun, she wondered if it really sounded like that, or whether it was just her body unable to process whatever sound it was making, the auditory centers of her brain sparing her the pain and madness of the creature's true voice.

Now she kept her eyes ahead, running blind in the blackness. Behind her the cracking continued. Then her ears popped as there was one huge bang. She slipped and fell forward, not tripping this time but being pulled from behind by an invisible force. Arms wheeling as she grabbed desperately for any kind of handhold, Liv looked over her shoulder.

The outer hull of the XK72 had been breached, the multitude of groping, adhesive tentacles tearing a gash in the side of the ship as the creature that had pretended to be Avery tried to pull its ever-increasing mass through the confines of the crawlspace. Air rushed out as the crawlspace—and the interior of the ship itself—became suddenly open to the absolute vacuum outside. As Liv watched, the creature tried to pull itself over the hole in the wall, but to no avail. There was a temporary restoration of pressure—enough for Liv's feet to once more make contact with the floor, causing her to topple forward under her own weight—then a *pop* as the creature's upper half was sucked into the gap.

Liv got to her hands and knees. Then her hand was pushed away as a small recessed nozzle extended itself from the floor.

Somehow, *this* was what really frightened her. Her heart hammered in her chest as, with a sharp hiss, the nozzle began to discharge a pungent yellow gas.

Liv glanced up and around, and saw more nozzles appear. It was an automated system, designed to seal a hull breach. Liv had just seconds before the yellow gas would solidify, first into a gel, and then that gel would in turn harden into a ceramic that was just as strong as the hull plates themselves.

Just then, the breach in the hull grew in size. Unable to withstand the pressure from the mass of the creature, the outer skin of the ship buckled, and blew out. The creature, now just an immense mass of anemone-like tentacles, was pulled out into the void. Tentacles grabbed hold of the edges of the hole to try to stop it being carried out on the evacuating atmosphere, but they weren't strong enough, and the regrowth of new tentacles to replace those pulled off the creature wasn't fast enough.

The creature shot out into the void, and Liv was dragged behind it, even as the automated system struggled to match the rush of leaking atmosphere with the yellow sealant gas.

Liv reached out toward the inner wall, hoping to grab a cable run or something else that might save her from joining the creature in the void. If there was an open wall panel close—there had to be, *had to be*—then she had a chance of escaping entombment in the sealing gel.

She screamed something—she wasn't sure what—

And then a hand grabbed hers, and pulled.

33

DON'T PANIC

Liv hit the deck on her back, rolling with the impact as her body sang in protest at the shock. Pushing herself up on her hands, she looked back toward the crawlspace. The gap in the wall made by the removed panels was already filled with a translucent yellow gel; as she watched, the transparent quality of the material began to fade, and that section of the crawlspace was filled with an opaque substance in a dark green that was almost as black as the insulating foam beyond it.

"Are you okay?"

Liv felt hands on her shoulders, and her muscles spasmed like she'd had an electric shock. She turned on the floor and stood in one swift movement, backing away toward the sealed wall, fists clenched. She blinked, her chest heaving with every breath, and was forced to kneel. She felt sick, her whole body sore and cold.

She took a shuddering breath and looked up.

"Deacon?"

The aux specialist held out a hand. Liv looked at it, blinking still. There was something wrong with her eyes, her vision cloudy and dim, sparkling at the edges. She rubbed her eyes, but it made no difference.

"Don't worry," said another voice. "You'll get used to it soon enough."

Liv jerked her head around to the other person she now realized was standing next to Deacon. She was almost as tall as Deacon, her white-blonde hair pulled back into a tight bun.

Astrid Healey, the missing engineer.

Liv moved her jaw up and down, but couldn't quite make her voice work. Deacon gave up waiting for her to accept his hand, instead reaching down to grab Liv's and pull her up himself.

Liv staggered on her feet, but didn't let go of Deacon's hand. She was staring at Astrid; then she glanced at Deacon. Deacon caught her fearful expression, and frowned.

"What is it?"

Liv stepped just a little farther back from the other woman.

"Is it really her?"

"If you mean, is she something pretending to be Astrid like that something was pretending to be Avery," said Deacon, "the answer is no. She's Astrid."

Liv felt dizzy. She felt cold. So cold her bones ached. Her vision sparked and swam so she closed her eyes.

"It took Deak awhile too," said Astrid's voice in the dark of Liv's mind, "so don't panic. Just breathe and focus on staying upright."

Liv nodded. The voice was right. It was Astrid. And Deacon. The two crew who had vanished, impossibly, from the confines of the XK72, stuck in the middle of a void. With her eyes still closed, Liv touched her earpiece, then realized she wasn't wearing it. She opened her eyes and looked at the others.

"Mirai," she said. "We need to get Mirai. She's out there—"

"We know," said Deacon, "but she's out of range now."

Liv stared at him, but he didn't say anything else. She was surprised by his coldness, but, she realized he was just being realistic.

Mirai was gone.

Liv wanted to say something else, wanted to scream and shout and rail against the universe and the hell that Colonel Redway had put them in, but almost on cue, her throat closed up. She tried swallowing, but nearly choked. She closed her eyes again, screwing them shut tight, like that would stop the world from swimming around her.

The dizziness passed a moment later. Liv opened her eyes and looked at the other two. Their outlines flared with shadows, but the world seemed to be getting more stable. Liv swallowed and rubbed her face; then she looked around. They were in an aft passageway somewhere. The ship was dark, the edges of everything moved when she blinked.

"I tried to get her," said Astrid, "but her velocity was too fast. This thing isn't that accurate." At that, she lifted her left hand and tapped the long, rectangular object strapped to her wrist. It was a computer link, identical to the ones from their EVA suits—and Liv realized it *was* from their EVA suits. More specifically, the third one, that had been mysteriously unsealed, but which they hadn't checked over.

Deacon looked at Liv, then Astrid. He nodded, quickly, almost to himself. "Okay, we're good, we're good, but time is ticking so if we—"

Liv ignored him, stepping up to Astrid. "Where have you been? We looked for you. We thought you were in the crawlspace. Hiding or stuck or injured . . ."

Astrid lowered her arm. "I've been right here, on the XK72. It was the safest place to be while I worked."

Liv closed her eyes again and just shook her head. In the swimming darkness behind her closed lids, she heard Deacon mutter to Astrid, "We really need to go, now."

Astrid said something in reply—Liv couldn't quite make it out, was she saying they still had time for something?—and then the engineer raised her voice, addressing her mission lead.

"Come on," she said.

Liv opened her eyes. "Where?"

"To the SLIP drive. I've got everything set up in there. I can show you."

The odd atmosphere was stronger in the SLIP drive module. The place was so familiar now to Liv, the machine at the heart of their problems sitting in the center under its mirrored cowling, marked on one side with a black streak courtesy of Deacon's earlier attempts at cutting it open. But right now, it felt so completely . . . alien. As Astrid moved around to the other side of the drive, Deacon parking himself by the hatchway, Liv couldn't hold back any longer.

"Why does everything feel so strange? It almost feels like—"

"Like you don't belong here." said Deacon.

Liv glanced at him over her shoulder. She worked her jaw a little, then said, "Yes."

"It's because of this place," said Astrid. "It's stronger here because we're deeper than the ship, but you can acclimatize. I don't think it'll have any long-term effects."

"Deeper than the ship?" Liv just shook her head in confusion.

"It's easier if I just show you."

Astrid moved to one of the consoles on the far wall, and picked up a data pad that was plugged directly into the system. Trailing the cable out, Astrid placed the device on the flat top of the SLIP drive.

Liv looked at it, then with a shock realized exactly what it was.

"You have Redway's data pad?"

"I grabbed it from the escape pod before they launched. I didn't know what Avery was doing, but I knew I'd need the data pad if I was going to figure out what to do." Astrid tapped on the pad and its 3D projector activator, shining a hologram into the air between them.

Liv rubbed her temples as she cast her gaze over the projection. "How did you get access without his passcode?"

"I borrowed some computer time and got the mainframe to bypass the lock," said Astrid. "Luckily I was done before you rebooted the system. That was a good idea, by the way. Exactly what I would have done."

Liv peered at the projected computer model on show. It showed three square, horizontal planes, arranged in a stack with a few centimeters separating each. A large green diamond-shaped icon floated above the center of the uppermost plane. The model was familiar, to an extent. It was part of the mission protocol, or at least a version of it.

"The XK72," she said, pointing at the icon, then she dropped her finger to indicate the three stacked planes. "Normal space, hyperspace. This mapping is the same as ours."

"Right," said Astrid. "The XK72 was to engage the SLIP drive, transit hyperspace for a few milliseconds of real time, then reenter real space. Mission completed, prototype drive tested, at which point we would return to Artemis control with the data." She reached forward and tapped the data pad. The green icon representing the XK72 lowered itself through the first plane and stopped in the gap between it and the plane below, then turned yellow.

"But we didn't transit hyperspace," said Astrid. "The Drop was initiated, we got stuck, and we're still here."

"Because Redway sabotaged the ship," said Liv.

Behind her, Deacon laughed. Liv turned and looked at him.

"Redway didn't sabotage the ship," said Astrid. "I did."

Liv spun back around. *"What?"*

"Hey," said Deacon. "We did consider that, remember?"

"Redway's orders were to take the XK72 deeper," said Astrid. She tapped the data pad again. This time, the hologram appeared to zoom out, the icon of the XK72 now a tiny dot between the two flat colored squares representing real space and hyperspace. As Liv watched, new squares appeared in sequence, building a huge stack of planes that stretched right down to the data pad itself. The XK72 was now right at the top of a very tall column.

"That can't be right," said Liv, hands on hips. "There's something wrong with the model. There's nothing *below* hyperspace. That doesn't even make sense."

"You're right," said Astrid, "but hyperspace itself is not 'flat,' for want of a better term. It has its own dimensions—call it *depth*. These planes—" she indicated the display, "—are just one way of visualizing it. With a powerful enough SLIP drive, you could drop far below the initial horizon." She pointed in the air, indicating the stack of planes in the holographic display.

"So where are we?" asked Liv. "You said we are 'deeper' than the ship."

"The XK72 is here," said Astrid, indicating the yellow icon on the display before tapping on the data pad to zoom the projection back in. "As the ship is stuck just under the horizon, we're casting a shadow downward."

Liv narrowed her eyes as she tried to process the information. Seeing this, Astrid continued.

"Put it this way," she said. "These planes don't exist, but they are each a horizon. Each layer casts a shadow onto the horizon below. The XK72 is stuck below the first horizon. Its shadow is cast onto the one underneath. That's where we are."

"In the shadow of the ship?" whispered Liv.

"Stable enough," said Deacon, "as the XK72 is so close to the surface. Farther down it degrades, becomes nothing more than mathematical probabilities."

"So *how* are we here?" asked Liv.

"I used the SLIP drive," said Astrid, raising her arm to show the wrist computer borrowed from the EVA suit. "It was a risk, but I helped design the drive so I knew it was possible, at least in theory. According to the math, it's actually very easy—and thankfully it worked. I didn't have much time to act."

"What's easy?"

"The SLIP drive has a field that encompasses the whole ship, but it can also be focused on people or even objects," Astrid continued. "That's why the outer skeleton of the ship is like it is—it's a focusing lens, allowing the field of the SLIP drive to be directed. And you can use that focus to cross from the XK72 into its shadow. Once I realized that Redway was going to go through with his mission, I knew I had no choice. I grabbed the wrist computer from one of the EVA suits, patched into the mainframe, then interrupted the Drop. With the ship stuck, I used the SLIP drive to phase into the X72's shadow, where I could work without interruption. I picked up Redway's data pad on the way."

Liv held up a hand. "So you know what Redway was doing? You know his orders—who he was working for?" Liv caught her breath a moment. "And who exactly do *you* work for?"

Deacon laughed. Liv shot him a look, and he fell quiet.

"Artemis," said Astrid. "Like all of us, except Redway. But the company had suspected something was up, had for a long, long time. Their military partnership had gotten worse and worse over the years. This whole thing"—she gestured to the shadowed chamber around them—"was supposed to be a collaboration. Instead, the military took our SLIP drive design, built it, then shipped it back and used their own team to install it. We never had a chance to inspect their work."

"That's not unusual," said Liv. "They pay for it, they want the data first."

"But it's a good way to hide something," said Deacon. "Something like a bomb."

Liv didn't respond—didn't quite know *how* to respond—so she looked back at Astrid. The engineer pursed her lips before continuing.

"I was seconded to the military by Artemis early on, not just to help with the mission planning and design, but to get inside, learn what was going on, try and find out what they were really planning. I was an undercover investigator, in the perfect position to gather data. What I found was another group, brought in to work on the SLIP drive. Military engineers, but not people Artemis had worked with before. But I cooperated, I worked with them, I got as close as I could, and eventually became part of that team. They were part of a . . . call it a faction, inside the military. Hard-liners, with their own agenda. Nothing ever recognized as official, not tied to any department. I dug as deep as I could, but there was a limit to how far I could push it without drawing suspicion."

Deacon folded his arms. "*That* I understand."

"Hard-liners?" asked Liv. "Including . . . who, Colonel Redway?"

Astrid nodded. "They needed someone they could rely on, someone to do their dirty work, no questions asked."

"Which is why our original pilot, Captain Jackson, was suddenly reassigned," said Deacon, barking a short laugh. "Enter Colonel Redway."

Liv ran her hand through her hair. "I don't understand." She dropped her arms and stared at the SLIP drive. "You're saying they planted a bomb inside the SLIP drive? How is that even possible?"

"Hey, that's not all they managed to get past Artemis," said Deacon. He walked over to the exposed crawlspace. The stripped framework beyond the gap in the wall was dull in the strange half-life of the ship's shadow, but the embedded crystal structures still glinted a little. "They fitted out the entire superstructure of the XK72."

"You called it a lens," said Liv.

"Yes," said Astrid. "It amplifies the induction field of the SLIP drive, making sure the signal is heard, loud and clear."

"A signal," said Liv, quietly. "For Avery. For the thing that *looked* like Avery." She looked at Astrid, looked at Deacon, scarcely able to believe what she was saying. "That's what the bomb is for."

"Set the bait," said Deacon, "amplify the signal to bring them in, then make a deep, *deep* Drop, then . . ."

Nobody spoke for a moment. Liv's mind reeled with the information and she struggled to put the pieces together.

"How did they even know these things are down here?" she asked. "Why attack them at all?" She paused. "Why haven't we encountered them before? Hyperspace travel isn't new."

"No, but the SLIP drive is," said Deacon. He spread his arms. "That's why we're here. The Single Linear Induction Pulse system is more powerful, more efficient. We can travel farther, faster."

"By going deeper?" Liv nodded as it came together for her.

"They discovered them in the initial phase of the project," said Astrid. "Right from the start, the military was hiding something in the data from the initial runner probes. They live between the horizon planes. Creatures, life forms, feeding on changes in the quantum state—essentially, eating the mathematical shadow of the plane above. Anything deeper than the first plane they can see and are drawn up."

"And the deeper we go," said Deacon, "the bigger the shadow, the more we draw these things up from the bottom." He paused and clicked his tongue. "The SLIP drive is a failure. We can't use it."

"Unless," said Liv, "you can remove the problem."

"Send down a bomb, problem solved," said Deacon. "Then you call it an accident, give out commendations to the brave Artemis crew who never came back, and the SLIP drive project continues."

Liv backed away from the drive until her back touched the wall behind her, then she slid down until she was sitting on the floor. She shook her head again, and she thought about Mirai, floating away from the XK72, impossible now to reach. Doomed.

Like them?

Like . . . *Redway*?

"You can't tell me that Redway was going to commit suicide, just like that?" Liv stared at the others. "He can't have signed up for a one-way trip. Nobody could be that fanatical, not even this . . . faction, you called it."

"You're right," said Astrid. "He's got a history—top test pilot, got himself out of a lot of difficult situations. It's all in his official record. A list of commendations as long as my arm."

"So," said Deacon, "committed to the cause, but too valuable to lose."

Astrid nodded. "He had an escape plan."

"Just one that didn't include us," said Liv.

"But one we might be able to use to get out of here," said Deacon. "If we can figure out what it was."

"I don't understand," said Liv. "The ship's mainframe is reset. Can't we initiate the Drop and resurface?"

Astrid shook her head. "I think it's too late for that. We've been here too long. The thing that took Avery's form got lucky, finding the escape pod and using it to climb to our level. But now more are coming. If we try a Drop, we might drag them up to real space—a place they are not supposed to exist in. If they survive by eating quantum probability, the consequences could be catastrophic."

Liv closed her eyes again. She brought her legs up and wrapped her arms around them, her chin resting on her knees. "And you're telling me," she said, "that you don't know what Redway's escape plan was?"

"Not yet," said Astrid. "There are protocols and instructions in his data pad, but nothing complete, at least that I've been able to find yet."

"That doesn't make any sense."

"Actually it does," said Deacon. "I've been over it. There's a lot of technical detail in his orders, but there must be something that only Redway knew about, or was briefed on in person. Until we figure out what that was, we're still stuck."

This was a lot of information to process. Almost too much. And as Liv thought about it, she felt a hot pricking behind her eyes, and when she blinked, she felt the tears begin to trickle down her cheeks.

All those years of work, for her, for the team, co-opted—*hijacked*—by a shadowy group of military hard-liners on a mission of their own, and damn anyone who happens to be in the way.

Already she felt the anger begin to grow. People needed to know. People needed to be brought to account.

People needed to *pay*.

She wiped her eyes.

Enough. Anger was good, yes—but only if she could direct it, use the energy it provided to find a solution.

To find a way home.

That was when she remembered what she had found attached to the ion drive. The device, the odd, rocket-shaped cylinder. She knew it had been familiar, somehow.

She opened her eyes.

"Okay," she said. "I think I know how Redway was planning to get out."

34

A GOOD WAY OF REMOVING THE EVIDENCE

The three remaining crew of the XK72 gathered around the data pad as Liv explained what she had found when she sabotaged the ion drive.

"That's it," said Deacon. "It's a SLIP core from a runner probe, just like you thought it was. Miniature version of this thing." He knocked the base of the SLIP drive with the side of his boot. "Same as the one in the probe we have loaded into the launcher." He paused, and rubbed his chin. "I'll need to see how it was connected—" he turned to Astrid, "—but Redway's technical readout makes a lot more sense now."

Astrid nodded. "Do you think you can reconnect it?"

"Like I said, I need to see it first, but I don't see why not."

"But how does it work?" asked Liv. "Surely we need the SLIP drive itself to resurface something as large as the XK72."

Astrid picked up the data pad from the top of the SLIP drive, turning off the projected display. She tapped at it as she spoke. "Ordinarily, yes, but like Deak said, now these readouts make more sense." She turned the pad around to show Liv a series of graphs and instructions in a text that was almost too small to read, even if Liv wasn't too exhausted to make sense of it anyway.

However, there was one chart that was easy to follow—an energy output reading that went beyond the bounds of the graph.

"An overload?"

Astrid nodded. "A controlled explosion. Overload the ion drive, rupture the fuel cell. Pump the output into the runner probe and activate it. It'll be destroyed as well, but the Drop is only milliseconds. A good way of removing the evidence too."

But Liv shook her head. "That still can't be enough."

"It can," said Deacon, "if you only take part of the ship with you. The XK72 is modular. You only use what you need. Ion drive module, passageway module. That would be enough."

Now Liv began to get it. She looked up at the ceiling. "Disconnect the ion drive module and the passageway. Blow the drive and use the runner core to resurface." She looked at the others. "Then sit in the passageway and signal for rescue?"

"Meanwhile," said Astrid, "the SLIP drive is engaged for a second Drop, one far deeper. The rest of the XK72 goes down and drags the creatures with it, as they follow its shadow as it crosses each horizon. And when it reaches a critical depth . . ."

"Boom," said Deacon.

Liv peered at the data pad again. It seemed logical, even simple, the way the other two explained it. They were both engineers, and Astrid knew more about the SLIP drive than anybody.

But was she right? Was this Redway's escape plan? Or were they just joining dots that weren't there.

More to the point, did they have any other option?

Liv paced the cabin, head bowed, as she thought it over. But after a few moments, she realized she wasn't thinking about anything at all.

Liv stopped pacing, and turned to the others.

"Let's do it."

35

ANOTHER CHIME, THEN A BURST OF STATIC, THEN THE VOICE

Astrid brought them back to the XK72 proper, controlling the focus of the SLIP drive's ever-present field with the EVA wrist computer.

As soon as they were back in the "real" ship, Liv felt warm and light-headed. She staggered on her feet, and the muscles in her legs ached and felt weak, like she'd just stopped running, even though she, Deacon, and Astrid hadn't physically moved anywhere at all. They were still in the SLIP drive module, but the cabin looked brighter, Liv's vision clearer now.

"Here." Astrid unstrapped the wrist computer and handed it to Liv. The plan was for Liv to get the XK72 ready while Astrid and Deacon worked on reinstalling the runner probe core in the ion drive. Liv's prep work involved isolating the module architecture systems—which, she now realized, she had seen Redway accessing after he had programmed in the new Drop sequence. Once Liv had accessed that system, they would be able to follow Redway's escape route by jettisoning the modified ion drive—along with all of the XK72 apart from the large module which formed the main passageway—and using the overloading runner probe core to resurface.

It was a risk, there was no doubt about it. A large risk. But there was no time to reconsider, not now. Each module offered basic but independent life support, and they could take some supplies—water, rations, the two remaining EVA suits, even though there were three crew now. Astrid had given Liv the wrist computer so she could activate both the module dumping and the Drop remotely, from the safe haven of the passageway.

As the trio stepped out of the SLIP drive module, Deacon and Astrid swung themselves up onto the ladder to access the ion drive above, while Liv headed for the flight deck. There, she headed straight for the module architecture controls and began getting the systems ready for an unorthodox, in-flight reconfiguration of the XK72. She only hoped the mainframe wouldn't try to stop her from what it would see as a catastrophic change to the ship's structure.

Her hands and fingers moved almost on automatic as her mind wandered, trying to process what had happened, what *would* happen—not just in the next few minutes, few hours, but when they got back home, back to Artemis.

Because . . . what the *fuck* was going to happen?

They had Redway's data pad, and the secrets it contained—proof enough of the deceit of Redway and his masters—but Liv couldn't even begin to comprehend how Artemis would react, how they would handle such a huge crisis of trust.

Then again, they had suspected enough to have entrusted Astrid with secret orders of her own.

And Liv felt . . .

No, no time for this. They could do all the contemplation, planning, panicking they liked while they were waiting in the passageway module waiting for rescue.

And then the nausea arrived, and quickly, as Liv's head began to spin. She closed her eyes and grit her teeth and told herself there was *no fucking time for this* and that the three remaining crew of the XK72 had a job to do.

Liv rolled her neck, then opened her eyes and sat forward as she began to check over her work. The module architecture system was fairly simple, and she programmed her new requirements with ease. She lifted her arm to check that the wrist computer was synched with the mainframe, thankful that the ship's computer didn't seem to mind what she was doing.

All systems green, green, green.

Using the wrist computer, she flicked on the internal comms, ready to report her progress to Astrid and Deacon.

Immediately the roar of static filled the flight deck. Swearing under her breath, her heart thudding in her chest, Liv flicked the channel off.

That noise. The same sound that had flooded the comms channels earlier, when the servodrone had been taken over by the entity.

But the drone was in pieces, the bulk of it presumably spinning out into the endless void along with Mirai.

Except . . .

Maybe it was her imagination, but Liv braced herself and brought the internal comms on again. The static roar ripped through the flight deck again.

And—there! A voice, buried in the noise, drifting in and out. But not the mechanized grind of the servodrone. This voice was human. Faint, but human.

Liv swung herself into the co-pilot's seat and, killing the volume to make the white noise bearable, began working on the comms control in front of her. As with the servodrone earlier, the system registered the signal coming from somewhere close by, but somewhere that *wasn't* the XK72.

Finally, Liv got a lock. A chime filled the flight deck.

"Liv! Open the—"

Then it was gone. Liv waited, breath held, hoping, *willing* the voice she knew so well to come through again.

Another chime, then a burst of static, then the voice, loud and clear this time, breaking through the noise.

"Liv! Liv! Open the airlock!"

It was Mirai.

36

ALL SYSTEMS GREEN, GREEN, GREEN

Astrid was already at the airlock by the time Liv got there, having heard Mirai over the comms, while Deacon kept working on the ion drive. The two women nodded at each other, Astrid's hand hovering over the hatchway controls.

Liv stepped up to the glass porthole of the hatch and looked through. Across the small chamber of the airlock itself, she could see through the outer window. There was a shape there, a bright orange blur bobbing around.

Liv opened her mouth to confirm to Astrid what she was seeing, that it was Mirai, that the airlock could be opened, but she stopped, catching the words in her throat.

Because was it Mirai?

The bright orange thing outside continued to bounce around, but that's just what it was—a shape, a form, a color. The voice over the comms *sounded* like Mirai, but then the thing that had walked around inside the ship had sounded (and looked) like Avery too.

Was it Mirai?

Or was it something else entirely?

Liv turned her body against the airlock, and looked at Astrid as the engineer punched the control panel.

"Astrid, wait!"

"Outer airlock opened," said Astrid. "I know what you're thinking, but it's her. It must be. Those things don't need our help to get inside."

"They tricked us with the escape pod," Liv said, hardly hearing her own voice. "They tricked us with the escape pod and with Avery."

"Maybe they did," said Astrid. She paused. "Your call, mission lead."

That was when the orange blob floating inside the airlock smacked directly against the porthole, the sudden collision sending Liv and Astrid jerking back in surprise. Recovering, Liv went back and looked through.

Inside the chamber, Mirai struggled with a disconnected oxygen hose from the EVA suit's compact backpack.

It was her, all right.

Liv brushed Astrid's hand aside and activated the control herself. The outer airlock door swung shut with a distant reverberation and the chamber began to pressurize. Liv went back to the window and counted the precious seconds until the atmosphere was equalized. Then—with Astrid's help—the pair pulled at the inner door.

Mirai almost fell onto them. Astrid caught most of her weight, and gently lowered Mirai to the passageway floor. The broken oxygen tube twitched against the grating, sputtering out the last of the suit's supply.

Liv fell to her knees, her hands sliding around the suit's neck as she struggled to find the helmet release clamps. Having finally located them, she pulled the locks free, then grabbed the helmet and gave it a twist. It came off with a slight popping sound.

Mirai gasped for breath, her eyes wide, her skin slick with sweat. Astrid helped her to sit up, and she and Liv waited a few moments as Mirai recovered. Finally, Mirai looked up, pushing her hair away from her face with her gloved hands.

"What happened?" asked Liv.

As she said it, Astrid jerked back, just a little, like she'd picked up a static shock from the EVA suit. She caught Liv's eye, but gave her a quick nod to indicate everything was okay.

Mirai coughed, then lifted the broken oxygen hose. "Newton's third law. For every action, there is an equal and opposite reaction."

Liv took the end of the hose from Mirai, and stared at it. It wasn't broken, it had been unscrewed deliberately from the EVA's backpack.

"Hey," said Mirai, taking the hose back, "it worked, didn't it?" She looked at Liv, then at Astrid. Now it was her turn to jerk back on the floor.

"Astrid!" She looked at Liv. "What's happened?"

In the Data Monitoring module, Liv, Astrid, and Deacon were watching the feed from the flight deck, which showed Mirai making preflight checks from the co-pilot's position. Deacon had reattached the SLIP runner to the ion drive in record time, allowing them a rare moment of . . . caution?

Because before they did anything else, they had to be sure.

After they had gotten Mirai out of the EVA suit and had made sure she wasn't injured, they'd briefed her on the plan to use Redway's escape route, and then Astrid had assigned her a list of tasks, the same set of routines that Liv had already completed. It was unnecessary work, but it kept Mirai busy and it allowed the others to observe her, from a distance.

None of them spoke. Deacon stood with his arms folded; whenever Liv looked at him, his eyes darted back to the screen, like he'd really been watching her all along.

"How do we know it's her?" Deacon finally asked.

Liv grit her teeth. She watched Mirai on the display.

It looked like her.

It sounded like her.

It was working like it was her, running through the pre-mission checks.

Liv sighed. "It's her." She only hoped she was right.

"Is it?" asked Deacon. "Mirai was blown out into the void. She couldn't have survived that long."

"The EVA suits are good for a hundred hours."

"She was using her oxygen supply as a rocket," said Astrid.

Liv stared at the screen.

"Liv?"

She knew Astrid and Deacon had a point. The chances of Mirai surviving her journey out into the void, of finding her way back to the XK72 even if she had managed to get her oxygen hose disconnected within minutes of being thrown off the ship's hull, were so infinitely small as to be impossible. And even as she thought this, the nausea returned. She thought she would throw up.

It was either Mirai or it wasn't. Her gut—her twisting, bubbling gut—told her she was real. But Astrid and Deacon were surprisingly cold and clinical as they assessed the new arrival. And that coolness made Liv doubt her own instincts.

It was Mirai, wasn't it?

They'd been fooled before. The escape pod had returned, also against almost impossible odds, and it hadn't brought back Avery Cormack.

It had brought back a monster. Something that had looked and sounded like Avery.

Just like the thing on the flight deck that looked like Mirai.

"We've got to make a decision," said Deacon. "And we have to make the right one."

Liv said nothing. She looked at the other two, but they were absorbed by the feed from the flight deck, their expressions flat, their eyes dark, staring.

Yes, she did have a decision to make.

Liv left the others to watch Mirai, and went to the ion drive module. She climbed the ladder and sat down on the decking. Being alone for a while was good, actually.

Because she had a lot to think about, and they were the kind of thoughts that went with the fact that next to her on the floor was the runner probe core she'd pulled from the ion drive, right where she had left it.

Deacon had never touched it.

Because Deacon had never been there.

Liv knew then when it had happened—oh, Mirai had come back all right. It was her. But she had brought something with her. Something which had first replaced Astrid (and Liv had *seen* it, that jolt, that shock, which now gave her a jolt and a shock of her own) and then, at some point, Deacon. When Astrid went to fetch him, insisting on going herself, not using the comms because the comms were glitchy and she didn't want Mirai to know what she was doing, she—*it*—had said.

So it was Liv and Mirai now. The two of them against an entire universe of horror.

Lifting her wrist computer, Liv accessed the module architecture system and started making changes. That task done, she brought up the SLIP drive master protocol and ran through the pre-Drop check sequence. A few minutes was all it took, and then everything was ready.

All systems green, green, green.

Then she got up and headed to the flight deck.

Mirai looked up from the pilot's position as Liv walked in, speaking not to Liv herself but to their twin reflections in the forward bubble of the XK72, beyond which the field of stars still shone. But the lights had not grown in size or number. It was like they were waiting. Watching.

Liv knew exactly what they were waiting for—the other two, the ones in the ship with her and Mirai, infiltrators who had found a way in and were ready to surface with the XK72 and bring the others up with them, giving them access to a universe of energy, an infinite feeding ground.

Liv knew that couldn't happen.

"All set," said Mirai.

Liv nodded, watching the window, watching the lights. Then something moved in the reflection, behind the two of them.

"We're ready."

It was Astrid. She had appeared on the flight deck silently and took a few steps forward—not from the direction of the main hatchway, but from the black void of the exposed crawlspace. Liv watched Astrid's reflection, willing herself to see some kind of difference, some way of recognizing the thing as not being one of them, some way of *knowing* it wasn't Astrid, but there was nothing. She would have to wait until it gave up the ruse itself and sprouted a head of many tentacles.

The thought made Liv laugh; she stifled it, but Mirai glanced sideways at her. The reflected form of not-Astrid didn't seem to register a thing.

Liv finally turned and nodded in acknowledgment to the thing that looked like Astrid, then moved to the co-pilot's seat. She sat down slowly, her eyes on the controls, her hands balled into fists to stop them from shaking. She looked at Mirai, and gave a nod.

"Acknowledged," said Mirai, perhaps answering for Liv, perhaps focusing on the task at hand to keep herself from running screaming from the flight deck. At least that's what Liv wanted to do. She squeezed her fists on her lap.

She reached forward and began the ion drive initialization, following the sequence Colonel Redway had planned on using to set off the overload.

Mirai looked up and read off the display. "Ion flow at eighty percent and rising,"

Liv nodded, but didn't speak. Mirai looked at her.

"Acknowledged?"

Liv didn't answer. She looked at Mirai, then glanced up as the thing that looked like Astrid moved behind the pilot's seat. Its gaze was fixed on the lights outside. It might have been Liv's imagination, but the thing seemed to be smiling, just a little.

Perhaps that was the confirmation Liv was waiting for, or perhaps that was just what she told herself.

"Acknowledged," said Astrid, instead of Liv. "Time to go." Finally, she dragged her attention from the forward view and looked down at Liv. "Module architecture ready?"

"All done," said Liv. "We can all go to the passageway module as soon as the master program is set. Mirai?"

Mirai entered a sequence on the console in front of her, her hands moving slowly over the controls. The system chimed and the panel readouts in front of Liv and Mirai changed to display the same simple text scroll.

Mirai glanced down. "Program initiated." She stood from the pilot's seat. "Ready to go."

"Acknowledged," said Liv. She glanced up at not-Astrid, the thing still standing there, now back to staring at the forward view.

Liv's mind was racing, along with her heart. A lot depended on certain things happening, on her *making* them happen, on everything going according to a makeshift plan in her head which, even now, she was beginning to second-guess. Because it wasn't just her life she was trying to save. There was Mirai, and Mirai didn't know anything about what was about to happen. But there was no way to tell her, to warn her, to do anything but follow the plan and hope it worked and that she and Mirai would be able to escape.

Alone.

Liv pursed her lips. "Where's Deacon?"

"Engineering," said not-Astrid, not taking her eyes away from the lights outside.

Liv watched her a moment.

Mirai looked between the two of them, almost bouncing on her feet. "Are we going to do this?"

"Yes," said Liv, her voice almost a whisper. "Let's go." She walked close to Mirai, resisting the urge to take the younger woman's hand in hers. Instead, she balled her fists again and walked toward the flight deck hatchway at a steady, calm pace, determined not to turn around, determined to stick to the plan, determined to get home.

She had reached the hatchway when she heard Mirai gasp. And then a voice spoke.

"You didn't really think this would work, did you?"

Liv turned around, her breath catching in her throat.

Mirai was facing her, standing in the middle of the flight deck. She was frozen in place, her face creased in pain, as Deacon

the thing that looks like Deacon the thing that looks like Deacon it's not him it's not him

who appeared out of nowhere in the flight deck

no, who had appeared out of the crawlspace just like Astrid had

had one huge hand wrapped around Mirai's neck. Next to him, the thing that only looked like Astrid had turned around, the stars in the void outside the ship now spinning in its eyes, like they spun in the eyes of the thing that looked like Deacon but wasn't him.

Liv jutted her chin out. "Let her go."

"Astrid's idea was a good one, I'll give you that," said the thing that only looked like Astrid. "She was a master engineer. The smartest person in this crew. Artemis clearly picks their crew well."

"Let us go, and we'll leave you alone," said Liv. "You don't want us. You want this ship. You want the SLIP drive. You can have it. We don't need it to escape. You can take it and feed off its shadow. That's what you want. Let us go."

Mirai gasped, her face turning red as she struggled to breathe.

"I knew almost as soon as you arrived," said Liv. "Mirai brought you back. You hitched a ride. Where are Astrid and Deacon? Dead, their bodies dumped in the crawlspace? Or did you do something else with them, like you did with Redway and Avery?"

Silence reigned. Mirai's eyes fluttered, and her arms, hanging by her sides, twitched. The thing that only looked like Deacon took a step forward and lifted its arm, raising Mirai up so her feet didn't even touch the decking.

"Let us go," said Liv.

The thing that only looked like Astrid shook its head. "It's not that easy."

"You have the XK72 and you have the SLIP drive. Let us go."

It smiled. "It's not enough."

"It's more than enough. Let us go."

"Why would we want your SLIP drive when there is so much more we can have, just out of reach," said the creature. "But not for long. You can resurface and we will resurface with you."

Liv took a step forward. Mirai gave another gasp, her chest heaving.

The thing that only looked like Astrid cocked its head. "We will just be the first. Once we cross the horizon, we can bring the rest of us up from the depths. Your world feels rich, plentiful. There will be much to feast on."

An alert chime sounded in the flight deck. Liv felt a tiny haptic vibration from her wrist computer. The ion drive was primed and ready to fire.

It was the last thing Liv planned on doing.

"Let us go," said Liv.

"No."

There was a muffled crunch. In not-Deacon's grasp, Mirai's body jerked, and her head lolled forward under his grip. Then the creature let her go, and Mirai dropped, lifeless, to the floor.

The world skewed sideways in Liv's vision. It was all she could do not to give up, right then and there. But she swallowed the bile that was rising in her throat and told herself that she wasn't doing it for herself. She was doing it for Mirai.

And Deacon.

And Astrid.

And Avery.

And it was now, or never.

Liv lifted her wrist and activated a preset sequence on her wrist computer, and disappeared from the flight deck.

Liv reappeared in the SLIP drive module, right on target, and pitched forward as her boots slammed into the decking, her arms wheeling for balance. As soon as she had regained her balance, she heard it.

Static white noise, quiet and growing quickly, the hurricane roar of the creatures of the void. Liv turned to the source—the gap in the wall, the crawlspace, where the focusing crystals glittered in the darkness, from where a cold wind began to blow.

They were coming for her.

All according to her plan.

Liv reset her wrist computer, selecting the second preset sequence. She knew she would have to be quick, but she had no idea *how* quick. Activate it too soon as they would find her again. Too late, and she would go down with them.

That was when something whipped at her feet—several somethings, slapping wetly, pulling at her boots, at her pant legs. Her skin beneath seared with cold as the green-blue tendrils of the void creatures flew out of the crawlspace and grasped for purchase on the decking, dragging the monsters behind them, all vestiges of human form now shed.

As a larger tentacle wrapped around her left calf, Liv activated two sequences at once. She transposed herself just a few meters, into the passageway beyond the SLIP drive module, and a moment later the hatchway slid closed.

Liv's left leg was numb, and the knee gave way, sending her to the decking. She rolled with it, ignoring the pain, landing on her back, the wrist computer raised in front of her. She hit the final preset sequence.

There was a heavy *ka-thunk*, followed by a series of smaller vibrations, as the SLIP drive module was detached from the main structure of the XK72.

And then there was . . . silence.

Liv lay on the floor, not daring to move, counting her breaths, willing her rib cage to hold it together as it felt like her heart was going to explode out of it. Her left leg began to return to life, the pins and needles sensation growing so strong she cried out in pain and forced herself to roll over, exercising her leg muscles to try to quell the sensation.

There, on her hands and knees in the middle of the passageway, she closed her eyes and listened to the silence, and then she yelled, as loud as she could, not words but just *feelings*. She yelled until her throat was raw and she could taste blood, but when she stopped she felt a hell of a lot better.

She opened her eyes and looked up, toward the two hatchways at the end of the passageway—the upper leading to the ion drive module. The lower to the SLIP drive module.

A module which was now no longer part of the ship—detached from the XK72, the Drop initiated a millisecond later, taking the SLIP drive down, down, down, and the creatures from the void with it.

Liv got to her feet, her ears ringing with the sound of her own blood.

She had to be sure. So she went to the flight deck. She stopped in the hatchway, and stared ahead.

The void outside the ship was completely dark. The lights—the creatures—were gone.

37

SHE WOKE HUNGRY AND THIRSTY

She woke hungry and thirsty and disoriented, and it took a moment for Liv to realize she'd fallen asleep in the co-pilot's position.

Sitting up, she rubbed her face. She felt—

Actually, she felt better. Much better. She glanced at the chronometer on the main console but the numbers were meaningless, as she had no idea when she had passed out. But that sleep, whether it had been long or short, had been very, very good, and free of dreams and nightmares.

What remained now was the nightmare of the reality she was in.

She gasped, nearly choking on the saliva in her throat, and pushed herself forward, leaning on the console as she coughed to clear her lungs. Then she fell back into the seat and closed her eyes, her chest heaving, as she remembered exactly where she was and what had happened.

Her heart thudded, and her head along with it, although the approaching headache was distant, intangible, more the result of the coughing fit than anything else.

Liv allowed herself a few moments to calm herself down, and consider her situation—not the big picture, *what the fuck am I going to do, I'm doomed* picture (time enough for that later), but something smaller, a challenge that could be easily overcome, the first small step to tackling the big, important stuff.

Hunger. Thirst.

No problem. She could break out rations. There was enough food and water to last for . . . well, for who knew how long, now that there was only one crewmember left.

Okay, *that* made her pause.

Mission Lead Liv Halliday. Last one standing.

She opened her eyes. Outside, through the bubble of the flight deck pod, the universe outside was black. There were no stars. No lights. Nothing. Just a blank, dark emptiness.

A void.

Excellent.

That was, she knew, a win. She slid to sit on the edge of the seat and checked the systems again, just to be sure, and . . . there it was. Or rather, there it *wasn't.* The ship's modular architecture system reported an error, which Liv cleared manually—the error being the SLIP drive module was missing. Liv checked over the rest of the system just in case, double-checking her hasty reconfiguration protocol hadn't accidentally deleted any other parts of the XK72.

But, no, it was all there. Including the bit she needed the most—the ion drive module.

Because Liv fully intended to follow through with Redway's escape plan. The ion drive module was still there, and inside that module was the runner probe core, just where Liv had left it.

As she thought about the work ahead, picturing the runner probe core, picturing the state of the ion drive's interior, she felt just a hint of panic begin to rise again.

She quelled that feeling. There was time enough to panic, to scream and shout and rant and rave. Put it on the to-do list. Check it off when it was done.

Liv laughed as she thought of it, and then she kept laughing.

When she was done, and her ribs ached, she lay back in the pilot's seat and fell asleep again.

Liv swore, and tossed the multitool to one side, and sat back, supported on her arms, her legs stretched out in front of her in the main passageway module. Between her knees was a silver box and a mess of circuit boards, all of them connected in what she thought was the right way, none of them working how she needed them to work.

She pushed away that by now oh-so-familiar sinking feeling, and reached behind her, not for the multitool but for another gold-foil-wrapped ration bar. She sat and chewed on it, not even registering the flavor—okay, so it was blueberry—savoring only the sustenance and energy the food would provide to keep her up and working for as long as she needed to.

For as long as it took.

The next job was to fix the control box of the runner probe core. It was a simple enough task, and she had a full spec sheet for every standard piece of Artemis equipment—two dozen models of hyperspace runner probes included—on her data pad. She had the tools, she had the skills, she had the instruction manual, but it was proving to be far harder than she thought. Even dragging half of the Engineering module out in the passageway to give herself more room hadn't made it any easier.

With a sigh, Liv pushed herself to her feet.

The XK72's mainframe was, indeed, very dumb, and offered no help whatsoever. Every query Liv entered, it spat out the same directive, to check the Technical Manual. And Liv was very keen to do just that, but there was the small problem that Avery hadn't submitted it yet.

Liv was on her own on this one.

She had, at least, been able to repair the runner probe control box, and was now ready to patch the core into the ion drive, but she hadn't paid much attention to the thing when she had disconnected it in the first place, and there was still the problem of the unbalanced ion drive itself. Even if she could get the core reconnected, she wondered if the ship's computer would let the drive operate for long enough to initiate the runaway overload. It was a vital part of the escape plan, and Liv also wondered why they hadn't thought of it before.

She took a bite of another fruit-flavored ration bar and got herself comfortable, data pad in hand, as she began to read through the ion drive's auxiliary power system specs, and not for the first time.

Also not for the first time, she wished the others were here. She wished for Astrid and Avery, and for Mirai and for Deacon.

But when she looked up at the reflection of herself in the forward bubble, the flight deck behind her was empty.

She got up and closed the main hatchway. As she passed the exposed black void of the crawlspace, she thought she could feel a cool breeze from it.

She told herself she would put the wall panels back at some point. But there were more important jobs that needed her attention.

Like how to get out of here, for a start.

Liv opened her eyes and tried to remember where she was, thinking for a moment that the flight deck was a flat metal plain under a flat metal sky.

As the flight deck swam into focus, she wondered what the noise was. The sound was electronic, low, but insistent, the tone steadily rising along with the volume.

Proximity alert.

Liv sprang up, falling out of the pilot's seat and onto the hard decking of the flight deck. Wincing, she pulled herself up and leaned on the console, a blue light on the panel in front of her pulsing in time with the alert, in time with the pounding of her heart, in time with the thudding in her head.

She looked up. Outside was nothing. A darkness infinite, featureless. A void.

And then—

A light appeared. Just a single point, slightly off-center.

And then another appeared beside it.

And then another.

And then another.

And then the lights were blocked out as something *moved* outside the bubble. At first it was a shadow, and then it moved again and it was a flash of orange, a silhouette of a person.

Knock-knock-knock . . .

Liv turned, slowly, wanting to close her eyes, her jaw muscles ached as she clenched her teeth together. As she turned, she willed herself not to look at the exposed crawlspace

don't look don't look don't look don't you fucking look

and when she was facing the closed flight deck hatchway she realized she had closed her eyes.

don't look don't look don't look don't you fucking look

The sound came again. From the other side of the hatchway, from somewhere else in the ship, the empty, empty ship.

Knock-knock-knock . . .

Liv Halliday opened her eyes.

ACKNOWLEDGMENTS

This book was a long time coming, and I'd like to thank everyone who made the journey with me over the years and helped get this dark little tale out into the world.

To my editor, Will Hinton, thank you for your incredible guidance in helping shape this adventure. Thanks also to the whole team at Tor/Nightfire: Oliver Dougherty, Jordan Hanley, Laura Etzkorn, Sarah Weeks, and Sarah Walker.

Thanks (an awful lot of them), to my crew: Michaela Gray, Sarah Miles, Chuck Wendig, Jen Williams.

Thanks to my agent, Stacia Decker. What a journey that was, eh?

And finally, thanks to my wife, Sandra, for everything, as usual. This one is for you. Love you heaps.

ABOUT THE AUTHOR

Lou Abercrombie

ADAM CHRISTOPHER is the *New York Times* bestselling author of *Star Wars: Master of Evil, Star Wars: Shadow of the Sith,* and *Stranger Things: Darkness on the Edge of Town,* as well as official tie-in novels for the hit CBS television show *Elementary* and the award-winning Dishonored video game franchise. Cocreator of the twenty-first-century incarnation of the Archie Comics superhero The Shield, Christopher has also written for the universes of Doctor Who and World of Warcraft, and is a contributor to the internationally bestselling Star Wars: From a Certain Point of View anthology series and the all-ages *Star Wars Adventures* comic. Christopher's original novels include *Made to Kill* and *The Burning Dark,* among many others, and his debut novel, *Empire State,* was both a *SciFiNow* and *Financial Times* Book of the Year.